Master of Freedom

Also from Cherise Sinclair

Masters of the Shadowlands (contemporary)
Club Shadowlands
Dark Citadel
Breaking Free
Lean on Me
Make Me, Sir
To Command and Collar
This Is Who I Am
If Only
Show Me, Baby
Servicing the Target

Mountain Masters and Dark Haven (contemporary)
Master of the Mountain
Doms of Dark Haven 1 (anthology)
Master of the Abyss
Doms of Dark Haven 2: Western Night (anthology)
My Liege of Dark Haven
Edge of the Enforcer
Master of Freedom

The Wild Hunt Legacy (paranormal)
Hour of the Lion
Winter of the Wolf

Standalone books
The Starlight Rite (Sci-Fi Romance)
The Dom's Dungeon (contemporary)

Master of Freedom

A Mountain Masters Novella

By Cherise Sinclair

Minou –
With love!
Cherise Sinclair

1001 Dark Nights

EVIL EYE
CONCEPTS

Master of Freedom
A Mountain Masters Novella
By Cherise Sinclair

1001 Dark Nights
Copyright 2015 Cherise Sinclair
ISBN: 978-1-940887-37-1

Forward: Copyright 2014 M. J. Rose
Published by Evil Eye Concepts, Incorporated

Author's Note

To my readers,

The books I write are fiction, not reality, and as in most romantic fiction, the romance is compressed into a very, very short time period.

You, my darlings, live in the real world, and I want you to take a little more time in your relationships. Good Doms don't grow on trees, and there are some strange people out there. So while you're looking for that special Dom, please, be careful.

When you find him, realize he can't read your mind. Yes, frightening as it might be, you're going to have to open up and talk to him. And you listen to him in return. Share your hopes and fears, what you want from him, what scares you spitless. Okay, he may try to push your boundaries a little—he's a Dom, after all—but you will have your safe word. You will have a safe word, am I clear? Use protection. Have a backup person. Communicate.

Remember: safe, sane, and consensual.

Know that I'm hoping you find that special, loving person who will understand your needs and hold you close.

And while you're looking or even if you've already found your dearheart, come and hang out with the Mountain Masters.

Love,
Cherise

Acknowledgments From The Author

Many thanks to the usual suspects, Bianca Sommerland, Fiona Archer, and Monette Michaels—crit partners extraordinaire. My wonderful Aussie buddy, Ruth Reid, helped with the story's psychology issues and beta reading.

A bazillion thanks to Lisa SK who suggested the heroine's occupation and tried to keep me on the straight and narrow as far as correctness. All errors are hers. (*Shoot, I tried. Okay, all errors really are mine.*)

While never sharing anything that breached confidentiality, the stories she gave me were simply hair-raising. People working in the prison system have my most profound respect.

And, on the subject of errors and prisons, an escape truly isn't easy at all. However, driving through fences? Yep, that does happen. (Thank you, Kevin).

I actually got out of my cave and attended some reader-author conventions this year—and was thrilled at y'all's enthusiasm. For those who attended, for those who brought me gifts or hugs or simply made me feel so, so welcome—you have my gratitude. Thank you!

Finally—I never forget that I'm creating these stories for you, my readers. And I hope you realize how much it means that you'll gift me with your time and trust. (Yes, that sounded very Dom-like, didn't it?) But it's honest, as well. Thank you, my dears.

Sign up for the 1001 Dark Nights Newsletter
and be entered to win a Tiffany Key necklace.

There's a contest every month!

Go to www.1001DarkNights.com to subscribe.

As a bonus, all subscribers will receive a free
1001 Dark Nights story
The First Night
by Lexi Blake & M.J. Rose

One Thousand and One Dark Nights

Once upon a time, in the future...

*I was a student fascinated with stories and learning.
I studied philosophy, poetry, history, the occult, and
the art and science of love and magic. I had a vast
library at my father's home and collected thousands
of volumes of fantastic tales.*

*I learned all about ancient races and bygone
times. About myths and legends and dreams of all
people through the millennium. And the more I read
the stronger my imagination grew until I discovered
that I was able to travel into the stories... to actually
become part of them.*

*I wish I could say that I listened to my teacher
and respected my gift, as I ought to have. If I had, I
would not be telling you this tale now.
But I was foolhardy and confused, showing off
with bravery.*

*One afternoon, curious about the myth of the
Arabian Nights, I traveled back to ancient Persia to
see for myself if it was true that every day Shahryar
(Persian: شهریار, "king") married a new virgin, and then
sent yesterday's wife to be beheaded. It was written
and I had read, that by the time he met Scheherazade,
the vizier's daughter, he'd killed one thousand
women.*

*Something went wrong with my efforts. I arrived
in the midst of the story and somehow exchanged
places with Scheherazade – a phenomena that had
never occurred before and that still to this day, I
cannot explain.*

Now I am trapped in that ancient past. I have taken on Scheherazade's life and the only way I can protect myself and stay alive is to do what she did to protect herself and stay alive.

Every night the King calls for me and listens as I spin tales. And when the evening ends and dawn breaks, I stop at a point that leaves him breathless and yearning for more. And so the King spares my life for one more day, so that he might hear the rest of my dark tale.

As soon as I finish a story... I begin a new one... like the one that you, dear reader, have before you now.

Chapter One

"You fucking..." As the inmate on the other side of her office desk alternated spitting and swearing, Virginia Cunningham fought to keep the expression from her face. Her years as a social worker had given her a fair amount of experience, but the past two months of working in a prison were sorely testing her skills.

She flattened her trembling hands on the desktop and glanced around her claustrophobia-inducing cement box of an office. Since the sole window was in the door, she'd tried to create a more spacious feeling by hanging vibrant posters of the nearby Yosemite mountains. Her favorite was of a man climbing El Capitan. She could almost feel the strain in his muscles as he moved upward toward the peak.

If only she could give him a boost. But the determination on his face told her he'd make the summit all on his own.

Now, if she could only transmit some of his resolve to the inmates she counseled. So many had given up hope. Or, like Mr. Jorgensen, were so filled with anger there was room for nothing else.

"Mr. Jorgensen," she said quietly. "When you—"

His voice rose to drown her out. "And those mother-fucking, cocksuckers..."

Lordy. Sometimes her job was simply to listen, however they chose to speak. Sometimes inmates would talk to her goldfish, Chuck, who lived in a small bowl on the filing cabinet. After they relaxed, she could move into active therapy.

Unfortunately, Mr. Jorgensen's ranting hadn't helped him one bit, and she had a feeling he wouldn't depart politely.

Although he had no history of violence, she'd been warned not to take chances—as if seeing unrestrained inmates without a guard present wasn't already risky. But it was what it was. She pressed the intercom summoning the correctional officer.

When the CO entered her room, she rose. "Mr. Jorgenson, our time is up now."

The prisoner spat at her. "And those fucking bastards…"

"Please escort him out," she told the officer.

"C'mon, let's go, Jorgensen," he said.

The inmate jerked around and saw the CO. Obediently and quietly, he stomped from the room.

As the door closed behind them, Gin sank back, turning her chair to avoid seeing the puddles of spittle. Thankfully, her desk was quite wide.

In the past when working with children and families, she'd been cussed out, yelled at, insulted. Teenagers especially were adept at the scathing put-downs.

But never had anyone spit at her.

She pulled in slow, calming breaths, although each inhalation brought the stink of Mr. Jorgensen's sweat mixed with the harsh cleansers used by the inmate workers.

Dear heavens, she was not cut out to work as a prison social worker. She should have looked before leaping into the position. Desperation surely did sorry things to a body—and she'd been so frantic to get away from her ex-fiancé that she'd taken the most distant job she could find.

Well, mistakes happened. And, so she'd carry on—and do the very best she could for the souls entrusted to her.

"The day is over. And I'm so out of here." Penelope's voice drifted in from the reception area.

What an excellent idea.

Jorgenson's had been Gin's last session of the day. She pushed to her feet, ignored her wobbly knees, and shrugged into her black jacket. The garment was loose fitting, as were her baggy pants and oversized, button-up, white shirt. The last thing she wanted was for an inmate to see her as a female, although her ugly attire didn't seem to affect the number of catcalls and whistles.

After a quick pat to ensure she had her body alarm and keys, she walked out of her office into the gray reception area. Two other counselors were preparing to leave. Flouting the suggestions for feminine attire, Penelope's flaming red, skintight dress accented every curve. Bless her heart, the woman obviously didn't have any problem with getting hit on by the inmates.

Near the door, Howard Slidell was pulling on his coat.

Gin nodded politely at him, then smiled at Penelope. "I'll walk with y'all, if it's all right."

"Sure, Gin," Penelope said. "There's safety in numbers, right?"

"Not with animals like these," Howard said sourly.

Gin bit down on her response. The overweight social worker was one of the most intolerant people she'd ever met. In his mind, the inmates were irrevocably bad. Unredeemable. With such a biased point of view, how could he help them?

Then again, maybe he'd never experienced the joy of improving someone's life. Lord knew, it wasn't easy to do, not here, but the chance to make a difference was what had called her into counseling. That's what she did.

* * * *

An hour later, Gin pulled open the heavy door to the ClaimJumper Tavern. The loud country-western music echoing off the rough log walls knocked her back a step. At a high enough volume, Johnny Cash's gravel voice could abrade skin.

Walking into a bar without a date surely could make a girl feel awfully lonely, and Gin paused next to the wall-mounted antlers serving as a coat rack. Despite being a Thursday night, the place was packed. With the summer season beginning for Yosemite Valley and the surround, the population of loggers, fishermen, and locals swelled with the influx of seasonal help.

She looked around unhappily. Her favorite brown cords and slinky silver-blue top with the intricate side ruching were definitely too dressy for the jeans and flannel shirt crowd. *Oops.* A shopping trip needed to happen in her near future.

More people entered the bar and spurred her into movement despite her desire to linger by the wall.

"Gin! Over here!" In the far corner of the room, a tall, curvy redhead stood and waved. Two other women were seated at the square wooden table.

Spirits lifting, Gin crossed the room, careful of the uneven floor in her high-heeled leather boots. Each breath brought her the scents of perfume and popcorn, beer and sweat, damp clothes and cologne.

"Gin, I'm so glad you came." Becca moved her hand in an all-encompassing circle. "Virginia Cunningham, this is Summer Aragon and Kallie Masterson Hunt. Summer is a nurse at the Bear Flat clinic. Kallie and her family own a wilderness guide business."

The pretty blonde in a golden cashmere sweater beamed across the rustic plank table. Definitely a "Summer." "Welcome, Gin."

"It's nice to meet you." Kallie was petite with dark, dark brown eyes, choppy black hair, and wore a flannel shirt over a tank top. She motioned to the pitcher of beer and held up a glass. "Do you drink beer?"

"Thank you—and y'all are lifesavers." Gin hung her suede jacket over the back of the chair and settled in. She took the beer Kallie had poured and downed a third. Cold and malty. "This is *just* what I needed."

"Rough day at work?" Summer asked with unfeigned sympathy, every inch the nurse.

"Sugar, you have no idea." Gin rolled her eyes and grinned.

"What do you do?" Kallie asked.

"I'm a social worker."

"With the county home health agency?" Summer asked, eyebrows pulling together. "Or do you have your own practice?"

"No." Longing for her old clinic made her swallow. "I work at the prison."

"Wow, I can't even imagine," Becca said.

"I've only been there about two months. It's very different from what I'm used to." Some of her associates had gone into prison counseling, so she'd thought she'd enjoy the challenge. Wrong. She stared into her glass, watching the bubbles rise to the surface. She'd dreamed of a fresh beginning, a brand-new life filled with rewarding work, a supportive community, and wonderful friends.

Instead, she'd been stunned silly by her job. And even worse, she missed her ex-fiancé, her friends, her city. In fact, she'd been more homesick than a child away at her first summer camp.

Moping around home and indulging in comfort food and old Western movies wasn't the way to start a new life.

After giving herself a good scolding, here she was, out having fun. *Gold star, Gin.* Happy noise surrounded her—laughter, clinking glasses, Alan Jackson singing *Good Time*, the popcorn popping. She smiled at the others. "I'm really glad y'all let me join you."

"Here, girl, have some essential salt and grease." Becca slid a plate of French fries over. "So what happened today?"

"Well, first there was a prisoner who...well, he feels so guilty about hurting a friend"—*about being the cause of his friend's death*—"that he's almost suicidal." And having Howard Slidell as his counselor in the past sure hadn't helped.

Could she pull him out of it?

She would. She had to.

"The next one"—she made a face—"he didn't want counseling as much as he wanted to...um, play with himself. In my office."

The shocked expressions of the others made her grin. "Then came the guy who was spitting and yelling at me through the entire session. His list of sexual endeavors was extensive, but I do believe some are not physically possible."

Kallie was giggling, Becca laughing outright.

Summer's smile faded. "Virgil—my husband is a police lieutenant—said a prisoner was murdered. Shanked?"

Gin's hands tensed on her mug. "It was *horrible*. The guard, I mean the *correctional officer*"—she needed to be better about remembering the correct title—"said an old con had sharpened a toothbrush handle and stabbed a new inmate." Gin took a deep drink. The young man had done cleaning and always had a polite word for her. And now he was gone.

"Oh, that's brutal." Summer patted her hand.

Kallie frowned. "Bet the warden's catching some grief over the death. People weren't happy when the state built the prison out here. They were worried about escapees and all that."

"No doubt. Although, the facility is awfully isolated," Gin said. "Have you been on the road to it? All those steep curves? I almost wet my pants the first time I drove it."

Becca laughed. "You should see the road to our lodge. And wait until it snows."

"I am so screwed," Gin moaned. "I don't know how to do snow. The highest peak in Louisiana is the levee."

"*Ah ay-im so sca-rewed,*" Kallie said. "I love your accent. And I'm being shallow, but you sound just like Scarlett O'Hara."

"I loved *Gone with the Wind* when I was little." Except the ending. Her smile flattened at the flash of memory. *Standing on the sidewalk as her father put his suitcase in the car. "B-but, Daddy, I'll try. I will. I'll do more…"* He hadn't stopped. Had driven away, just like Rhett.

"So you've been here only two months?" Summer asked.

"Mmmhmm. I might should have done more reading before I ran off to California."

"Hey, why ruin the joy of discovery?" Becca tilted her head. "But was there a reason you left too fast for due diligence?" Under Becca's genuine concern, the question didn't feel intrusive.

"My fiancé and I broke up. And I..." She'd hurt so badly and would have done anything to keep him. The realization had panicked her enough that she'd snapped up the most distant job offered. Possessing a California license from years ago let her start immediately. "I didn't want..."

"To ever see his face again?" Summer nodded. "I know the feeling."

"Men." Kallie refilled Gin's glass. "They can be such bastards."

"Dumb too. There are moments I'm not sure they're any smarter than stumps," Summer agreed.

"So true." Becca grinned. "Except for our husbands, who only occasionally descend to the maggot-IQ levels."

As alcohol buzzed through her veins, Gin realized she should have eaten before drinking. She grabbed a French fry. "Husbands, huh? So, you won't be out partying and picking up men?" *With me?* She didn't want another man, but how could she give up dancing?

And sex. Surely a girl could find a man who'd be a good lover without wanting anything more.

"You've never seen territorial men like ours." Becca grinned. "My husband would tan my ass if I tried."

"Uh-huh. Sure he would." Gin snorted.

"Oh, Logan has paddled my behind before," Becca said.

What...seriously? A thrill shot through her at the thought of *spanking.* Lord, have mercy, she'd certainly been reading too many erotic novels.

Becca waved her hand at the others. "Jake and Virgil would too if their ladies misbehaved."

"Becca." Summer frowned at Becca.

Kallie chimed in. "This isn't a topic for general conversation."

"Let me tell you how I met Gin." Becca grinned at her friends.

Gin choked on her beer. "No." But she was coughing too hard to be understood.

"It was in Pottery and Pages. Would you believe Mrs. Reed set up a

WHAT TO READ AFTER 50 SHADES display?" Becca nodded at her shocked friends. "Truth. Anyway, Gin had picked up a Lexi Blake/Shayla Black book, a Fiona Archer, and a J. Kenner."

Gin considered crawling under the table. True, she and Becca had hit it off, but still...she'd just met these others. Nice, normal women who lived in a small, small town. She was doomed. And her blush must be approaching crimson.

Summer shook her head. "Becca, you're embarrassing her. Did you mention we're into the same kink?"

"Of course... Oh God, I *didn't*." Becca turned to Gin. "You must think I outted your reading habits to the Christian ladies sewing circle, right?"

Gin managed to pull in a breath. "Uh, actually, yes."

Across the table, Kallie and Summer were giggling themselves stupid.

Kallie held up a hand. "None of us are, like, in the 24/7 lifestyle, but we do play. In fact, I'm leading a wilderness tour this weekend for people wanting instruction about BDSM. My husband and his friend are teaching it."

Beer. Drink some beer. Gin took such a big gulp that she choked. Again. Her face not only felt hot, but now her whole body had entered the sauna. "Wait," she said hoarsely. "You mean the romances are for real? BDSM is real?"

Becca's eyebrows lifted quizzically. "Well, yes."

Oh. My. Stars. "My ex-fiancé said the stories were just hot fantasies made up to sell books." People really did that stuff? Gin leaned forward to whisper to Kallie, "And you take people and teach them how?"

Kallie tilted her head. "Mmmhmm."

Wow. Wow, wow, wow. "I never thought..." Her insides were quivering. Fantasies couldn't truly exist in physical form...right?

"You know," Kallie said slowly, a slight smile on her lips, "I could use assistance with camp chores. You want to come and see?"

She shouldn't. *Bad, bad idea.* "Yes." The excitement racing through Gin's veins made her body shake...until her common sense resurfaced. "Uh, maybe. Can I simply watch and see what's what?"

"That's all that will happen. The guests are all couples—and monogamous. You couldn't play even if you wanted to." Kallie grinned. "You in?"

It was real. The craving to see for herself was too overwhelming to be put aside. "Yes. Please. I'm in."

Chapter Two

In the twilight, Atticus Ware finished rubbing down Festus. He turned the buckskin into a roughly constructed corral with the Mastersons' pack animals.

A long stretch eased the ache in his shoulders, and a slow breath cleared the shadows from his mind. Sometimes even a small mountain town like Bear Flat contained too much civilization. At intervals, he needed to escape, to inhale the crisp, clean air, to hear the thud of horse's hooves on a dirt trail, to watch an eagle soar over the evergreen forest. Nature kept his spirit whole, no matter how depressing the world he worked in became.

A job in law enforcement could be fucking grim.

A scent drifted to him, and his eyebrows went up. Was that bread baking? Here? There was no oven available.

As he crossed the mountain meadow, he noticed new green sprouts were poking up through the dead brown grass. A gurgling stream crossed through the valley, under a split-rail fence, then behind the row of one-room log cabins. Just past the cabins was the roof-only "pavilion," holding the bricked-in grill on the left, a fire pit in the center, and several rustic picnic tables. Two outhouses hid in the trees.

Everything looked good. The Hunts and Mastersons had done a fine job turning Maud's Creek meadow into a permanent spring camp. And it worked extremely well for BDSM classes.

On Friday—yesterday—Jake and Kallie Hunt had brought their students up; last night, the new Doms should have received their first lessons. Tonight, Atticus would take the couples further into the lifestyle.

Nothing was as fun as teaching bondage. And, despite the still chilly evenings, the fire pit should give off enough heat to let them have fun.

He dumped his sleeping roll and saddlebags in an empty cabin and strolled toward the pavilion. With any luck, coffee might still be on the fire. Damned if he couldn't use some. Although this was his day off, a massive car accident in the early hours had all hands on deck, even a detective.

His mouth twisted. Ugly scene. Flashing lights, blood black on the pavement, twisted wreckage. All because some asshole decided his manhood might take a hit if he admitted to being too intoxicated to drive.

Struck a little close to home, dammit, because he'd kept envisioning his brother as the belligerent drunk and their friend Ezra as the white-sheeted body on the ground.

Sadness moved through him. He missed them both. Ezra had grown up on the neighboring Idaho ranch, one year younger than Atticus, two years older than Sawyer. The three had run wild as youngsters, until Atticus had been forced to grow up early. But once Sawyer had reached high school, they'd all fought together, rode rodeo together, even scored women together.

Now Ezra was dead, and Sawyer was deteriorating in prison with a DUI manslaughter conviction.

Idaho seemed very far away.

"You all right, Atticus?" Jake Hunt called from the pavilion.

He blinked and shook himself. Staring like a statue at the bubbling creek. *Dumbass.* "Just moving slow."

As he stepped under the pavilion roof, he glanced at the fire pit. It was already giving off a good amount of heat, as was the grill. "How many people am I teaching tonight?" he asked Jake.

Jake Hunt and his brother owned a forest lodge catering to alternative lifestyles, including BDSM. Partnered with the Mastersons' wilderness guides—one of whom was Jake's wife—they occasionally conducted instructional camping trips. "Only three couples, all married. A great group."

"Good enough. They ready for bondage?"

"They're looking forward to tonight." Jake tossed a steak on the grill. "I tried to find you a decent partner, but the submissive already had plans."

"Jesus, Hunt, I told you I'd find my own subs. Is *butt out* not in your vocabulary?"

"Nope." Jake grinned, then sobered. "Logan and I are damn well going to find you some better submissives since you don't seem capable of doing it yourself."

"Butt out, Hunt." He'd heard that married women often set up their girlfriends, but matchmaking wasn't a word that should be used in the male zone. *Ever.* "Got any coffee?"

"Should be some left." Jake nodded to an old-fashioned percolator on the grill and returned to tending the sizzling steaks. In the ashes to one side, foil-wrapped potatoes formed silvery mounds. More coals buried a Dutch oven.

Atticus sniffed. Fuck, that smelled fine. "Did Kallie make bread somehow?"

"Not a chance." Kallie approached from the rear. The tough, little black-eyed brunette—like a Hindu version of Tinker Bell—hugged him firmly. "Good to see you, Atticus."

"And you, half-pint," he said, just to rile her some.

She hated being called short, and her fist hit his belly with a solid thump.

Enjoying her, he gave an exaggerated grunt of pain and bent over holding his stomach.

She laughed.

A low giggle came from someone else.

Straightening, Atticus saw a woman next to Kallie. About five-five. Gorgeous green eyes held flecks the same golden-brown as the freckles sprinkling her cheeks. A long braid of dark auburn hair rested on one softly curved breast.

Very, very nice.

Her gaze fell in a beautifully unconscious display of submission.

"Hi there." He waited to smile until she looked at him again.

Red touched her pale skin. "Hello."

"Virginia, this is Atticus," Kallie said. "He's the bondage instructor tonight."

"Virginia." Atticus held his hand out.

"It's *Gin*, please. A pleasure to make your acquaintance." Her slow, liquid drawl made him think of mint juleps and mansions. She gave him a crooked smile, the right side higher, creating a tiny dimple at the corner of her mouth.

"Same here." Her delicate fingers were decorated in a subtle silvery blue. Did she wear matching undies under her dark blue jeans—ironed, no less—and a form-fitting green thermal Henley? He'd bet the brand-new clothes were bought just for this trip.

Why did he find that charming?

Didn't matter, since she wasn't available to play. The only women here had come with their partners, and he wasn't a man who poached.

Gin's heart beat disconcertingly fast as the man studied her with intent gray-blue eyes.

After a second, she realized he still held her hand, and she jerked hers away, then flushed. *Smooth, Gin.* But the way he'd touched her… Could a man express sexual interest by holding a woman's hand? Without moving?

But his hand had been warm, the palm and fingers extremely hard and callused. And big too. Wasn't it strange how when his hand had engulfed hers, she'd felt safe?

He was over six feet tall, and the battered cowboy hat added more inches. Some men wore hats to cover up baldness, but his thick brown hair reached past his collar. His face was angular, his nose long, and a neatly trimmed beard accented the square strength of his jaw. He could have stepped from one of the cowboy movies she loved.

The men who'd tamed the west wouldn't have any trouble taming a woman…and neither would this one. A shiver ran through her.

His eyes narrowed. "Are you cold, sweetheart?" he asked softly, his voice low and rough.

Like she'd admit he'd made her shiver? "Yes."

"Virginia." His disapproving expression made her stomach plummet. "First lesson for tonight: be honest. Even—and especially—when the answer makes you uncomfortable."

Her mouth dropped open. "B-but, I'm not—"

"I know you're not my submissive to correct, but I'm an instructor. Both your Dom and I must be able to trust you to tell the truth. Alright, pet?"

"Yes. Of course." She took a step back. "But I—"

His eyes, stern and intent, zinged every thought from her head. "No buts."

"I… Would y'all kindly excuse me? I need to make the salad." She walked with dignity to the cooking table, knowing she was totally fleeing. But why? Over the years, she'd managed the criminally insane, convicts. *Teenagers* even. And now she ran from a perfectly normal man?

Only he wasn't normal at all. He was...unsettling.

Off to one side, Kallie had her hands over her mouth, smothering laughter. And Jake was grinning. *Well, honestly.* Couldn't they have corrected the man? Gin shot them a scowl, which made Kallie laugh louder.

As she chopped vegetables, she tried to concentrate. Except...he was watching her, that cowboy Dom. The feeling shivered over her skin and up her spine until she had to put the knife down before she took off a finger.

* * * *

With the supper cleanup finished, Gin perched on a picnic table in a shadowy corner, well away from the lanterns and firelight illuminating the rest of the pavilion. Well away from the heat of the fire pit too. The air held the tang of frost, and the table was cold under her bottom. Shivering, she pulled her knees against her chest and wrapped her arms around her legs.

Jake and Kallie had taken off to settle the horses for the night and enjoy time alone. Gin felt a bit envious of their open affection for each other. If Kallie was within reach, Jake had his arm around her. Kallie was more discreet, but she'd stand on tiptoe to plant a kiss on Jake's jaw and end up plastered against him as he took more. Maybe they'd been married a year and a half, but their honeymoon sure wasn't over. Lucky Kallie.

Near the fire pit, Atticus sat on top of a picnic table, well lit by the lanterns hanging from the rafters. His boots were planted on the bench, his forearms on his knees. His hat lay beside him, and he'd rolled up the sleeves of his flannel shirt. The three couples sat at an adjacent table.

"How did your practice sessions go after Jake's class last night?" he asked them.

Two couples professed themselves extremely pleased.

Natalie, the third submissive, wasn't as thrilled. "I wanted Pete to just...just take complete charge, but he kept stopping to ask if I liked each thing he tried." Her brows drew together. "I mean, I want him to care, but *not* to care."

From her perch off to one side, Gin played with her braid and considered. She'd had the same complaint about a couple of lovers. Wanted to kick them into gear and say, *take me already.*

"Domination is a balancing act, especially if you haven't worked with your partner before," Atticus said to the men, not singling out the unhappy Dom. "And with some timid submissives, checking-in isn't a bad idea. For the rest, make sure they know their safeword, and then the onus is on you to read their expressions, muscle tension, and breathing.

"I hear what you're saying"—Pete pulled at his blond mustache— "but I'm not sure I know what to look for."

"Fair enough. Let's have an assessment lesson before we start on bondage." Atticus raised his voice. "Jake?"

No answer.

After a brief wait, Atticus said in a dry voice, "Apparently they're...occupied."

The group laughed.

Atticus straightened, looking around. "Let's see..."

When his gaze hit Gin's, her table seemed to slide downward a couple of feet.

"Ah, Jake left me an assistant," he said. "Gin, come over here, please."

"What?" She shook her head. "No. I'm not supposed to be part of...of the lessons."

Atticus glanced at the others. "See how her arms tightened around her knees? I'd guess surprise and a little fear." His baritone voice lowered even further. "I need your help, Virginia."

"Shi-*sugar*," she said under her breath, realizing she didn't have much of a choice. Not and be polite. After all, Kallie had been generous enough to let her be part of the weekend. How could she tell the teacher no? Her reluctant feet carried her to the Dom.

Why did being rude seem like a worse offense than a nice, simple murder?

He held his hand out to her, waiting until she gave him hers. "Cold little fingers," he said to the others. "Is she chilled—in which case we need to warm her up—or is she frightened?"

Still holding her hand, he regarded her thoughtfully, his eyes dark in the flickering firelight.

She frowned at him.

"Easy, magnolia. I'm not going to ask for anything dire." Smiling slightly, he drew her up to sit beside him on the picnic tabletop. When he put his arm around her, the heat from his body felt like a blast furnace, and she couldn't help but lean into him.

"Got yourself chilled over there, didn't you?" He pulled her closer, his body all muscle against her side, and massaged her chilly hands.

She needed to make things clear. Somehow. "I'm not here to play."

"No problem, darlin'." The laugh lines beside his eyes deepened. "I'm just going to use your body for a bit—this won't be a real scene."

"Excuse me?" Her breathing went into its own hissy fit.

His lips quirked, and he lifted her chin with a finger. "Gin, these Doms need to see what I'm talking about. I need an assistant here. Can you help us out?"

Oh, his question was purely manipulative. She recognized the technique and still couldn't find it in herself to refuse. She nodded.

"You're a good sport. Thank you, sweetheart." When he smiled at her, her insides swirled right into a gooey mess.

"What do you need me to do?"

"I'm going to have my hands on you—above the waist only. Your only job is to keep your eyes shut and not talk unless I ask you a question. Can you do that for me?"

He'd touch her. Above the waist. Her breasts. To her dismay, her skin tightened as if her breasts were totally onboard with the idea. "Okay." She closed her eyes and braced herself.

"Her cheeks flushed when she thought about being touched," Atticus was saying to the others. She heard something slide on the table. Then he put a set of headphones on her, destroying her ability to hear him.

Her eyes popped open. "Wait."

Atticus grinned. Damn, the little subbie was cute. He'd been aware of her sitting over in the corner, all big eyes. Jake'd said she was a sweetheart, so Atticus had observed as she cooked, served, and waited on the group during supper, bustling about to ensure everyone was well fed. She'd beamed at their reaction to her food. The need to please was a bright light in her.

And now, although clearly uncomfortable, here she was...because he said he needed her.

He touched the corner of her eye to remind her of his order.

Her reluctance was obvious, but she closed her eyes.

"All right. Submissives, get rugs from the pile and spread them out on the far side of the fire pit. Then either sit or kneel over there and wait for us."

As the women left, Atticus turned to the Doms. "Gentlemen, tell me how you know Gin's not a happy camper now."

The men all studied the redhead.

"Her fingers are clamped on the table."

"Mouth is tight."

"Jaw too."

"Good," Atticus said. "Notice her shallow breathing as well. Let's upset her a bit more and give you a wider area to observe." He unbuttoned her fluffy cardigan, then the light shirt beneath it. Inch by inch, he drew both garments down her arms and off.

She was as fair as the snow-tipped mountains, and he'd been right—her lacy bra was a silvery blue. After a second of appreciation, he got himself back on task. "See her struggle to keep her eyes closed. How she swallows because the worry has dried her mouth." He tipped her chin up with two fingers and pressed his fingertips lightly on the side of her neck. Fuck, she had soft skin.

"You can touch your submissive's throat here to check her pulse. Another location is here." He flattened a palm over her sternum...above her breasts since he didn't want to send her into cardiac arrest.

"Virginia's heart is hammering, by the way."

Grins appeared.

"Obviously we have a scared little submissive here." He waited a few seconds to let the men grasp the lesson. "Let's see if I can calm her down." He put an arm around her, drew her to his chest so she could absorb his warmth and feel his even breathing.

She was definitely a tempting armful. The way she struggled to obey his orders, despite her nervousness and newness, tugged at every dominant instinct he possessed.

After he moved her braid out of his way, he ran his right palm up and down her back in long, slow strokes. Nudging her headphone top aside, he rested his cheek on top of her head. She had silky hair.

"See how her breathing slows? The positioning of her hands?" Her small fingers were curled over his left forearm. Despite her nerves, she was holding on to him.

He gave her hand a reassuring squeeze and, with surprising reluctance, released her to sit alone. "Isn't it cute how her shoulders straighten as she braces for what I do next?"

He checked his audience. The Doms were leaning forward attentively, which boded well for their own submissives. Atticus glanced toward the fire pit. On their rugs, the women talked quietly. Good.

He turned his attention back to the Doms. "Before, during, and after a scene, what you need to watch is...everything. Skin color—and not just in her face. Breathing. Observe the muscles in her arms and shoulders and belly. Especially check her hands." He paused. "Each submissive is different. Do any of you play poker?"

Nods from all three men.

"This is the same as reading your opponent's tells. Actually, what you learn here will serve you well in poker." He grinned and brushed a finger over her chin.

A tiny wrinkle appeared between her brows. She gave a small shrug as if to dislodge an annoying insect.

"Now, did you see the little line that said she was worried?"

Two nodded. One had missed it.

Atticus tapped her lips this time, and the line reappeared. Then he rubbed his knuckles across her cheek, reassuring her again. "See which way her head tilts? Does her body move toward me or away? Is she welcoming my touch?"

Atticus pulled his hand away, and Gin tipped her face ever so slightly toward him.

"Damn, the reaction is subtle, but it's there," Ralph muttered.

"These are the types of clues you study during a scene. Again, each submissive is different." Atticus flattened his hand on Gin's stomach, enjoying the slight roundness, even as the muscles beneath flinched. "See the reaction. I'd call that surprise at an unexpected touch."

He didn't move, letting the heat of his palm reassure her. "And again, she relaxes back into me. Check her eyes, her mouth. See how her muscles have softened, her fingers opened."

She was damn pleasing to watch.

"Now, I hate to do this, but..." He gave her stomach a light, stinging pinch and pointed out her gasp. How her lips pressed together again, the worried line between her brows. "Her shoulders are knotted now."

A brush of his finger had her belly muscles flinching, had her whole body swaying infinitesimally away. "See how she flinches from my touch now? She doesn't like being pinched."

"Neither would my wife," Ralph muttered to general agreement.

"When it comes to inflicting pain, even if for pleasure, you'll need to acquire more assessment skills," Atticus told the Doms. "But for this evening's rope play, you've got what you'll need. And you'll get better with practice."

He pulled Gin back into his arms, partly to reassure her, partly for his own enjoyment. "Any time you're unsure of what your submissive is feeling, step back and study her. She's under your control; she's not going anywhere. Take your time and read her body language." Atticus grinned. "And know that an intense scrutiny will increase her excitement more than you thought possible."

All three Doms wore thoughtful expressions.

"Dismissed. Hydrate your submissives and take them for a bathroom break. When you come back, we'll begin the bondage portion of the evening."

As they left, he regarded his little armful. He pulled her headphones off. "You can open your eyes, Virginia." Her preferred "Gin" suited her personality, but he liked how her full name rolled off his tongue when he wanted her attention.

She blinked and tipped her head up. Her pupils were dilated in the darkness, turning her eyes a deeper green. Her gaze wandered over his face, then she gave her head a shake and looked around. When she noted the absence of students, she asked, "Are you done with me?"

Not even close. "Thank you for being an excellent assistant." He kissed her lightly.

Soft body, soft lips, generous spirit. And she had a worried line between her brows again.

"I'm sorry I had to pinch you," he said.

"It wasn't a problem." Her hand flattened on his chest as if to shove him away, but she didn't. And her next inhalation was deeper. Liked touching him, did she?

"You're welcome to stay for the bondage part of the class." He smiled slightly. "Jake and Kallie will be back to help which means you can just watch."

Her eyes lit up. "Wonderful. I've always wanted to"—she caught herself—"to *see* what it looked like." Flushing, she jumped down, grabbed her clothes, and started back toward her corner.

"Virginia."

She pulled on her shirt first, then turned.

He pointed to a picnic table beside the fire pit, but out of the way. "Sit there. The corner is too cold for you."

Wordlessly, she stared at him, mouth open. "I... Well, thank you."

As she obeyed, he frowned. He'd been giving her orders; a new one shouldn't startle her. Surely, she wasn't surprised that he'd noticed she was chilled.

* * * *

"They all did well," Atticus told Kallie later.

Two of the couples were enjoying the more...intimate...finales to their scenes. The third, more inhibited, couple had retreated to their cabin for privacy.

The bondage lesson had gone well. Each new Dom had secured his submissive as instructed, each had been careful to keep the ropes snug, but not overly constrictive. Then Atticus had taught predicament bondage, and the submissives had been whimpering delightfully within five minutes.

"Nice class," Kallie said. "I love the either-or bondage you came up with. At the same time, I hope Jake never tries it on me."

Atticus grinned. Tonight's setup would let the submissive bend to ease the pull on her nipple clamps, but that movement would tighten and drag the rope positioned directly over her clit. There was nothing like giving a submissive a choice between two evils. After a couple of minutes, she'd have shed the day's worries and would be focused totally on the two uncomfortable choices.

Speaking of submissives, one had disappeared. "Where's our little redhead?"

"Gin?" Kallie nodded toward the two couples. "She didn't want to be a voyeur."

"Ah. How did she happen to join us this weekend?"

"She was curious about BDSM. So in return for assisting me with camp chores, she got a chance to watch the lessons."

"No Dom or boyfriend to bring?"

"From what she said, I think she's unattached," Kallie said.

Excellent. It had been a long time since anyone intrigued him as much as the little redhead did. He'd enjoyed flustering her. He'd like to do more. To arouse her. To see what it would take before she lost control. Her lovely drawl said she grew up in the Deep South. Would she have the inhibitions that came with being raised in the Bible Belt? Overcoming those would be a fun challenge.

He fucking loved reducing a female to the point where she thought of nothing except what he was doing to her. He asked, "She only wanted to watch? She's that new?"

"She'd never even met a Dom before. In fact, she thought the BDSM fiction she read was invented to sell books. You can't get much newer."

"Mmm." A newbie. He usually avoided them, but hell, he was an instructor. It would be a shame not to provide some…education. "You mind if I yank her out of her cabin and see if she wants some hands-on participation?"

"Atticus, I don't want you scaring her." Kallie frowned before her lips curved into a smile. "But if you can lure her into enjoying BDSM, well, she'd be a great addition to our gang."

"Far be it from me to deprive you of a new buddy. I'll see what I can do."

In her cabin, Gin heard the laughter from the pavilion.

What a weekend. Last night, Jake had taught the new Doms how to dominate their women. And despite hearing him explain exactly how to make a woman submit, she'd still found watching to be incredibly hot. And had longed to be one of the submissives.

Tonight…well, tonight had been even more fascinating. Even more disconcerting.

Atticus had taught the Doms how to choose rope, how to ensure the safety of the submissive, how to turn simple knots into restraints. Then the two experienced Doms had helped the beginners tie their women in different ways.

Gin had found her breath coming faster. Just from watching. The mere idea of giving a man so much control over her was terrifying. And so, so sexy.

Now she'd added in the memories of Atticus touching her. Every place his fingers had brushed still tingled—her cheek, above her breasts, her neck, her stomach. His hand had felt huge when he'd flattened it over her belly, and when he'd embraced her, the warmth of his body had sunk right into her bones.

His easy voice had held an underlying steely command. And with each order, her attention had narrowed to a pinpoint focus.

How had he made her obey so quickly?

She chewed on her lip and considered the squareness of his shoulders, the straightness of his back, the way he held his head. Ex-military, she'd bet, and he'd commanded others. He wore authority as easily as his hat.

He was definitely a Dom. And according to those BDSM books, she was certain she'd be considered submissive. He'd surely treated her as if he thought so.

Her response to his confident control didn't rest too easily in her memory. After she'd planted her butt on the picnic table, she'd obeyed him without thinking. Following his orders had felt good and as natural as...

As if she was a square peg, and after years of being surrounded by round slots, she'd found a square slot. It had her name on it and fit her perfectly. That there was purely worrisome.

She had also noted that the word *submissive* wasn't nearly as appealing as *dominant*.

But Kallie was submissive. Yesterday, bless her heart, she'd gone from obeying Jake to tossing out orders when setting up camp. Anyone calling Kallie a pushover would find her fist in his tummy.

Gin grinned at the thought.

These people certainly lived in an interesting world. But no need to worry herself about the lifestyle. She'd only ventured here to get her questions answered, and she'd achieved her goal.

Now she'd enjoy a quiet evening in a mountain cabin, snuggled down in a warm bed with a new novel. That was romantic enough for her.

She picked up her book—a Civil War romance. In the beginning, the heroine possessed a satisfying personality, but two chapters in, she'd descended into wimpdom. The girl needed a good kick in the posterior or, as the inmates said—*to grow a pair.*

Poor southern belle. Truly, in the south, females had a tough time acquiring big brass balls. Mama had emphasized appearance over aptitude, courtesy over competence. Gin had been able to do flawless makeup, hair, and nails, dress attractively, and graciously hostess a dinner party, all before she reached eleven. And then her father had walked out.

Life had become difficult. In addition to the financial woes, she'd had to tend to Mama, who went through men faster than Sherman burned through Georgia.

But she'd also discovered the rewards of standing on her own two feet. Maybe she lacked big brass balls, but she'd learned independence and acquired courage the size of...oh...marbles.

Unfortunately, her bravery hadn't survived Atticus. Being studied by that Dom with the steely blue eyes was awfully intimidating. And hot.

Yesterday, Penelope noticed a big brute of an inmate and said, "I'd do him in a heartbeat." Gin felt the same way about Atticus, and wasn't that a sorry thing to know about herself?

Pfft. Enough. She turned her gaze back to her reading.

A chapter later, the heroine had rediscovered her backbone, when approaching footsteps caught Gin's attention. The steps changed to thuds as the person crossed the tiny porch. *Her* porch.

There was a tap on the door. Before she could answer, Atticus stepped into the cabin.

"What are—" Gin tossed her book aside. "I do believe you're in the wrong cabin. This one is mine."

"I know, darlin'," he said. "I came to find you." His gaze swept over her, making her all too aware of the lowness of her décolletage. "Gorgeous nightie, pet, but you quit the evening a little early, didn't you?"

"It seemed appropriate when everyone grew…occupied."

As he crossed the room, everything about him was cowboy sexy. Those long legs, battered boots, black hat, and bucking-horse belt buckle.

He went down on his haunches beside the bed, putting their eyes at the same level, then took her hand. "Listen, *Gin.*" He grinned, his white teeth framed by the dark brown beard. "Isn't that a harsh-sounding word for such a pretty woman?"

Oh, he shouldn't smile at her. It was too distracting. And he'd called her pretty.

"Gin," he said again. "You wanted to learn about BDSM. Came all the way here. True?"

Under his penetrating gaze, her chest turned as shivery as if she were inhaling tiny bubbles with each breath. *Stop melting and think.* She put a chill into her voice to remind him of proper decorum—which didn't include cabin visits to a woman in her nightwear. "It may be true, but I do not believe my interests are your concern."

An unexpected dimple appeared on his right cheek above his beard. "If you want to freeze me out, that accent of yours ruins the effect. It's like listening to warm honey."

She gave an exasperated sniff and tried to free her hand. "Go on back to your students, please."

"All done with them. They're Jake's now," he said. "The way I see it, I owe you a class for helping me earlier. Let's go to the pavilion where you'll have some backup, and I'll give you a taste of what you missed."

"No." The word jumped right out, but…lacked any conviction whatsoever.

And oh, he could tell. He didn't move. Didn't speak. His intent blue gaze stayed on her face.

She mustn't. Shouldn't. Actual participation would be insane. Stupid. Foolhardy.

But he'd said they'd go to the pavilion. Kallie'd rescue her if needed. Kallie and Jake might be friends with Atticus, but neither would permit anything abusive.

She'd scolded the heroine in her book for cowardice. Was she any braver? If she wanted to learn about BDSM, what better opportunity would she have?

Only…he'd touch her.

How badly she wanted his hands on her was disconcerting. Her swallow was loud in the quiet cabin.

Amusement lit his eyes.

Despite her inner quivers, she gave him a nod.

"Let me hear a yes from you."

"Yes," she whispered.

"Atta-girl." His strong fingers rubbed warmth back into her palm. "I plan to do a bit of bondage." He paused, his gaze holding her. "I'll leave your clothing on—but might move it some."

She managed another nod.

"And then I'll use my hands on you. But nothing else, Virginia."

"Use my hands on you." Oh, my, yes. Heat rolled across her skin despite the chill in the cabin.

"I see you like the idea."

How could she be so obvious? Yet he forestalled her sense of humiliation by squeezing her fingers and adding, "I like the idea too, pet."

She struggled to behave as if she wasn't a complete ninny. "Um. Should I have a safeword?"

His knuckles ran down her cheek, like the burning trail of a meteor. "Not this time, sweetheart. You'll have enough to think about without having to remember a word. *No* will mean no."

Would she even be able to speak if the Sahara Desert in her throat grew drier? "All right."

"Then we're good to go." He used her hand to tug her right out of the bed.

His gaze raked over her, from her breasts, which seemed woefully exposed by the form-fitting lace bodice, to where her nightie stopped at her upper thighs. Thank goodness she'd worn the matching lacy bikini panty.

"I like how the color matches your eyes."

The surprising compliment kept her from diving back under the covers.

Girl, pull it together. She was a tough, experienced social worker, not a historical romance heroine.

Before she could continue scolding herself, he slid his fingers behind her neck and gripped her hair, preventing her instinctive withdrawal. "Listen, Virginia. Every time your mind wanders from the here and now, I'm going to do something to drag it back."

She stared up at him, feeling his strong grip, the utter confidence in his deep voice. Seeing only the resolve in his blue eyes.

"Yeah." His lips curved. "Much better."

Before she could respond, he scooped her up into his arms.

"Oh my goodness, put me down." She punched at his arm, appalled, dizzy, terrified.

"I have you, sweetheart." He hadn't completely closed the cabin door, and he nudged it open with a boot and walked out into the dark night as if he was treading a well-lit hallway.

Kallie and Jake looked up as he entered the pavilion. The rest were *busy*. In the middle, Ralph had tied his wife to the picnic table and was teasing her with a vibrating toy. On the far side, Sylvia was tied forward over a post so her husband could take her from behind.

"Oh my stars." This was way, way, way more than the students had done last night. "Let me down," Gin demanded, even as her arms curled around Atticus's neck.

"Easy, baby." He turned so she got a far-too-good look at the activities. "Does anyone there appear worried about spectators?"

"I… They…"

He made a warning noise, as if to say, *look before you talk.*

One woman was giggling. And the second…climaxed then. Gin's cheeks heated. "I guess they're fine," she muttered.

With a masculine chuckle, Atticus rubbed his chin on top of her head.

Jake strolled over. "Found yourself a pretty play partner, I see." He gave an approving nod.

"More of a student," Atticus corrected. "She'll feel more at ease if you promise to keep an eye on her."

Jake's blue eyes—a shade less gray than Atticus's—softened. "We'll watch out for you, Gin," he said gently. "Being careful is good. Anytime you don't know the Dom, play where you have buddies around."

She nodded.

"Atticus, your bag's on the table there." Jake gestured to the other side of the fire pit. "Kallie thought you might return."

"Appreciate it," Atticus said. He carried her across the pavilion with a detour to avoid the older couple in the center. Ralph was alternating spanking with teasing his wife with a sex toy. Her cries coincided with the fleshy smacking sounds.

Don't look. Gin set her forehead against Atticus's shoulder and heard him laugh again.

At the picnic table, Atticus set Gin on her feet. "Stand right there, Virginia." Atticus's relaxed voice couldn't conceal the power beneath.

Gin's knees shook as she waited, and she couldn't tell if she were chilled...or scared. She knew darn well she was excited though.

How many times had she imagined herself in a book heroine's place? And here she stood.

Lord have mercy.

After laying the shaggy six-foot rug on the ground, he shrugged off his flannel shirt. The black T-shirt beneath stretched over contoured chest muscles and hugged his flat stomach in a way that made her mouth dry.

He opened his bag, draped a thick blue rope over his arm, and tucked blunt-tipped scissors in his jeans pocket. He studied her, standing close enough she could feel his body's heat. "Injuries? Medical problems? Any past circumstances or triggers that might make you panic?"

The questions were reassuring. He was being careful. "No. Only— you won't use a gag, will you?" Just the thought made her heart rate increase.

"Gags are for people who know each other," he said. "I need you to tell me if anything is painful or too frightening." He ran his finger over her lips. "The *ropes* shouldn't hurt you, babe."

Her next breath came a little easier...until her mind focused on the slight emphasis he'd given "the ropes." Would something else hurt? She held back her question. The Doms in her books required their submissives stay quiet.

Annoying Atticus might not be a smart idea.

He was still standing there. Watching her. When her eyes lifted to his, he gave a nod, as if satisfied, then walked around her. Touching her. Running a hand down her bare arm. Across her lower back. Moving her hair to fall down her back. He stroked down her spine, as if assessing her vertebrae. His fingers massaged her left shoulder, then the right.

His hand was warm and callused. Firm.

"You're a beautiful woman, Virginia." He unbuttoned her nightie, letting it hang open. "I'm going to tie a modified karada—a rope web for the torso."

Her hands closed into fists as she kept herself from moving. She was still covered, she reminded herself. The silky material caught on her peaked nipples, making her think of the old question, *Are you cold or glad to see me?*

She had an uncomfortable feeling that Atticus already knew the answer.

He draped the rope behind her neck, the ends dangling in front. Slowly, but without hesitation, he began to weave the rope around her, above her breasts, below her breasts.

With the first knot, she tensed. He stopped. His gaze on her was steady, revealing no irritation or impatience. Jake and Kallie liked him, she could tell. She'd seen him work with the other people here and how he emphasized safety and honest communication. Everything about the man said he was in control. He wasn't a little boy—he was a man, an honorable one.

"We'll stop if you need to, but you can trust me, baby," he said quietly.

"I know. I do."

The appreciation in his gaze said he knew she'd offered him a gift. "Thank you, sweetling."

She felt slight tugs as he created a series of diamond-like patterns down the center of her body. Gradually a latticework of rope snugly formed around her torso, and the sensation of being enclosed was oddly comforting. Back when she'd worked with children, some of the autistic ones could be settled by firmly wrapping a blanket around them, as if the sensation of being hugged would subdue their nerves so they could process the world's input more normally.

This was...nice. Under the slight scrape of the ropes and the sure movements of Atticus's hands, she felt her pulse slow. He never left her, always kept a hand on her somewhere, as if she might float away if he let her go.

"You take rope well." He grasped her upper arms. "I want you on the ground now."

She started to reach for him for balance...and couldn't. While she'd been daydreaming, he'd bound her arms. Tipping her head to examine her left arm, she saw an enthralling gridwork running from her wrist to over her elbow, like a woven sheath, all attached to the blue ropes patterning her torso.

Wiggling, she tried to move her arms out, and nothing budged. Her heart rate kicked up a beat and increased exponentially as she struggled. She couldn't *move*

A strong hand closed on her shoulder. "Easy, Virginia, easy. Look at me now."

Her breathing felt too fast, but she was fine. Wasn't panicking or anything. Much. It was just...she couldn't move.

He cupped her chin and got right into her space, his blue eyes trapping hers. "Take a slow breath, babe. Another." His voice was easy and low, like the rumble of thunder in the distance.

She inhaled.

"Good. You knew this was what was going to happen. This isn't scary—you're just surprised at the feeling, I know. Very normal." He was close enough she inhaled his crisp pine scent with each breath.

"I'm all right," she decided after a minute.

"Of course you are," he said. He bent and kissed her gently. "Mmm, nice." He took her lips again—longer, but still lightly, leaving her wanting more.

What would it feel like if he really kissed her?

"Now, let's try this again."

As she bent her knees, he scooped her up and squatted down to lay her on her back.

Oh, boy. The blue rug was fluffy-soft, the ground hard beneath it. She wiggled. The knowledge she'd have trouble rising with her arms pinned to her sides was a bit worrisome.

"You look gorgeous in rope." Still on one knee, Atticus rested his forearms on his thigh. His gaze was warm, approval gentling his lean features.

She managed a smile. "It's kind of nice. So is this it?" Would he release her now, having given her the "taste" he'd talked about? She wasn't sure if she was disappointed or relieved.

"'Fraid I have more in mind." He pulled another rope from his bag, this one a dark red.

"More?"

"It would be a shame to leave half your body without decoration." With competent fingers, he created an amazing ropework of knots running down her left leg, then lifted her knee and secured her ankle to the blue rope around her hips. He repeated the process on her right leg.

Flat on her back, knees bent, feet widely separated. The provocative posture seemed as if she were waiting for a guy to settle over her. Another flush ran over her skin. Thank goodness, she still had her nightie and panty on.

"Better." He surveyed his work, and a dimple dented his right cheek before he tugged on her baby doll top. Under the ropes, the silky material slid apart as he bared her breasts completely.

"Wait—" She moved to pull her nightie shut, and the ground fell away beneath her as she realized she couldn't. Couldn't prevent anything he wanted to do.

And anyone could see her. "They'll—" Her voice died away. He'd positioned her behind a picnic table, which partially blocked any view of them.

"Figured you might be a tad modest, especially coming from the Bible Belt." He rubbed his knuckles over her cheek. Still on one knee, he loomed over her, darkness behind him, firelight flickering over his tanned face. His cheekbones were high—his features sharply chiseled.

There was nothing soft about the man. He exuded a dominance that said things would go his way and all the control was in his hands.

"But hiding behind a table is all the modesty I will allow you," he said in an even voice, holding her gaze with his. And then he traced along the rope covering her chest.

"Atticus," she gasped. Her breasts swelled, and the nipples puckered to jutting points in the cool air.

His finger never stopped as it followed the ropes above her bared breasts and then below.

"Now, darlin', you stay silent unless you really have to talk," he murmured. He wet his fingertip and circled one nipple, the cooling wetness making it harden further.

Her toes curled under and a throbbing started between her legs. She realized she was extremely damp down below.

He stretched out beside her, propped up on one elbow. His free hand gently molded her right breast while his thumbnail scraped over the nipple.

She gasped as the exquisite abrasion shot straight to her clit.

"Nice." He bent and nuzzled her cheek, his beard soft against her skin. And then he claimed her mouth, his firm lips taking charge. Surprised, she resisted for a second, then her lips parted, opening to him. His tongue swept inside. Deliberately, he explored her mouth in a long, drugging kiss. His hand continued to stroke her breast.

Her body craved more. As she wiggled, wanting to touch him, she realized again she couldn't move. Couldn't fend him off if she needed. He could do...anything to her.

More heat shot through her, and a moan escaped.

"Mmmhmm. The southern magnolia likes bondage."

No. Surely not. But truth was truth. She'd never—ever—been so aroused. Thank goodness she still wore her bikini panty.

Only as he lifted his head, he ran his hand down her bare stomach and under the tiny excuse for coverage.

Oh my stars. She gave a cry—half protest, half desire.

He paused. Waited.

She should object. Nothing came out.

The sun lines beside his eyes crinkled...and he continued. When his fingertip grazed her clit, her hips jerked.

"Atticus," she whispered.

One side of his mouth tilted up. "What did I tell you about talking?" His voice held both laughter and sternness. And without warning, he stroked right over her clit, his fingers slick and hot and firm.

Her cry drowned out the crackle of the fire.

"Mmmhmm." He sounded as if he were taking notes, although his intent gaze contained enough heat to warm her skin. His finger teased her, up and around the increasingly swollen and sensitive nub. As if he had all the time in the world, he simply...played. Circles and taps, firm rubs, light caresses.

And each touch sent pleasure lancing across her nerves until need vibrated through her system.

Then he moved his hand away.

Her whine of protest made him smile.

"Soon, sweetling. First, let's find out how you feel about pain."

She stiffened, a tremor of anxiety running up her spine.

"Not to worry," he said with a huff of laughter. "I'm not a sadist. But pain can be a rewarding tool if used right." His hand stroked up her stomach, palmed a breast, and plucked at her nipple. This time the sizzle was stronger, as if her awakened lower half was unable to fend off the urgent call for sex. After teasing both nipples, he rolled one between his fingers.

Heavens above, the feeling... His fingers were warm, scratchy, and created a disconcertingly pleasurable pressure. Her eyes closed as her back arched upward.

"Look at me, Virginia."

Half dazed with sensation, she opened her eyes.

He trapped her eyes, held them, as his pinch compressed and the overwhelming pleasure edged into pain. Everything inside her turned liquid.

Sweat broke out on her skin as her legs trembled.

"Oh yeah, baby," he said softly. "You're fun to play with." He released her nipple and even as the blood rushed back in with a wave of heat, his attention turned to the other.

Pleasure, pain. The entire pavilion seemed to shake with her growing need.

Before she could recover, he lowered his head. His tongue trailed over her throbbing breasts before he sucked on one nipple.

His fingers trapped her clit. A light pinch there shocked her and her hips jerked upward.

He stroked the sensitive nub, working one side, then the other, and she swelled, tightened.

Each touch, each sucking tug on her breast, drowned her in sensation. Her body gathered, the pressure coiling deep inside. *Wait. Here. No.* And then the inexorable orgasm rolled over her, shook her loose from her mooring, and propelled her straight out to sea.

Nice. Atticus set his hand over the little submissive's pussy—playing fair by keeping his fingers on the outside—but he could feel her cunt spasming. Under his palm, her jutting clit was softening. She'd grown even wetter.

Fuck, she came beautifully, and he damn well wanted to send her over again.

However, he'd pushed her enough for one night, even though he'd given her opportunities to quit if needed. She had been a bit unnerved near the end—but her body had won out over her mind.

He loved when that happened.

As he withdrew his touch, she made tiny enjoyable whimpers, then opened her eyes, still looking dazed.

He held her gaze and put his slick fingers in his mouth. Luscious honey, much like her voice. "Mmm."

A second later, she understood what he was doing and an adorable redness rolled from her breasts up into her face.

Would she turn that same embarrassed color if he licked the taste straight from the source? If so, he'd have to make sure her hands were tied so he could enjoy himself at leisure.

When the last of the treat was gone, he ran his wet fingers over her rosy nipples, enjoying the way they pointed again. Yep, arousable more than once. A man would be able to take her over and over. Make her come her head off.

There was more than one kind of sadism, after all.

But not tonight, unfortunately.

"Let's get you out of these ropes, sweetheart." He unknotted the ties from her hips down. Sure, he could have cut through them, but...hey, he wanted the excuse to run his hands over her some more. Soft and fragrant, enticingly rounded, with skin like the smoothest of satins.

Been a long time since a submissive delighted him so well.

Her voice had gone husky, but the liquid smoothness was still there as she said, "Um, thank you, but this was awfully one-sided. I mean..."

Oh, he knew exactly what she meant. His cock throbbed as if it wanted to burst its own restraints. "This night was for you, Virginia." He rolled up the rope and tossed it onto his bag. Gently, he straightened her legs, massaging her hips and knees, hearing the cute suppressed mewls of enjoyment she made. Inhibited and yet not. Interesting contradiction.

"But..."

He stood her on her feet so he could undo the rope around her waist and breasts. "BDSM is a give and take sort of play, but doesn't have to happen all at once. There are some times I take and take and take." Not many, he'd realized after Jake and Logan had pointed out what an idiot he was. "Sometimes I give. And sometimes it's both."

As he tugged at the knots, his knuckles brushed over her breasts. So fucking soft.

"But you must be, um, hurting."

Wasn't she a generous little cutie? "Yep, but I'll survive. Was worth it to see you enjoy yourself." After unwinding the rope from her waist, he tossed it onto his bag with the other to be cleaned later. Cupping her cheek, he kissed her lightly. "You've been a good girl. Why don't I get you a glass of wine while we watch the others finish up?"

Chapter Three

She couldn't believe how much the temperature could drop in these California mountains. When she'd left her cabin this morning, there'd been a frosty haze on the meadow grasses. Gin shivered and stood closer to the bricked-in grill as she stirred the gravy.

Only the clients were still in bed. An hour ago—sometime near dawn—Jake had lit a fire, so Gin could cook over evenly hot coals. The biscuits in the Dutch oven should be done soon.

Kallie'd made the coffee, and Atticus had gone to feed the pack animals.

Unable to resist, Gin checked out the corral. Again.

The Dom was simply heart stopping. His sheepskin jacket made his shoulders even broader. His jeans snugged over a really fine ass. Ignoring the food and water, the horses crowded around him, wanting his attention.

He gave it in full measure just as he had with the students last night. Why did his unstinting generosity make her go all gooey inside?

As the fragrance of bacon rose in the air, Gin popped a crispy strip into her mouth. *Yum*. Everything tasted better in the mountains.

So...was the great outdoors why her orgasm last night had been off the charts?

Or was it because she'd been tied up?

Or because the person who'd wrapped her up like a macramé project was a drool-worthy hunk? An experienced, forceful Dom?

Or all the above?

Her lips curved. Perhaps, she should research the subject, since—hey, every female in the world wanted to know the answer. She'd start with sex in the wilderness without bondage, and advance to non-wilderness sex with bondage. Either way, she didn't see a downside.

As for the drool-worthy hunk—and powerful Dom, well… Gin shook her head. Finding comparable subjects might be difficult.

After her "lesson," Atticus had ignored her excuses, put his fleece-lined flannel shirt on her, and they'd joined the group around the fire. Classes over, the students and instructors were all having a good time. Atticus had served her a glass of wine and kept a comforting arm around her. Whenever she'd look up, his gaze had been on her. Studying her. Oh, she knew from her romance books he was just being a good— would he be called a *top?*—and performing *aftercare* stuff and making sure she wouldn't have a bad reaction.

Yet, the way he paid attention when she spoke, how he'd attended to her needs and cared for her, had made her feel important. Beautiful and intelligent.

Worthy.

Later, he'd walked her to her cabin and…*mmmhmm*…pressed her against the door and devoured her mouth until she was weak-kneed. To her regret, he'd steered her into the cabin and bid her good night as if they'd been on a perfectly ordinary date.

This morning, she'd given herself a talking to about how one-night stands—one-night *scenes?*—were not to be taken seriously.

Whatever the phrasing, *one night* was the operative term she'd told herself sternly.

And then she'd seen the remnant of a rope mark on her ankle, and her panties had dampened as if she'd devoured an entire erotic romance. One perfectly good scolding totally wasted. She wasn't listening to herself at all.

"Those biscuits smell fantastic." Kallie walked over to steal a piece of bacon. "You can ride trail with me any time you want." With a quick grin, she strolled out to the cabins and yelled, "Five minutes to breakfast."

Gin blinked. The woman had a shout rivaling a prison guards'.

The doors banged as people emerged.

A few minutes later, Gin put a giant bowl of scrambled eggs on the table.

Atticus patted the empty seat beside him, so, feeling like a starstruck teenager, she joined him. In the morning sunlight, his eyes were bluer than blue, and his beard was dark against his tan skin, giving him the appearance of a pirate.

He smiled, tugged a loose strand of hair, and released her from the bondage of his gaze.

Conversation was drowned out by the clatter of utensils as the crowd helped themselves. As people dug in, silence ensued.

"I haven't had biscuits and gravy like this since I left home," Atticus said eventually, juggling his second biscuit.

The mere sound of his deep, rough voice sent her heart into a set of flip-flops.

"You're a fucking fine cook, Gin." His praise and the chorus of agreement warmed Gin better than any sweater.

Even as she smiled her thanks, she studied Atticus. In the daylight, he seemed oddly familiar, as if she'd seen him before…although no woman in the world would forget meeting him. Then again, Bear Flat was so small she might have caught sight of him in the grocery or something.

"Gin, I think you have a volunteer to help with the leftovers." Jake motioned toward something behind Gin.

She turned to see a black dog with sorrowful brown eyes sitting at the edge of the pavilion. A big Labrador, with every rib showing. She could see the hunger—and hope—in its eyes. "Oh, the poor baby. He's starving."

Kallie frowned. "Isn't that old Cecil's new bird dog? Um…Trigger?"

"You think?" Jake studied the animal. "You figure no one picked him up when the old guy died?"

"Cecil didn't have family," Kallie pointed out. She started to rise.

"I'll do it. I've got some food here," Gin said. She crumbled a biscuit into the empty egg bowl and poured some bacon grease over it.

"Gin," Ralph said. "Be careful. The beast looks dangerous."

No, he just looked hungry.

Before she was halfway across the pavilion, Atticus had joined her. She eyed him.

"Just in case, sweetheart. The guy's been on his own for a while."

"I'll be fine." Yet, having someone looking after her was comforting. And unfamiliar.

Atticus stood silently as she knelt a few feet from the dog. "Hey, buddy, would you like some breakfast too?" she asked quietly. With the bowl beside her, she reached out her hand.

The dog stood quickly, and she held her breath. What if he did attack? But then he padded forward, neck extended to sniff her fingers. After a second, she was able to stroke his head, ruffle his fur.

"Oh honeyboy, look at you," she crooned. "No one's been caring for you, have they?" She nudged the bowl forward. "Time for breakfast, boy."

The Lab began to lower his head, then waited, gaze on Atticus.

"Go on, buddy. Help yourself," he said.

And exactly like Gin last night, the dog obeyed the big Dom.

After watching for a minute, Gin let Atticus pull her to her feet. They returned to the table.

"No, we can't take him in," Jake was saying to Kallie. "Thor won't share territory with another male dog. We're lucky he made an exception for your cat."

Kallie *pffted*. "Mufasa would have clawed his face off."

"Like owner, like cat," Atticus said and winked at Kallie.

As everyone laughed, Kallie rolled her eyes. "Anyone up for taking in a dog?"

The guests shook their heads, offering excuses ranging from no-pet condos to allergies to a houseful of cats.

"How about you, Atticus?" Jake asked.

"Not a good time. Lost my old hound last month; I'm not ready for another yet." Atticus looked away.

Bless his heart, he'd loved his pet, hadn't he? Gin squeezed his arm in sympathy.

His gaze settled on her, and a dimple appeared. "When I grew up, the last person to speak got stuck with the chores. Looks like you won yourself a dog, darlin'."

"*What?* No. No, no." She drew herself up. "You're very funny, but I can't—" Her mind spun, trying to think of why she couldn't.

His grin was drop-dead devastating, darn the man. "Got other pets? Kids? Family? Allergies? No-pet living quarters?"

The little mountain town had very few apartments, and she'd ended up renting an actual house. She thought frantically for a minute and reluctantly answered, "No."

When he ran a finger over her lower lip, heat touched his eyes, then disappeared as he said, "Cute pout, sweetling."

Bite him. Show the dog how it's done.

Atticus's grin widened as if he could hear her thoughts. He tapped her lip lightly before removing his hand to safety.

Darn.

"You like dogs, sweetling. He likes you too." He jerked his chin to the right.

She turned.

The Labrador sat behind her, looking ever so obedient. His brown eyes held a hope she couldn't rebuff.

"I think you've been claimed." Atticus put his hand over hers. "He needs someone—and nothing is as straightforward as the love a dog can offer."

Gin had always wanted a dog, but her mother hadn't allowed any animals; a strand of animal hair might mar Mama's perfection. Preston had refused to consider pets—he hadn't wanted to share her with anyone or anything.

When younger, she'd visit her pet-blessed friends and discovered that purring cats and wiggling dogs were more addictive than any drug.

A bubble of anticipation rose. Her gaze slid to the Lab. "Trigger? You want to come home with me?"

He licked her hand.

"Fuck, that was too easy," Atticus muttered to Kallie. "She's a pushover."

Grinning, Kallie winked at Gin and changed the conversation to the day's plans and the route they'd take back to the wilderness tour headquarters.

"So I simply...take him home?" Gin whispered to Atticus.

"That's right, baby." He rested a hand on her shoulder, his blue eyes tender. "Take him home. Feed him. Walk him. Love him."

Atticus smiled down at the little submissive. Her face showed everything she felt, and the wonder there was that of an orphan seeing Christmas tree lights for the first time. She could break a man's heart.

He wanted to spend some time with her, and the fact she'd sat beside him pleased the fuck out of him. Unlike some awkward post-scene mornings, he was enjoying the woman's company.

Despite her clothes. Seriously, who wore gorgeous lingerie in a log cabin? And designer jeans and an expensive, curve-fitting sweater in the wilderness? Over it, she was wearing his flannel shirt from last night—and damned if he didn't like that.

High-maintenance women were usually piss-poor company. But...this one was a mass of contradictions. She wore no makeup.

Although she'd pulled her hair back in some fancy braid on both sides of her head, the rest tumbled down her back freely. And she didn't fidget with it. Her only jewelry was a necklace with a golden pendant: *"If you can imagine it, you can achieve it. If you can dream it, you can become it."*

She was a romantic. And she was going to adopt a bony Labrador. Yeah, he wanted to get to know her better.

Although the fact that Jake would approve was annoying as hell.

With a couple of bites, Atticus finished off his biscuit and grabbed another before Jake could get there.

At Jake's low curse, Gin giggled.

Atticus turned to her. "Thanks for making my kind of food. When I helped at one of Kallie's gourmet camp cooking weekends, I swear, the chef taught people to make a salad of two lettuce leaves topped with something gooey and a single raspberry. Jesus."

She wrinkled her nose. "No gourmet from me. I'm all about southern comfort food."

"Works for me," Jake said, joining in. "I hope you come on more trips. We could expand our menus."

"I'd like to join you again," Gin said. "I love cooking for others."

Jake glanced at Atticus. "See? She has the attitude you should search for."

Atticus stiffened. "Don't recall asking for your opinion."

The Hunt brothers could be as tenacious as wolves on carrion, and Jake ignored him to say, "Those 'do me' submissives you pick up aren't worth the time."

"What's a 'do me' submissive?" Ralph asked, keeping the annoying topic going.

Jake smirked at Atticus. "Much as there are Doms who are only interested in getting *serviced*"—he added air quotes around the word—"there are selfish submissives who care only about getting their needs met. They want to be taken under command for a scene, to get their rocks off…so to speak…and then they're done. In a good relationship, each party—whether Dom or sub—has as much desire to please the other as to receive."

The guy from San Francisco nodded his understanding. "That selfish attitude is found in vanilla relationships, too." The man kissed his wife's hand. "Before Sylvia, I might not have understood what a difference a generous heart can make."

Atticus glanced down at Gin.

She was listening with interest, although he doubted she fully understood.

"The Dom/sub dynamic can confuse people. Sometimes it's difficult to sort out what's going on," Kallie said to the guy, then turned to Atticus. "For example, *you* have a super-take-charge and protective side that disguises your over-the-top need to make your subs happy."

"Interesting. Super-take-charge and a need to please. I bet you were the oldest." Gin tilted her head. "And maybe you needed to take on adult status before your childhood peer group did?"

Atticus stared at her, brows drawing together. "Where the hell are you coming up with that?"

"Gin's a social worker at the prison." Kallie added for Gin, "Atticus works with Summer's husband at the police department."

A social worker? Like edged steel, the words sliced into his brain. He couldn't move for a second. Sawyer'd mentioned last week that his counselor was a pretty Southerner.

Counseling, my ass. Last winter had revealed to him the truth of prison "counseling." It'd been in the prison reception room. Sawyer had his elbows on the steel table, his shoulders hunched like an old man, as if each day drained more of his endurance. After the so-called therapy had started, he'd almost stopped talking. Unable to tolerate the silence, Atticus had to fill in with talk about his week.

When he'd complained about a perp arrested for the third time, his brother had muttered, "*He's a total fuckup. Like me.*"

"*Bullshit.*"

"*Fuck, Att, even my therapist says I'm not worth the food I eat. The air I breathe. That I'm a waste of skin.*"

Their stepfather'd tried to convince Sawyer he was worthless. This counselor had damn well finished the job. *Damn her.* She'd appeared so softhearted; seems her generosity didn't extend to convicts.

As the students' conversation drifted to overcrowded California prisons, Atticus turned to Gin and lowered his voice. "You like working with inmates?"

"Not as much as I thought I would." His frozen voice and expression must have registered. Her head tilted. "Even though you're in law enforcement, you have a problem with people who work in prisons?"

No. He had a problem with shrinks in general, like the one who'd medicated a teammate into a coma, the one who'd let his stepfather loose after his so-called "therapy," and definitely this one in particular. "Yeah."

She flinched.

He wanted to apologize...until he remembered his brother's spiral into hopelessness. *God, Sawyer, fight it.* Frustration chilled his voice even further. "Yeah, I do."

Her expression went blank, and she bent to pet the dog.

Unaware of the discussion, Jake was refilling coffee cups. "Atticus, did Kallie give you an invite to the party in a couple weeks? Some of the Dark Haven members from San Francisco plan to come. And guests are welcome." Jake glanced at Gin and raised his brows.

No fucking way. "I'll be working." Whatever night it was.

Chapter Four

"Sawyer, I want you to think about what I said. Be ready to talk about your thoughts next time." The prison social worker waited for him to respond.

Sawyer Ware scowled. What the hell did the woman want anyway? He'd fucked up his life—nothing new there—and his screw-up had killed his best friend. He didn't need counseling to acknowledge his guilt and to know he wasn't worth shit.

Never had been; never would be. His abusive asshole of a stepfather had made that clear. If he hadn't learned the lesson, Mr. Dickwad Slidell had ground it in further. The counselor had told him repeatedly he deserved to be in prison, shouldn't be alive, should have died in the crash instead of Ezra.

His nightmares said the same. Night after night. Sawyer would hear his best friend yell, would jerk his attention back to the dark highway, squint into the glaring oncoming lights. Wrong lane. Rip the wheel to the right—overreacting. Car fishtailing, tires screeching, losing traction. At the edge, the tires caught only gravel, lost traction. The car slid right off the road—and rolled down the steep mountainside.

The memory had his fingers clamping onto the chair arms. *Why couldn't it have been me who died?* Every minute he lived was a minute Ezra should have had.

He shoved up out of his seat.

The pretty counselor watched him with concern. "Sawyer—"

"Done here."

Where Slidell hadn't hesitated to tell him he deserved every moment of misery, this one worried about him. She'd even asked if he'd considered suicide. He'd thought about it, truth be told. There was no way he could pay back what he'd done, although, at one time, he'd had a forlorn hope of doing something to settle up. But now…exerting the effort to off himself would take more energy than he could summon.

Slidell was a shit therapist, but at least the bastard hadn't nagged at him for answers. This one wanted too badly to help him.

On the plus side, Ms. Virginia was nicer. Smelled better. And her slow, southern drawl was soft on the ears. Yet, as he nodded to her, he realized how far gone he was. Even after this long in prison, a curvy female rang no bells.

After regarding him steadily, Ms. Virginia rose. "All right." He vaguely remembered how she'd set out her guidelines…including saying if he needed a session to stop, he could tell her. Considering how Shit-for-Brains Slidell had kept him there no matter what, always hammering at him, Sawyer did appreciate the chance to escape.

Escape, hell. There was no escape. Not for him.

As the correctional officer fell into step to escort him back to his cell, Sawyer felt as if he were walking through sludge, through a world of shadows and despair.

Gin chewed on her lower lip as she watched Sawyer Ware depart. His self-hatred had him mired so deep he wasn't seeing any light. His previous caseworker had made it worse.

Howard Slidell. Bless his heart, the counselor himself needed therapy. He had some serious issues. Maybe making his caseload feel guilty was effective with some, but inmates like Sawyer already had enough guilt to drown them.

Ex-military, suffering from PTSD, he'd not adapted back to civilian life well, then he and his best friend had overindulged and the friend had died. Sawyer'd barely missed felony charges, but, as if to compensate, the judge had given him the middle sentence of two years in a state prison.

Unlike many inmates, Sawyer felt as if he deserved incarceration and anything worse the world could throw at him.

If only she could get through to the man. His despair was tangible…and worsening. He sure wasn't listening to anything she said. Maybe because she was female; maybe because she'd never been to war.

Who knew?

She frowned. Who else might have an impact on him? Did he have family she could call in for a session? Or maybe a friend?

The mental health secretary could do some research and find someone since there'd undoubtedly be paperwork Gin didn't know how to do. The warden was a bit of a slacker, but the California Department of Corrections & Rehabilitation did like its regulations and rules.

Typing quickly, she sent the secretary an e-mail with the request. If having a family member in didn't work, she'd figure out something else.

Giving up wasn't in the job description.

Truly, these inmates were quite a test of her skills—some had diagnoses she'd only seen in textbooks—but she'd always liked challenges.

But this might not be the best place for her. She could now see that her years working with adolescents might have had a greater impact on them than she'd realized. Her inmates were showing her how a youthful intervention might have set them straight and kept them out of prison.

She wanted to go back to that. And, oh, she really did miss working with children.

Then again, some guys here could simply break her heart. Like Sawyer Ware. She wanted to scold him like a big sister, to ask him, "What were you thinking?" then slap him upside the head and tell him to get over it.

He needed help so badly—and she would *darn well* get through to him somehow—yet, true healing would have to come from within him.

Just like she had to bring about her own cures.

Homesick? She was pretty well past that.

Lovelorn? She studied her hands, watching how they flattened on the desktop. At least the BDSM weekend had given a fast shove to getting her over her ex-fiancé.

Lonely? Well, in only three days, Trigger had relieved much of the loneliness, which had been the main reason she'd missed Preston. Her lips quirked.

Sad to say, the dog was far better company.

If only Trigger didn't remind her of Atticus. If only she could stop dreaming about the sexy, commanding Dom and that amazing night of stars and crisp mountain air, of wood smoke and his piercingly blue eyes. Of rough rope and her inability to move away from hard hands intent on giving her pleasure.

If only that night hadn't been followed by a morning of harsh words and open dislike.

When she'd talked with Kallie and Becca on Monday, she'd told them how much she'd enjoyed the BDSM lessons. She'd spoken the honest truth. Thank goodness they were still new friends or she wouldn't have managed to dodge their questions about Atticus.

She shook her head. Watching Westerns made a girl believe that the heroic cowboy was supposed to fall head over heels in love, win the heroine, and ride off with her into the sunset.

Instead, her big cowboy had got shed of her like he'd discovered a booger on his boot. So much for romantic tales.

At least she wouldn't have to see him again. Considering his antipathy to prisons, Dom Atticus Whoever probably avoided this facility like the plague.

Chapter Five

One week later, seated behind her sterile steel desk, Gin watched Sawyer walk into her office. She could swear he moved slower each week, as if every movement and thought was being dragged out of a hole.

With a grunt, he sank down into the facing seat and frowned. "What's with the extra chair?"

"You noticed. That's something, at least."

A tap on the door caught her attention. Gin looked up and felt as if she'd run smack into a tree trunk. "You," she breathed.

"Gin." Atticus stood in the door, and her world shifted sideways as his steely blue eyes met hers.

What in the name of heaven was he doing here? In her office? Where she worked? Trying to hide her reaction, she clasped her hands on the desktop.

He still looked at her as if she'd killed his prize horse or something.

Her anger sparked to life like a misfiring Bic lighter.

"Excuse me, but I'm in the middle of a session." She had to be pleased that her voice remained even.

"I'm aware," he said politely. "But the e-mail you sent indicated this time and this room."

E-mail. The secretary had arranged for Sawyer's brother to attend the session today. "You're... You're not brothers."

"Yep." His voice sounded like an iced-over gravel road. "Atticus *Ware.*" Without waiting for her invitation, he hooked the empty chair with his boot, moving it so he could sit beside his...brother?

Seriously? But now she saw the similarities between the two men. Atticus had collarbone length, dark brown hair; Sawyer's was the same color, clipped short. The dark blue eyes were the same, as were the strong jawlines and long noses. Sawyer had more bulk in the shoulders, Atticus was slighter taller and leaner and far more tanned.

They were *brothers*. No wonder Atticus had looked familiar.

After a second, she realized he hadn't been surprised to see her today. Not in the least. She straightened. "You *knew*. You knew that morning that I'd been assigned to your brother."

She had a mind to throw her chair at him, the good-for-nothing snake.

"Sawyer mentioned his therapist was from the south," Atticus answered curtly.

Humiliation washed through her, heating her anger further. She'd trusted him to tie her up. He'd touched her intimately, given her an orgasm. They'd shared something. But because she worked in a prison, he thought she was scum.

Even worse, he hadn't explained who he was. "You didn't think I should know you were Sawyer's brother?" Her voice came out as sharp as the shards of betrayal ripping through her.

"Nope." His unrelenting gaze stayed on her as he settled himself with his long legs extended.

When Sawyer snorted, she glanced at him. *Hmm...* Rather than his usual slumping posture, he'd tilted back in his chair, legs stretched out in front of him like Atticus's. He was watching the...show. Nothing before had caught his interest. She'd even gone back and reviewed security tapes to see if anything had ever roused the man.

But now...

"Well, then, let's begin." She gave Atticus a stony look and folded her hands on the desk. "I've worked with Sawyer for a few weeks and—"

Atticus straightened. "You mean months."

"No. I mean weeks. I've only been in California for about two months now."

Atticus's eyes narrowed as if he thought she was lying. Slowly, the animosity disappeared from his face. "Hell," he muttered, rubbing his hand over his beard.

She remembered the feel of his beard and how... She gave her head a shake. The past was over. And she didn't give a flying hoot what the man thought.

He wasn't important and neither was she. Her concern was Sawyer. Soldiering on, she said in a cool tone, "Mr. Ware, I believe Sawyer feels condemned by everyone for what he did. He thinks he's hated by anyone who knew Ezra."

She set her emotions aside and opened herself to anything that might point her in the right direction. "Am I right, Sawyer?"

The animation faded from Sawyer's face, his shoulders slumped again, and he angled away from his brother.

It was like seeing someone die.

She turned to Atticus and saw shock and dismay on his face. Then his mouth compressed and raw anger lit his eyes.

He surged to his feet.

Oh hellfire, what had she done? "Atticus—"

His glance of warning seared the words from her throat. Seizing Sawyer's prison shirt, he leaned in to force a face-to-face confrontation. "You stupid dick."

Sawyer's face drained of color. He stared at his brother like a rabbit waiting to be slaughtered.

"You. Fucked. Up." Atticus shook him with each word.

Gin started to rise, then realized Atticus was in total control. All anger had disappeared, leaving only resolve behind.

Hurried footsteps came down the hall, and the door opened. Gin held up her hand to stop the guard. Someone must have heard the shouting.

"You were drunk. And stupid. And driving," Atticus grated out. "But Ezra's alcohol level was even higher. If he'd taken the wheel, he'd have been as messed up."

Sawyer's eyes were wide and alive with emotion. "I killed him," he said hoarsely.

"You made a choice. If you hadn't swerved off the road, a family would have died," Atticus said. "Remember what Mom said when we screwed up? 'Nobody escapes this life without making mistakes. Some of them will hurt others.'"

"Yeah." The single word was guttural and yet held a dawning hope.

"Yeah. After a screw-up, you fix everything you can, grab hold, and do better next time. That's the mission, bro." Using the shirt he'd fisted, Atticus thumped his brother against the back of the chair. "Am I clear?"

"Fucking Dom," Sawyer said under his breath.

"Am. I. Clear?"

Sawyer wrapped his fingers around his brother's hand, which still held his shirt, preventing another shaking. "Oorah, jarhead."

"So says the SEAL." The corner of Atticus's mouth tipped up. "For the record, asshole, I don't hate you; I love you. Don't forget it again."

He released his brother and straightened. He glanced at his empty chair and shoved it out of his way with his boot. The look he shot Gin was unreadable. "Interesting sessions you have, Gin. I'll be seeing you again."

Before she could respond, the door closed behind him.

See him again? The slimy dog had known she was Sawyer's counselor. Had thought she was incompetent. After pulling in a furious breath, Gin looked at Sawyer. And stilled.

He had tears in his eyes.

Okay. Okay. Even if she'd only managed to speak once and hadn't directed the long session she'd planned, Atticus had—had done the job.

Her brows drew together. How would she react if she believed someone had messed up her sister—if she had a sister? Considering how little Sawyer talked, maybe his brother hadn't known about the change in counselors.

Putting Atticus out of her mind, she sat back in her chair, eyes on Sawyer, and watched the intervention start to work.

Chapter Six

Spring was in the air. Friday had arrived, and Gin was free for the weekend. She rolled down her windows, letting the brisk mountain wind erase the pervasive stench of the prison.

For hours after she returned home, she could smell the place, as if every inhalation held the suppressed anger, despair, and hopelessness.

With a grunt of frustration, she kicked on her ride-the-roads playlist with Roger Miller's *King of the Road* and let the music flow around her.

Heavens, but this had been a nasty day. Sex offenders. Of all the inmates, she found them to be the worst. And the one she'd had in session today had shown no remorse at all. He didn't think he'd done anything wrong in raping a child.

It purely made her nauseous.

Trying to escape the feeling, she stomped the accelerator, whipping around the curves and glorying in how her low-slung car clung to the road.

As forest gave way to small farms, she slowed. Everywhere she looked was color. Vibrant spring-green grass had sprung up along the road shoulder. Leaves were filling in the deciduous trees. Tiny lupines created purple swaths across a pasture. Yellow flowers in the ditches were bright enough to rival the sun.

In town, a banner strung high across the intersection proclaimed: BEAR FLAT WILDFLOWER FESTIVAL. Below it, sawhorses blocked off Main Street.

Gin's mood lifted at the sight of colorful booths lining the street and on the boardwalk. A band at the end was playing a country-western tune of Willie Nelson's.

An SUV pulled away from the curb, the back filled with children who waved cheerfully at her. Laughing, she waved back and parked in their spot.

Once out of her car, she frowned down at her clothes. Since the recommended prison attire was "baggy," Kallie'd given her some of Jake's old sweaters. The oversized man's sweater she wore was perfect for the prison, but way too blah for a spring festival.

But if she wore only the tank beneath it, she'd freeze.

Hadn't she left something in the trunk?

She had. She peeled off Jake's sweater and donned the green, three-quarter sleeved cardigan. The open knit draped nicely around her. And surprise, she had a figure again.

After slinging her purse over one shoulder, she locked her car and headed toward the fun.

"Gin." Her name was called in a deep baritone voice. Atticus was exiting a Ford Taurus, which he'd parked in the street. In the very center.

Typical arrogant police officer, right? Even his walk was strong, almost predatory.

And yet…her body quickened at the sight of him. She sternly told it to behave. The man—even if he should be polite for a change—was Sawyer's brother and, by Department of Corrections' policy, off-limits to her.

Having watched Gin changing clothes, Atticus smothered a grin as he left his unmarked vehicle. Couldn't blame her for not wanting to look like a box—the recommended style for women entering a prison. He'd far rather see her in something that showed off her curvy figure and brightened her moss-green eyes.

He'd hoped to run into her.

Three days ago, she'd orchestrated the "intervention" which had turned his brother around. Because Sawyer was different. Sure, he wasn't back to the light-hearted, gung-ho person he'd been when they were growing up. But since his TOD in Afghanistan, he'd grown increasingly withdrawn.

He'd never gotten drunk though.

No, Ezra had been the one who'd enjoyed being blitzed. He'd

probably goaded Sawyer into going past his usual limits. Like Atticus, Sawyer didn't like giving up control to anyone or anything. He'd been a control freak even before the SEALS. After his discharge, he'd consumed even less.

Being the man he was, Sawyer would blame only himself.

And the canny counselor had figured it out in the few sessions she'd had with him. God knew, the asshole previous shrink hadn't managed dick.

Sawyer had been almost himself this morning. Had made a few jokes. Reminisced. Asked after their younger brother. Even mentioned that he was trying to figure out what he'd do when he got out in another year.

Atticus sighed. The little submissive counselor had done well, and he'd treated her like crap. Guilt was a lead weight in his gut. When people judged him by bad interactions they'd had with other cops, he considered them idiots. Look who held the idiot label now.

And even when he'd thought her an asshole shrink, he'd wanted her. Her body, and even more, her submission. Her trust. Her generous spirit. The sweetness in her that made her enjoy cooking for others. That made her feed a starving dog and give it a home.

But his behavior had burned his bridges with her. Just now, her eyes had lit up—and then turned blank. He'd probably taken up permanent residence on her assholes-of-the-world list.

She braced her feet and raised her sharp little chin. "Can I help you, Officer?"

"Not Officer. It's Detective," he said.

"What? Oh. Detective Ware. Right."

"And yes, you can help me by slowing down. You ran your ass through a speed trap halfway up the mountain."

The surprise in her eyes was delightful. Made him want to create it again when she was under his control in a scene. When she was naked and... *No.*

"I did?"

"Mmmhmm. I told the uniforms I'd take the responsibility of warning you." Damned if he knew why he'd volunteered. Damned if he knew why she was stuck in his brain.

"Oh. Um. Thank you."

"Your thanks can be observing the speed limit. The prison section of road is known for patches of ice. And for the number of people who've died. I don't want to be the one pulling your body from that

POS car of yours—because when it hits a tree, the frame will fold like an accordion." Like the last accident he'd seen. His gut knotted at the memory.

"I—" Her gaze took in his expression and her eyes turned soft. "I'm sorry, Atticus. I never thought about how horrible dealing with accidents must be for law enforcement. I'll be more careful."

Why did she have to be so likable? Tenderhearted? *Desirable?* "I'd appreciate it." He stepped closer.

She backed up. "Well. Excuse me then."

Atticus grinned as she walked away. The little magnolia couldn't quite manage to put a frost into her southern sweetness, could she?

As she disappeared into the festive crowd, he shook his head.

Diversion was done. Time to force his ass over to the climbing wall. The Search and Rescue guys had been surprised when Atticus volunteered to help out, since they'd seen his reaction to climbing higher than five or so feet.

But damned if he'd keep acting like a pussy. Only way to lose the fear would be to keep at it. Maybe today, he could haul his ass up higher—without a flashback. Without freezing or losing his lunch.

* * * *

An hour later, Gin had managed to stop thinking about Atticus…mostly. She'd scored sexy bookmarks from Pottery and Pages, had on a leather wristband from the camping store, and had munched Parmesan popcorn from the diner's booth. At the Hunts' Serenity Lodge table, she'd nibbled homemade brownies and won Becca as a companion when Jake shooed her off for a break.

As they strolled down the boardwalk, Gin smiled at the bright yellow daffodils filling the wooden barrels. Over her head, purple pansies spilled over the sides of hanging baskets.

A girl darted past, pigtails bouncing, her face decorated with stars and moons. Her little brother gave chase, his cheeks an adorable pink under yellow tiger stripes.

At their giggling and happy yells, Gin felt homesickness sweep over her. There was none of this joy inside a prison. How could she have known she'd miss having children around so, so much?

"I know you ate a brownie. But would you like some non-bazillion-calorie food?" Becca gestured to the barbeque at the volunteer firemen's booth.

Unfortunately, the scent of grilled meat reminded Gin of the camping trip. No, face it; everything these days reminded her of Atticus. Darn the cop for being the sexiest man she'd ever met. And she might have been able to put aside a simple physical attraction. But, his utter self-confidence—his power—attracted her like a lemming to a cliff.

And he was just as deadly.

"Sure, we can grab some food." Past the firemen's booth, a small crowd had gathered around a tall...thing. "What in the world is that?"

Becca followed her gaze. "A climbing wall. The Search and Rescue guys run it to raise money for their equipment. Logan might be there; he loves mountain stuff." Becca shook her head ruefully. "Me? I can't even cross a stream without spraining an ankle."

Gin eyed the twenty-five-foot monolith. Colorful handholds poked out everywhere as if it had contracted a disease. Amazing. "I've never seen one in real life. Can we go watch?"

"Sure." Becca led the way, skirting the crowd to come up on the side, almost at the base.

Perched on the wall, a little girl was reaching for a handhold.

Gin froze. "Oh my stars, she can't be more than ten. She's going to break her neck."

"You've got what Logan calls the 'mommy sees disasters' syndrome." Becca waggled her eyebrows.

"What?"

"A *worst case* imagination." She shook her finger at an imaginary child. "'If you run with a stick, you'll poke out your eye.' 'Slow down on those steps or you'll split your head open.' 'Don't eat too fast or you'll choke to death.'"

Gin's snickering disappeared when the girl on the wall climbed another foot. "We worry because those things happen." If the child hadn't been above Gin's reach, she'd snatch the girl down.

"In this case, no worries," Becca said. "With a safety harness on, she can't get hurt even if she jumped."

After studying all the ropes and gear, Gin started to relax until spotting Atticus Ware beside a man working the ropes.

Oh no. No, no. Seeing him once today was one time too many. She didn't like feeling all quivery inside; it surely wasn't healthy. Maybe she was allergic to him?

She dragged her gaze away and back to the contraption.

The little girl stretched toward a peg with her free hand. She couldn't quite reach it.

The audience yelled encouragement.

Her face crumbled when her fingers touched and slipped off the handhold. "I can't," she wailed. "I can't do it."

"You can." Atticus strolled closer and looked up. "Never limit yourself with a *can't* word." With appalling ease—and no harness—he climbed the wall, looking like the most devastatingly handsome Spiderman ever. Once at the girl's level, he secured himself with a hand on a peg and touched the child's cheek lightly. "Take a breath, baby."

Under his steady gaze, the girl did.

"That a girl." Atticus's low rumble barely reached Gin. "Look at the peg to the right of your foot. If you move there, you'll be able to reach the next handhold. And then you can figure out the rest."

Upper lip pulled between her teeth, the girl studied his solution. "I see it!" Eyes bright with delight, the girl shifted her weight, carefully gripped the peg Atticus had indicated, and then charged upward right to the top.

Cheering broke out.

Atticus had followed her for a few more pegs and then...stopped. Gin squinted at him. Was he sweating? His shoulder muscles looked bunched with tension; his fingers were white on the handholds.

Perhaps he was worried about the girl? Yet she'd already reached the top.

When she waved her little fist in victory, he grinned.

Gin's heart gave a wrenching tug. Why did seeing his open pleasure in the child's success make her want to laugh and cry and hug him? This man was something special.

Behind her came a high scream.

Startled, she spun around.

On the boardwalk, the preschooler with the tiger stripes had fallen. As blood ran down his knee, he wailed loudly. The little girl with him burst into tears of sympathy.

"The Bassinger kids." Becca said. "Their mother lets them run wild." She nudged the gawkers to one side and sailed through.

Gin followed. "I'll take the boy."

As Becca knelt beside the girl, Gin sat down next to the little boy. "Oh, honey, you've got yourself a boo-boo there, don't you?"

Without further invitation, he flung himself into her arms, almost knocking her over.

"Well, sugar." Half laughing, she set her purse down, snuggling and rearranging him on her lap. "Let's take a look then, honeyboy." Not more than a shallow abrasion, she decided. Pointing to the barrel of bottled waters, she lifted her voice to the surrounding people. "Will someone fetch me one of those, please."

A second later, she heard a bottle cracked open, and the chilled plastic was placed in her hand. "Thank you," she said without looking up.

A dowsing of water washed away the dirt from the scrape and made the little boy whine. His head stayed firmly buried against her shoulder.

As his skin dried, she used her free hand to dig in her purse. She hadn't removed her mini first aid packet from when she worked at the family clinic. There. A quick glance showed the options. "Honey, do you want a butterfly or a Transformer on your knee?"

The boy's head popped up. He solemnly studied the Band-Aids she held up. A shaky finger pointed to the Transformer.

"Excellent choice, darling." But she couldn't reach his knee with both hands. "Let's move you—"

His arms squeezed her waist. He wasn't going to budge, was he?

"Well, then..."

A low chuckle came from above her, and Atticus knelt beside them. "You look like you've been in a battle there, soldier," he said. "How about I cover your wounds up?"

A thumb in the mouth prevented any reply, but big eyes watched the cop as he plucked the Band-Aid from Gin's hand, tore it open, and applied it fast and easy. Only a little squirm showed the child had felt anything.

"Well, there, don't you look fine?" Gin kept her gaze on the Band-Aid, not on Atticus's lean fingers. Was the man good at everything? Ropes and orgasms...and Band-Aids. "Can you thank the detective?"

His *thank you* was garbled by the thumb still in his mouth.

"There's their mother." Becca set the girl down and pointed toward the grocery store.

"Mama!" The girl dashed across the street.

The boy scrambled up, almost tripped again, and followed his sister, all owies forgotten.

Grinning, Gin watched as the two barreled into their mother, almost spilling her sack of groceries. Shaking her head, the woman bent to examine the owie. She might not watch them as closely as she should, but there was love there.

"All fixed." Becca glanced at Atticus, then Gin. "I'm going to grab some barbecue. I'll get you some too, Gin." Without waiting, she headed across the street.

While Gin was still staring after her, Atticus smoothly rose to his feet. He grasped Gin's upper arms and pulled her up. "You did a nice job there, counselor. You're good with injured soldiers."

The compliment warmed her heart and left her at a loss for words. "Ah, thank you."

He regarded her thoughtfully, making her too, too aware of his size and the strength in the fingers still curled around her arms. He was holding her in place. The knowledge sent a shiver up her spine.

"Gin," he said softly. "Seems like we're not done with each other."

What? "But—yes, we are."

He touched her cheek, watching her intently. Could he see the way she melted inside?

He could. "Liar. I won't push you...here. But I'll be at Jake and Kallie's party tomorrow night."

When she couldn't manage more than a stare, she saw his smile, sharp as a scimitar. "That's an invitation to play, pet." He ran a finger down her cheek, then sauntered away toward the climbing wall.

After a second, Gin realized she was gulping breaths. She glanced around. Two teenage girls gave her envious stares before turning their attention back to Atticus.

Becca was in line by the firemen's grill and hadn't been watching.

Breathe slower, Gin. Most difficult to do. Because Atticus wanted her at a BDSM party. Because he'd said, "*I won't push you here,*" meaning he'd push her there.

If she went.

Going to the party would be a really stupid idea.

Not because he'd been a jerk. She'd already forgiven him. After all, he'd thought she was the incredibly incompetent Howard Slidell, who'd messed up Sawyer.

No. She shouldn't go because she shouldn't have anything to do with Sawyer's relative.

She stepped around a man who was encouraging his son to try the wall. Trying things was good.

Maybe not this party though.

Even if there were no ethical issues involved, she would hesitate. It was too easy for her to fall into defining herself by a man. Especially this man. The sexy Dom detective could take her over without even trying.

But...she honestly did want to learn more about the BDSM stuff, and opportunities in this area would be few and far between.

What would happen if she went to the event? She could do a scene or two. After all, playing with a Dom at a party wasn't like actually dating. Show up, do something together, leave the man where you found him.

Attending a BDSM event might be a bit like visiting a lending library of men. Borrow a guy for a limited time—a scene—and put him back for the next user.

But, Atticus would be available for other *borrowers*. Her gut gave a tiny clench. She'd have to watch him play with other women?

Yet, better she experience a little discomfort than get involved with him herself.

Okay then. She'd visit Jake and Kallie's lending library of Doms and do some sampling. But she'd leave the Atticus book sitting on the shelf.

Chapter Seven

This isn't a good idea, Gin. Truly not a good idea. Sure it was Saturday night—but she should have just stayed home. Gin followed Becca into the rustically decorated Serenity Lodge and up the flight of stairs to the private floor where Becca, Logan, and their baby lived.

"Kallie and Jake had the other half of the top story, but when they moved out, we remodeled," Becca said. "We expanded our living room, kept theirs as a playroom, and turned their bedroom into a nursery."

Women filled the living room, and Gin froze for a second, remembering every miserable moment of being the new girl in school. Her executive father had relocated the family three times. After he left, her mother had moved them another three—each time she hooked up with another man.

As a social worker, Gin was comfortable meeting new people. But being a new person in a circle of old friends wasn't exactly the same. *Just shoot me now.*

She summoned a pleasant expression and followed Becca.

"Hey, you made it!" To Gin's relief, Kallie was present. Seated on a lounge chair, the brunette waved. "I'm so glad. Virginia—known as Gin—meet Rona and Abby from San Francisco."

Abby had fluffy blonde hair and a flawlessly white complexion. The huge leather couch she occupied seemed to engulf her. She gave Gin a welcoming smile. "It's nice to meet you."

"Welcome," Rona called. She stood in front of the fireplace holding a black-haired baby a few months short of a year. A scarred-up German shepherd rested his weight against her legs.

"A *baby*." Delighted, Gin walked across the room.

The dog rose in warning.

Uh-oh. Gin stopped and held her hand out, wondering if her fingers would get nipped right off. "Hi there. May I have permission to visit the baby?"

"Thor, it's all right," Rona said.

The dog ignored Rona and sniffed Gin's fingers. Finally, its tail wafted back and forth. *Permission granted.*

"Thor, it's all right," Becca called belatedly. "Gin is a friend."

With a light whine, Thor sat back down.

Obviously Becca's dog. Gin studied the baby's black hair and blue eyes, then turned and asked Becca, "Is this *your* baby?"

"He's my munchkin, Ansel," Becca said, beaming. "Doesn't he look just like Jake and Logan? He's a Hunt male from head to toes."

"And he's a charmer." Rona motioned toward Becca. "Like his mother—*not* his father."

Although Becca laughed, Gin frowned. What did that mean? Was Logan nasty?

"Here, why don't you hold him?" Rona passed Ansel to Gin. "I need to finish dressing, and you look as if you could use a baby fix."

"Oh, there's never a question." Gin gathered the little boy closer.

Gurgling happily, Ansel bounced and reached for her loose hair.

How she'd missed holding babies. Gin kissed the top of his head, inhaling the baby powder fragrance. "Aren't you a little honey?"

Rona opened a jewelry case on the coffee table and pulled out earrings before glancing over. "That's not a Virginia accent I hear, is it?"

Gin pouted. She'd thought her accent was fading. "I was born there—hence my name—but grew up mostly in Georgia and South Carolina." Then Louisiana and Alabama after her father had walked out.

"Ouch." Rona reached over to pat her shoulder. "It's difficult to be moved around so much, isn't it?"

At the ready sympathy, Gin's last discomfort faded. She should have known that Becca would have nice friends.

"Here, I'll take the monster child while you get out of your coat." Kallie lifted Ansel and blew bubbles on his bared tummy, making him squeal with laughter.

Gin dragged off her knee-length coat and took the baby back. "Did the nasty woman call you a monster-baby? What was she thinking?"

The silence registered. She looked up. "What?"

All eyes were on her attire. Becca frowned.

Gin's heart sank. Well, spit. Even after days of trying to decide what to wear, she'd obviously picked wrong. But, how could she not? She owned clothes suitable for nightclubbing in a big city. But this party was going to be held in a barn. And yet, Kallie had said to wear something sexy.

Honestly—a barn?

Gin had managed fairly well, she'd thought. Her best lo-riders were paired with low-heeled boots—barn, right?—and a frilly, somewhat cowboyish, shirt.

Trying not to pout, she checked the women's attire. The corsets and bustiers showed off breasts. Kallie had on a short, short skirt; Becca's was ankle-length, but slit every few inches so ample amounts of skin teased the eyes. Rona wore fishnet stockings and a skintight, leather skirt that molded her ass.

Gin's gaze turned to Kallie. "I do believe our perception of what constitutes *sexy* must be worlds apart."

Every woman burst out laughing.

"Becca." A tall, black-haired man strolled in the room. "Are you ladies about ready to leave

At first, Gin thought he was Jake, but no… Jake was easy-going, his attitude relaxed. This man was the opposite. In fact, he could give the hard-faced inmates a run for their money in sheer intimidation. Surely this wasn't Becca's Logan.

As if in answer to Gin's concern, he curved his arm around Becca.

Becca was still frowning at Gin. "I'm going to need another fifteen minutes—someone needs better clothes."

"No," Gin protested. "I don't."

Ignoring her completely, Becca confided in her husband. "You know how much I love to dress people up."

A brief smile transformed Logan's face as he squeezed his wife. "Sugar, you must not have had enough dolls as a girl."

To Gin's dismay, he turned to look at her. His steel blue gaze did a slow head-to-foot of her clothing—and he was obviously unimpressed. He walked over. "Logan Hunt. And you're Virginia?"

"Um, yes. But it's Gin." Just being friendly, he was as terrifying as Atticus in a bad mood. She had to force herself to meet his gaze. "It's very nice to make your acquaintance." *Lie, lie, lie.*

He took his son, ignoring the tiny fist bouncing off his chest. "Your first BDSM party?"

Oh no, he wanted to talk? She gulped. "Aside from the camping trip, my first everything."

Not only did his face have scars, so did the powerful hands holding the baby. Yet, Ansel chortled and kicked with no fear of his father. "I heard you had an introduction to rope. Would you like me to set you up with Atticus again?"

"No!" When Logan's eyes narrowed, she realized she'd been overly emphatic. "It's really fun to meet new people."

"Is it now." His tone said he knew she was bullshitting him.

Lordy, Atticus should be his brother instead of Jake.

"Well, pet, since I'm one of those in charge of the party, why don't you tell me what you're looking for in a play session and—after Becca dresses you up—I'll help you find someone."

"I..." Talk about being put on the spot. Shi-*sugar.* "No rope."

"You didn't like being bound?"

Oh, but she so had. She could still feel how Atticus had trailed the ropes over her skin, his gaze watching as her whole body roused. The way he'd wound the strands around her, taking more of her will with each binding, returning pure sensation. She shivered.

An eyebrow went up, and Logan smiled slowly. "But not this time, I see. Perhaps something simple. Flogging?"

She shook her head.

"Spanking is about as basic as it gets."

Her cheeks turned flame-hot. Dear heavens, she didn't even know him, and he asked if she wanted to be spanked? Even worse, her thoughts had immediately gone to Atticus. Of being held... *Stop that.* "Um..."

Logan waited her out, second by second, until she nodded.

"It's a start. I'll help you negotiate a scene with someone." As he left the room without waiting for her answer, Gin gaped. His statement had sounded more like a threat than a promise.

Too late to go home. "Oh, dear," she said faintly and dropped down onto the couch next to Abby.

Abby took her cold hand. "I know how you feel. The first time I met Xavier, he told me he wanted my breasts and showed me what nipple clamps were all about."

Gin stared at her. "Seriously?"

"The funny thing was..." Abby tilted her head. "The clamps didn't fluster me nearly as much as my first experience with a Dominant."

Across the room, Rona was nodding. "Exactly. After talking with

Simon the first time, I almost tripped trying to retreat. Needing to get my head back on straight."

Gin felt the muscles in her shoulders relax. "I'm glad I'm not alone."

"Not even close." Abby patted her hand. "As for the clothes, Becca dressed me up the first time I came."

"Me too." Kallie grinned at Becca. "Besides, there'll be city submissives there, flaunting their fetwear at us backwoods types. We have to pull out the stops to keep up. So you can't let the home team down, right?"

"Well," Gin said. "When you put it like that..."

* * * *

Atticus had commandeered a corner of the barn to think and watch the BDSM scenes from a distance. Apparently, Gin wasn't going to take him up on his invitation. He hadn't wanted to pressure her after he'd been such an asshole, but maybe he should have tried harder. Dammit, every time he saw her, he wanted her more.

If he showed up at her house and asked her to accompany him here, would she shut the door in his face?

Undoubtedly.

Then again, nothing chanced, nothing won. The worst she could do would be say no.

Before he reached the door, he was intercepted.

"Atticus. It's good to see you again." One of Dark Haven's most powerful Doms was accompanied by another man.

"Simon. Did you bring your pretty wife?"

"Of course."

Of course would always be his answer, Atticus knew as they shook hands. Simon's love for his submissive was a legend among the Dark Haven people.

Simon motioned to the man beside him. "I don't think you've met Xavier Leduc. He owns Dark Haven."

Atticus had heard of the owner of the BDSM club who was called *my liege* by the San Francisco submissives.

"Good to meet you," Xavier said. He stood a good couple of inches over Atticus's six-two. With black eyes and hair braided almost to his ass, he probably had Native American ancestry. His bearing said he knew his way around a fight.

"Heard a bit about you. I hope to get a chance to visit your club someday." Atticus held a hand out.

"You'd be welcome." Xavier shook his hand. "I appreciate the assistance you gave deVries and Lindsey last winter."

"Part of the job. It's good when things come out right." And kidnappings so rarely did. Atticus glanced at the well-populated barn, seeing Doms and subs he didn't know. "I see you brought a number of your members."

Xavier smiled. "We all enjoy getting out of the city."

"Some of our submissives hoped for a introduction to you, by the way," Simon said.

Atticus grinned. "You on babysitting duty tonight?"

"Always. As is my Rona." Simon studied him. "So, are you free this evening?"

Atticus hesitated. Although he'd noticed several pretty submissives, he didn't have any interest in taking them under command. He'd rather talk a southern magnolia into—

The barn door opened, and Logan escorted in five women, all flushed with laughter. Their bright spirits lit the area. Kallie and Becca came in first, then Simon's wife and a blonde submissive he didn't know, then…Gin.

The women pulled off their coats revealing corsets and bustiers, fishnet stockings and high heels, skimpy skirts.

Atticus waited impatiently for Gin to unveil.

Now that was worth the wait. She'd gone with leather, and not the brightly dyed kind, but in natural shades. A dark brown bustier with matching short skirt. Leather wrist cuffs. High-lacing sandals with his favorite kind of heels. When a man bent a woman over something—like a hay bale—the extra height tilted her ass just right for entry.

His dick stood up and shouted for attention.

Simon nodded to the group. "I see Becca has picked up another nervous stray." After a second, he added, "My Rona likes her."

Atticus studied them and agreed. From the way the women clustered around Gin, teasing her, fixing her hair, giving gentle pats, they all liked her. Of course, Kallie's wilderness tour clients had liked the little Southerner as well. She did have an appealing sweetness.

That sweetness would be his tonight.

But when he straightened, the motion caught her attention. Her eyes widened. She retreated an involuntary step, nodded at him briefly…and turned her back.

"Fuck," he muttered.

"Did you upset a little submissive?" Xavier asked in amusement.

Hell. With a grunt of frustration, Atticus manned up. "Seems so. I did a scene with her. She's new, but the chemistry was fantastic. Then I discovered she's a counselor—and I judged her by old shit and kicked her to the curb. Made a mistake."

"Most counselors are good people," Simon said mildly.

"You took her trust, got her vulnerable, then dumped her." Xavier summed up the story brutally and succinctly.

"And then blindsided her at her work. I screwed up." He needed to apologize. But a frontal approach would get him blasted down, especially since she was braced to rebuff him.

"Let her ease down." Xavier confirmed his thoughts. "Give her time...maybe enough time to play with another Dom."

When Atticus scowled, Simon nodded agreement with his friend. "It's a risk, Atticus. But if there's chemistry between you, she'll feel the lack with someone else, and that might give you a chance. If not, then maybe she's not the one you need."

Let someone else touch her? His gut tightened.

And yet, the advice was excellent, no matter how unpalatable.

* * * *

Bent over a hay bale, Gin rested her forehead on her hands. She'd asked for a breather from being spanked. This sure wasn't any fun.

Everything here seemed unreal, as if she'd wandered into one of her kinky books. The location added another dimension of unreality. This was a *barn* complete. Straw was scattered on the ground, adding its fragrance to the scent of leather. Rather than the sounds of horses, the building was filled with gasps and moans and an occasional scream and the smack of implements on bare flesh.

"Ready for more?" Garret's voice drew her attention back.

When Logan had started introducing her, she'd shot down his first two choices. Then, when he was called away, she'd found this Dom named Garrett who had appeared less intimidating—if anyone could say that about a man who'd spank a woman.

Garrett flattened his palm between her shoulder blades again and pressed her chest onto the straw bale.

His hand hit her bottom and she flinched. Lordy, her butt was getting tender. He continued—and she heard her own bare flesh being struck and it still didn't seem real.

She gritted her teeth as the Dom spanked her faster. The stinging grew to a red-tinged pain, and tears filled her eyes.

When he eased off to rub her bottom, she pushed upright and wiped her eyes.

"You can cry, girl," he said, his voice gruff. "That's the point for a lot of submissives."

No. She firmed her chin and shook her head. She didn't cry in front of strangers. In front of anyone.

This spanking stuff wasn't what she wanted. None of it. She'd been wrong. Inside she ached, as if her spirit were being compressed into a tiny fishbowl of sadness and frustration.

Anger whirled up from nowhere, as if her body was finally reacting to being hurt. To being trapped.

She took a step away from the hay bale, relieved she hadn't let him tie her down. "I'm done now."

"Done?" When Garrett touched her arm, she pulled away. "Gin."

"I'm fine." She controlled her voice. "Thanks for the time."

"Let's go over to the corner and talk then. Girl, you—"

"No." She took two more steps back and bumped into a man.

Turning, she recognized Rona's devastatingly handsome husband. The Dom was in his forties, with silver flecking his neatly trimmed black hair. A submissive stood on his left.

Master Simon curled his right hand around Gin's upper arm, preventing her from further retreat. "Garrett, Jacqueline watched you play with Gin and hoped you'd give her some time." He smoothly guided the submissive toward Garrett while moving Gin away. "I have somewhere else Gin needs to be."

"You'll make sure she has aftercare?" Garret asked.

"I will."

Moving on, Garrett looked down at the thirty-something submissive. "What did you have in mind for a scene?"

As she was led away, Gin felt her anger fade, leaving her empty inside. Time to go home.

"Did you enjoy your spanking?" Master Simon asked.

Compared to his confident baritone, her voice came out thin and shaky. "It was fine."

He shook his head, stopped her right in the center of the room, and tilted her face up to him with a finger under her chin. "Has no one ever told you not to lie to Doms?"

"*First lesson for tonight: be honest.*" Atticus's voice spiraled down the well-worn path in her memory and brought tears to her eyes. She'd wanted Atticus to be the one to spank her and how stupid was she?

"I'm sorry." Her voice shook slightly. "I guess I'm not cut out for this BDSM stuff. I-I thought it was worth a try."

"You're cut out for it, pet," Simon said gently. "You merely picked the wrong Dom for you." He looked over her shoulder at someone behind her. "Atticus, I'd say she needs a good cry. You have my permission to spank her until she does."

Gin whirled around—and right into Atticus's solid body. His arms closed around her, trapping her. It really was him—Atticus. For a moment, she sagged into him, staring.

Oh, her memory hadn't been nearly adequate, had never blown this stunned feeling into her chest. His eyes were still a mesmerizing dark blue; his black sleeveless T-shirt showed off a body ripped with muscles. Colorful tats covered each deltoid.

When his gaze released her, she managed to inhale...and realize why he held her. She glared over her shoulder at Simon. "You-you don't have the right t-to give me to someone. Your permission isn't..." Her brain misfired, messing up her words.

"Thanks, Simon. I'll take care of her." And then, as he had before, Atticus scooped her up like a baby.

Oh, the sensation of being wrapped in his rock-hard arms was like coming home. Thrilling at his strength, her body softened into his.

No, she mustn't feel this way. "Put me down."

"In a minute." He walked over and sat on one of the hay bales lined against a wall. Her bottom rested on his thighs, his jeans abrasive against her tender skin.

She struggled to stand.

Holding her with one arm, he cupped her face in his rugged hand. "Before we begin, I want to apologize."

The surprise halted her fight.

His intense blue eyes bored into hers. "I was a dick to you. And, even worse, made your job harder."

She pulled in a shuddering breath and gathered her composure. She was a professional. A social worker. *Act like one.* "You were," she agreed. "You thought I wasn't helping Sawyer. But...why do you have it in for the whole counseling profession? Was there a psychologist who hurt you or someone you care for?"

His eyes narrowed. "Got your shrink hat on, I see."

"I don't like that word, okay?"

He heaved a sigh. "Sorry again. All right, it's like this. Some of my boys in the Marines came home fucked up and didn't get shit for help from the pros."

"Well, I know the V.A. system is over-burdened and understaffed, but still—I'm sorry. It's not right." Where was a better place to put money than in treating the soldiers who'd served their country?

"Then the last prison shr—uh, therapist did more than not help my brother. She messed up his head."

"His last counselor was male," Gin muttered, making him blink.

"Either way. Sawyer wasn't bad off when he got here, before getting '*help*.' But he got worse with every so-called session. I complained to the prison administration and was blown off."

Gin closed her eyes as sympathy and a kind of guilt assailed her.

"I'm sorry, Gin. I was wrong to take it out on you."

True. Still, she understood needing to protect family. Being angry for them. So she shared. "I guess no one told you that Mr. Slidell was removed from Sawyer's case."

"Seriously?"

She nodded. "So your complaint was heard. Eventually. In admin's defense, I have to say they're so used to inmates drowning the system in complaints and grievances that they probably didn't move very quickly—especially since Sawyer didn't say a word."

"They brought you in to repair the damage."

"I'm trying." Not always succeeding. Her sense of urgency and frustration with Sawyer and her other cases pulled at her again, filling her head with everything she should be doing. Not sitting here and—

"Whoa, look at you disappear." The voice came from— "Eyes on me, subbie."

The rough-edged command whipped every thought from her head. She blinked and met Atticus's intent gaze.

His dimple showed. "Fuck, you're cute."

Her expression of disbelief and disgust made him chuckle.

"Simon gave me orders. Since I see where he's coming from, I'm going to follow them."

Orders? What… Make her cry? Her mouth fell open.

"Virginia." His hand curved over her jaw, holding her so she was forced to look into his blue, blue eyes.

A girl could get lost in those eyes. In his face that said strength and honesty.

"Sweetling, I watched you and Garrett. You wanted a spanking but didn't trust him enough for it to work. Can you trust me?"

The nod happened before she could get her lips around the word *no*.

"This time, you have a safeword. It's red." Even as she processed the words, Atticus lifted her, and a second later, she was belly-down over his muscular thighs. A caress of cool air hit her buttocks as he flipped up her tiny leather skirt, and then…right where she was already sore…a hand like concrete smacked her bottom.

"Ow!" She shoved up, kicked, rocked. Her right hand tried to shield her ass.

He bent her arm, pinned her right wrist to the hollow of her back, and held her there as he continued. *Smack, smack, smack.*

The burning grew, familiar this time, taking her over until each bite of pain thrust her closer to losing it. Tears filled her eyes and spilled over as she choked back her cries. The pain of controlling them was worse than the burning on her skin.

He stopped to rub her bottom. His other hand rested on her lightly as she struggled to maintain control. Inside her head, she could hear herself saying the safeword, but her jaw gripped the word too tightly to escape.

"Sweetheart," he said gently. "Let go. Trust me with those tears."

But to cry would mean…opening up. She could feel the dark, impenetrable barriers that kept her safe. That imprisoned her emotions.

To her dismay, he started again. Stinging, painful slaps hit her bottom, her upper thighs. It hurt… The pain increased, filling her head, crushing any resistance before it.

Inside her chest, the ball of sobs grew, cracking the barriers, breaking through until she couldn't hold back. Until she was crying and crying, loud and jagged.

"There we go, baby." He gripped her waist, lifted her, turned her, and set her on his lap. As he pulled her close, his fingers threaded into her hair to bring her cheek against his wide chest.

She cried.

The sobs spilled out like a river in flood, uprooting her emotions. Anger and frustration and bitterness and sorrow were scoured clean.

A lifetime later, she realized she'd stopped, and only hitching breaths were escaping. Her face lay against a shirt soaked with her tears.

Warmth radiated from Atticus. His hold on her was like his ropes, snug and secure and unbreakable. With growling, soothing noises, he stroked her shoulders.

She'd cried all over the man.

Surly she should feel embarrassed, but only found…quiet. She was emptied, mind and soul, as if a brisk wind off the high glaciers had blown everything away, leaving only crisp, clean air behind. She pulled in a bigger breath and felt his hand pause.

"Back with me?" he rumbled.

Each movement took an age, but eventually, she lifted her head.

One corner of his mouth tipped up as his gaze moved over her face. Oh lord, her makeup must be running down her face. He shifted her so he could grab a tissue from a box on the hay bale.

"Hay bales are sprouting tissue boxes?" Her voice came out husky.

"Simon brought one over." He ignored her hand and wiped her cheeks and under her eyes.

"Thank you." None of Gin's lovers had…cared…for her. Not like this. She'd never felt so cherished in her life. "Sorry for…" *For bawling all over you like a baby. For doing it for such a long, long time. For—*

"Sweetheart, I *made* you cry." His hand lay along her cheek; his thumb stroked her chin, her lips. And then his lips grazed hers before he said in an even voice, "If you hadn't, I'd have kept spanking you."

His level look said he spoke only the truth. He really had wanted her to cry—and so had Simon. "B-but, why?"

He tilted his head. "How do you feel now? Stressed? Upset? Conflicted?"

Cleaned out. "Oh."

His lips quirked, and he ruffled her hair. "Time to get fluid and food into you."

As he set her on her feet, her legs wobbled. He steadied her with an arm around her waist…and she almost started crying again.

When they moved into the open area, she spotted several women standing nearby, carefully not watching, yet sending flirtatious looks at Atticus.

Gin bit her lip. Considering the way he looked—and how darned dominant he was—she'd bet he was extremely popular. "Um. I can…can manage by myself. You don't need to concern yourself."

"I don't, huh?" He stopped midstride. "What's going on in that head of yours, babe?

"I know you probably have others to see," she said reasonably. "Simon didn't give you any choice, but I'm fine now on my own."

Hearing Gin's words, a twenty-something brunette slid smoothly into their path. Her skintight mesh revealed lush breasts and a shaved pussy. "Atticus, I'm free whenever you are."

Gin stiffened. As she'd feared. Now she knew where she stood. She started to pull away.

Fucking-A. Atticus tightened his grip around the little submissive he intended to keep and stared down at the one he'd enjoyed last winter. Only enjoyed wasn't the right word, considering how full of demands and *I-wants* she'd been. Tanya had taken and given nothing back.

His brows drew together.

A snorting laugh came from the left where Logan and Jake were blatantly eavesdropping.

Atticus shot them an irritated look. Jesus, he hated when the bastards were right. But they were. He'd let his standards lapse. True, he enjoyed giving, but a too-permissive Dom wasn't good for anyone in the lifestyle. And this kind of behavior from a submissive was plain disgusting.

His attention returned to Tanya, who smiled as if she'd been cute.

"Did I ask for you?" His tone was icy, and he felt Gin flinch.

"Um." Tanya took a careful step back. "No."

"Did you interrupt a conversation I was having?"

"No. I mean yes. Sir. I-I'm sorry, Sir."

"Interrupting anyone is rude. A submissive butting into a Dom's conversation is inexcusable. Who the fuck trained you?"

Someone cleared his throat. Xavier had joined Jake and Logan.

Seeing him, Tanya went corpse-white and dropped to her knees.

"Tanya is a member of Dark Haven," Xavier said. "If you care to reprimand her, I can watch over the other one." When he nodded to Gin, the little social worker edged so close to Atticus that he could feel her every curve.

Amusement glinted in Xavier's black eyes, and Atticus smothered a smile.

Xavier finished, "Or I can assign Tanya to someone who'd enjoy reinforcing proper protocol."

Atticus kissed the top of Gin's head, inhaling her delicate fragrance. "This one is mine. Do what you will with the other."

"I rather thought that's what you'd say." The Dark Haven Dom fisted Tanya's hair, pulled her to her feet—not roughly, but ruthlessly—and walked away.

All right then. Atticus held Gin a minute, thinking over the past few minutes. To have a beautiful woman unsure of her appeal was refreshing and yet unacceptable. "Virginia."

He waited until she lifted her head.

"Just so you know, Simon knew I planned to hook up with you. He simply lent a hand."

She blinked. And then he saw what he'd hoped for. Delight.

God, he liked seeing her happy.

Rubbing his cheek against her soft one, he murmured, "Let's get some food—and if you want to protect me from any other forward submissives, you have my permission."

When she gave a husky laugh, he rewarded her—and himself—with a slow, long, deep kiss.

* * * *

Gin hadn't noticed—after all, crying took a lot of work—but the atmosphere of the barn had changed over the evening. A few scenes continued, but the earlier intense anticipation had disappeared. In the "social" area, sweaty, glowing submissives sat on blankets or rugs at their Doms' feet. To Gin's surprise, it felt…nice…to be one of them. Who ever thought Ms. Professional would enjoy sitting on the ground between a man's knees while he fed her tidbits from his plate. How strange.

Hmm. Did submission fulfill some sort of deep-seated need in a woman? Or maybe… She shook her head. Not a good time for psychological evaluation, let alone reality testing.

She'd accept—for now—that Atticus's behavior wasn't humiliating as much as it was claiming, as if he was proclaiming she had a place where she belonged.

One where she felt safe. Cared for. Wasn't this what everyone wanted?

When he stopped to stroke her hair, she noticed his plate was empty. Rising gracefully—and wasn't she proud of not tripping?—she took the dish from him. "Can I get you more food or some coffee or anything?"

His smile was a satisfying reward. "You learn fast, sweetheart. Now, pretend you're in the military and tag a 'Sir' on the end when you talk to a Dom. For politeness."

Heavenly stars, she'd seen what happened to submissives who

weren't polite. Xavier had restrained Tanya in the center of the barn. With her hair tied to a dangling iron hook, she'd stood and watched everyone else having fun. After a while, another Dom had released her, making her crawl behind him as he talked to other Doms.

"Yes, Sir," Gin said softly, earning herself another warm look.

"Very nice. And I don't need any more, but thank you."

She disposed of the paper plate and returned, expecting to sit back at his feet. Instead, he pulled her onto his lap, chuckling when she winced. Her bottom was going to be extremely sore tomorrow.

"Atticus." From two hay bales down, Logan tossed across a tube. "I keep this on hand for my redhead."

"Thanks." Atticus lifted Gin to her feet. "Bend over, baby."

"What?" He couldn't possibly be serious. They were surrounded by people and—

His jaw tipped up infinitesimally.

Oh no, he'd given her, like, an order. Her face heated to scalding, but she turned. Everyone had seen her butt before, after all, only not— not like this. Her knees shook as she bent.

Without any hesitation, Atticus lifted her leather skirt and spread the lotion on her stinging buttocks.

Ow!

Callused hands didn't go well with tender skin. Even the coolness of the gel didn't help. It *hurt*. She tried to step away—and was stopped short by his grip on her skirt.

"Nice try." His hand didn't pause, just continued the excruciating torture until he was satisfied. After tossing the tube to Logan, he tugged Gin down onto his lap.

"It still hurts, you know," she muttered.

"Yep." He took her face between his hands and held her as he claimed her lips, as his tongue tangled with hers, as he took everything she offered. When he lifted his head, she'd forgotten her sore bottom.

"About the pain." He brushed her cheek with his bearded jaw. "The lotion decreases bruising. Doesn't help with pain since it isn't the kind containing an analgesic."

"What's the point in cutting the pain?" Logan asked. He tugged on Becca's hair with a blade-like smile. "If I spank a little rebel, I want her ass to hurt afterward."

Becca wrinkled her nose but rubbed her cheek against his fingers. Obviously, she wasn't feeling abused at all.

I'm so glad she has a loving relationship. No one deserved it more than

Becca.

As various conversations whirled around the group, Gin let herself snuggle against Atticus. Nothing had felt so right in a long time. Enjoying the sensation, she idly looked around the barn. A flogging was happening in one corner, and she liked how the Dom had used the stall boards to restrain his submissive. Along the back wall was—

Oh. My. Gin stiffened.

In full sight of everyone, a Dom had his woman in a leather swing with her legs chained out of the way and was fucking her forcefully. *Wow.* And she'd thought the sex was kinky at Kallie's wilderness place.

"Problem, pet?" Atticus asked. He followed her gaze. "Ah." His eyes were very blue as he regarded her thoughtfully. "Now, if I was doing the scene, I'd have you in the air, but use only rope for the suspension." The dimple at the edge of his beard appeared. "You'd be naked, so there would be no barrier to my hands. So I could touch you where I pleased."

Heat rushed through her like someone had turned a heater on high. She glanced at the couple again. Suspension with ropes—no swing? Swaying up in the air with no control? In bondage?

"No. No way. Never." *Never, never, never.* If he messed up one knot, she'd end up on the floor.

His eyes narrowed as he assessed her face, her shoulders, her hands. "It does take a high degree of trust to let someone bind you *and* suspend you. Maybe that's why I enjoy doing it so much."

The mere thought brought on the shivers. She felt her head shaking a *no* even as she tried for a light tone. "I suppose the sex part is a side bennie?"

He didn't answer but a smile lightened his face.

This Dom could get females anywhere he went. The knowledge made her feel even more unsure of herself. She shoved aside the dismal attitude. She was pretty and smart and nice, with a good figure. Educated. Held a job. She wouldn't let herself feel unworthy because her "date" for the night was past scorching on the hotness scale.

Relationships got corrupted when one party didn't feel worthy. He—or she—would denigrate the other to feel better, to assure himself that no one else would want his significant other. She'd seen it often enough. One poor person—usually the wife—ended up feeling like dog meat because her beloved cut her down all the time.

Or, in Gin's case, she'd work her ass off to prove she was worthy.

"Interesting thoughts going through your head." Atticus drew her attention back with a touch on her cheek.

"Uh, no. Not really." Under his level gaze, she blurted out, "I was reassuring myself I wasn't dog meat."

His stare of surprise made her laugh.

She might as well say it. "You're very hot, Detective Ware. I feel outclassed."

"Thank you." His grin could stop traffic—especially if the drivers were female. "But, you're off base. There isn't an unattached person in this place who doesn't envy me." He stroked her hair for a second. "You're beautiful, magnolia, but a Dom wants more than merely physical attractions. You have kindness, intelligence, and an unexpected sense of humor." He bent and his lips against her ear whispered, "And your willing surrender has a beauty I can't explain."

His words left her breathless. "But…"

"Or did you want to know that any Dom here would enjoy bending you over a hay bale."

"Don't be crude." She considered thumping him and decided against it. The punishment might be bad. Being tied up in the center of the room—she'd probably die of humiliation.

"What was that thought?"

Snoopy Dom. But she didn't mind sharing some of what she'd thought. "I'm rather uncomfortable with doing everything in public, you know," she admitted. "I'm not like that."

"Ah, baby." His smile turned gentle. "The out in the open play isn't merely for those who like being watched. It's also for new play-partners. Having monitors on duty"—he indicated Logan and Jake— "makes it safer when people are getting acquainted and want to do some scenes. It's a bad idea to take a stranger to your bedroom and let him tie you up."

Jake had said the same thing. She nodded.

"And then some people aren't out to play in public, but they like to socialize. Of course, some do enjoy being on display." He nuzzled between her breasts, making her heart skip a beat. "Now I happen to like putting a submissive up in ropes. Sharing her beauty. And once she's in such a vulnerable position, it's tempting to go ahead and do more."

"More?" she breathed.

He traced a finger over her lower lip. "I'd tilt you down so you could use that mouth on me…and then tilt you the other way at an angle to fill you with my cock."

My stars. His bluntness was appalling…and she felt herself dampen.

"I…"

His palm settled over her breast under her bustier. "Your heart is pounding, pet."

Her world narrowed to the warmth of his hand and her own surging lust. "From fear. Sir."

"Some. Not all." Rather than touch her more intimately, he moved his hand to her waist.

Oh, she wanted more than anything to feel the slight abrasion of his callused fingers on her bare skin.

"You should be a bit anxious, since I intend to get you up there eventually."

"Not a chance." She grasped his wrist to move his hand. He was immovable and the evidence of his sheer strength had her breathing in deep, trying to get the fog of need out of her brain. "Listen, I shouldn't be with you at all. You're the brother of one of my cases. This isn't…"

"Baby, if you were dating an inmate, CO, or the warden, I could see the problem. Me, not so much."

No, really, she shouldn't be with him, even if logic said there was no threat to Sawyer or the prison. Atticus was a law enforcement agent, after all. But her brain wasn't working too well because her hormones had taken over. Every cell in her body wanted to merge with his.

At her lack of answer, his brows drew together. "It honestly is a problem for you? I don't want you to get in trouble."

"There are regulations, you see." Her voice came out hoarse.

"Got it." He released her, holding her as he rose to his feet. "Then why don't we go somewhere more private to finish talking. And if nothing happens, that's all right too." He kissed her lightly and raised his hand to the chorus of voices bidding them goodnight.

Chapter Eight

His idea of private was taking her to his place. When she'd told him her stuff was at Serenity Lodge, he laughed and said his house was "next door" to the Mastersons' ranch and down from the Hunts' Lodge.

A few minutes later, he stopped her on his porch to point to the west, higher up the mountain. "You can see the Mastersons' second floor lights through the trees. Their property butts up against mine." He unlocked and opened the door. "That's how we got to be friends."

On the other side of his house, white board fencing shimmered in the moonlight. "Do you have horses?"

"Gotta have horses." He held the door open.

He was such a cowboy. Smiling, she stepped into the living room. The décor was rustic, with Native American accents. In a wall of stone, the fireplace still held a few glowing coals. A red, brown, and white geometric patterned rug warmed the dark hardwood floor. Red pillows on the squashy-looking leather couch matched the brick-red armchairs.

The six-feet wide flat-screen TV said a man lived in the place.

Atticus kissed her cheek and walked through the small dining area, past the bar island, and into the kitchen. "Beer or wine?"

"Wine would be wonderful." As she slid onto a leather-covered barstool, he opened a bottle and poured. His big hand made the wine glass look absurdly delicate as he handed it over and poured one for himself.

"You have a comfortable home." She sipped the full-bodied cabernet and nodded to the black and white photograph over the fireplace. "Is that you and Sawyer?"

"Good eye." The two mud-streaked teenagers held their horses' reins, while behind them unfolded the action of a rodeo arena. "We were at the Cody Stampede. I was in ROTC in college and planning to head into the Marine Corp; Sawyer was still in high school. Few years later, when I was in the military police, he enlisted in the Navy. Didn't come out the same person."

Her heart ached for the innocent boys they'd been. A decade and a half later, they wore the self-possessed, dangerous look of men who'd seen death. Who'd dealt death.

And Atticus had a cop's cynical eyes that said he'd seen the worst of human nature.

What was she doing with him? As his gaze lingered on the picture, she studied him. So tough. Yet, the lines at the corners of his mouth and eyes were from laughter.

He could be gentle.

She'd seen him reassure the little girl on the climbing wall. *"Take a breath, baby."* And then he'd encouraged the child to do more than she'd thought possible.

Gin had seen his love and loyalty to Sawyer—and his ability to say he loved him.

Yes, this man was special.

And she wanted him more than she'd wanted anyone before. She frowned into her drink, and when she looked up, he was watching her, sipping his wine, and waiting.

With some of her dates, she'd felt their impatience, as if they tired of wading through the getting-to-know-you phase before they could get some. Atticus displayed no urgency, just the quiet patience of a very experienced man.

The knowledge increased her low-key arousal.

Far, far sooner than she should have finished, she drank the last of her wine.

"Nervous, pet?" he asked.

She nodded. Although the air was chilled, her body felt like a heat pump, and her stomach quivered with nerves. She hadn't had many lovers and no one since meeting Preston. No one after.

He studied her for a moment, eyes narrowed. "Talk about mixed signals," he said. "I can take you back to your car, sweetling, if you like. Or I can light a fire, and we can sit and talk."

"Or we can go for the third option." She set her glass on the island, grasped his hand, and pulled him down the dark hallway. Hopefully his bedroom was at the end of it. "Let's get this out of the way."

"You make sex sound like a trip to the dentist."

"There have been—" Her mouth snapped shut. Blushing, she stopped dead, not believing what she'd started to share.

"I see." His chuckle was low. "I'll try to make this feel better than a long, hard drilling."

The suggestive words delivered in his deep baritone sent tingles over her skin.

With his hand on her stomach, he backed her into a room, even as his mouth covered hers, taking possession. The minute her arms wrapped around his neck, he curved one hand under her ass and pulled her up on her toes. His thick erection pressed against her pelvis.

When he lifted his head, she was breathless.

Her skin simmered with heat. She glanced at the bedroom and saw no interesting kinky shackles or piles of rope or handcuffs. "So we're going to do this the old-fashioned...um, vanilla...way?"

"Mostly." He undid her bustier. "I'm not going to tie you down, sweetheart. Not until you know me better."

"Oh. Okay." That surely wasn't disappointment she felt. The sensation of his scarred knuckles brushing each newly bared inch washed the emotion away.

She glanced up at him and saw his half-smile and the comprehension in his expression. He knew...

Flustered, she lifted her hands to undo his shirt. "You're overdressed."

He caught her wrists and eased her arms down. "Hands stay at your sides, pet."

His voice didn't raise—not an iota—but the ruthless quality made the hairs on the back of her neck rise. Her arms went limp.

The Dom didn't need ropes to bind her.

Without a second's pause, he unzipped her skirt and tossed it onto a chair. "Now stand right there, Virginia. If you move, I won't be happy."

Why did the growled, almost threat, make her so wet?

He disappeared to her left, and she heard the strike of a match as he lit one candle. Another and another, until their soft glow filled the room.

When he opened the window, a breeze billowed the drapes, and the candles flickered. The lush fragrance of the pasture grass wafted into the room. The swishing of wind through the trees joined the rumble of thunder in the distance.

"Storm moving in." He returned to stand in front of her and simply look at her. She was completely naked; he was fully dressed. The contrast made her feel exposed and so, so excited. Her heart was trying to bang right out of her chest.

"Tonight, I want you to remember two things, baby." He caressed her breast and made her toes curl. "One: I'm going to take what I want from you, and you'll have no choice but to please me...so don't worry about disappointing me. Two: a clear *no* will stop me; nothing else will."

Her knees almost buckled. "Atticus."

"Mmmhmm." With a hand between her breasts, he moved her backward until the backs of her legs hit the bed and her butt landed on the old-fashioned quilt.

From a sitting position, she looked up at him.

"Put your hands under your ass."

She blinked. And he waited. *Oh. Okay.*

When she shoved her hands between her still tender bottom and the quilt, her weight pinned them there.

Bending over, he set her feet on the edge of the mattress so her knees were raised. Firmly, he pushed her knees down toward the mattress until the bottoms of her feet were forced together. Opening her.

Heavens above.

"This is new," he murmured, tracing a finger over her bare pussy. "I rather thought I saw shaved skin earlier."

Her face felt bright red—again. "Um, yes. For tonight. Kallie said a lot of Doms prefer...bare."

His jaw turned stern. "Right here, your only concern is one Dom."

"I..." She'd imagined him touching her with every swipe of the razor. "If you don't like it, then—"

"Oh, little counselor, I do like it," he said. "You can keep your beautiful pussy just like that for me."

He liked it. Thank heaven, he liked it. She'd seen how the heat in his gaze increased, and yet he didn't move, just studied her.

As he stroked a finger up and down her damp, clean-shaven skin, the sensation was strange. Intense. What would it feel like when he actually took her? Her clit throbbed a demand, and she wiggled slightly.

He smiled and went down on one knee. His hand curled around her feet, keeping the soles together, as he leaned forward and ran his tongue up one outer labia, over her mound, and down the other side.

Her pussy engorged to achingly swollen between one heartbeat and the other.

He licked her again and again until she throbbed with anguished need, and then he nipped her inner thigh. The sharp sting made her jump, and her legs tried to move—and his grip didn't budge. He had her pinned down and held open. The feeling of being controlled made her moan.

His tongue washed the tiny hurt before he bit her on the other side, laved it away. He nibbled the crease between her hips and pussy, then circled her clit with unerring precision and teased the infinitely sensitive area under the hood. The whole area swelled to the point of pain.

The strength ran out of her arms and she realized she'd fallen back, hands still trapped beneath her bottom.

His tongue flicked over her clit again.

"Oh, Atticus." The words came out in a moan. "Please. I need—"

"Uh-uh, sweetheart. You need what I will give you when that time comes, and not a second before."

Fuck, she was a beauty. Her skin gleamed in the candlelight, sheened with a light moisture. Her rosy nipples had spiked into dagger points with need. The cords of her neck were rigid, her eyes holding nothing but him and what he was doing.

He licked over her clit, pleased with the shiny pink pearl, fully out from the hood and straining with need. Under his hand, her legs trembled.

Time to send her over...for the first time. Ever since the camping weekend, he'd craved seeing her come again, this little uptight submissive who looked so surprised that she had needs.

With a smile, he slid his finger through her swollen, drenched folds and inside, imagining how the hot silk would feel around his cock.

She gasped; her hips jerked upward.

"No, baby, I won't let you move." Holding her feet in place, he squeezed his hand. Reminding her that she was under control.

And the way her cunt spasmed around his finger made him chuckle.

Finding a submissive who turned him on and who suited his needs was like a gold miner discovering a giant nugget in his pan.

He bent and teased her clit, enjoying the slick taste of her on his tongue, the delicate muskiness.

In the tender area near her hipbone, he smelled her body lotion.

Vanilla and light lavender, he decided.

When she moaned a plea, he lingered there, brushing his lips against her skin. Such a beautiful voice. He'd enjoy gagging her someday—but here and now, he wanted to hear how her liquid southern accent thickened when she said his name.

He could feel her trembling and straining upward, so he pushed two fingers inside her cunt and curled his fingertips forward to the puffy ridged area inside the enveloping hot satin walls. Mercilessly, he rubbed the small spot, taking a moment for a few thrusts, then rubbing again.

Her quivering halted as her muscles tensed.

Almost there. Her face was flushed, her eyes closed, right there with him. He drew the moment out because he could. Because he wanted to. Fuck, she was gorgeous.

Be nice, Ware. With a sigh of resignation, he leaned down and pinned her clit between his teeth, flickering his tongue right over the top. *No escape, sweetheart.*

Her hips lifted, her breathing stopped, and the squeezing spasms began around his invading fingers. "*Atticus.*"

Yeah, that accent could make a dead man rise. His cock fucking wanted to be inside her right then.

Before she could recover, he rose and grabbed a condom from the bedside table. Opening his jeans, he sheathed himself and planted one hand beside her shoulder on the bed. "Look at me, Virginia." He waited until she opened dazed eyes. After swirling his shaft in her juices, he pressed in.

Not fast and rough the way he wanted—not until he knew how well they'd fit—but slow and steady.

Her eyes widened delightfully. "Atticus." Her neck arched sweetly as her pussy stretched to accommodate him.

Finally, he was buried to the root, and her cunt gripped him like a hotly oiled fist. "Jesus, you feel good."

She swallowed, eyes a little shocked. "You too." Her words sounded strained.

"Been a while, pet?" She wasn't a virgin, but damn, she was tight.

Her nod confirmed his supposition, and he tried to suppress his satisfaction. Instead, he lifted her hips. "Hands out, Virginia. I'd like to feel them on me."

Her lips curved with pleasure. She didn't hesitate to run her palms over his arms, his chest. She liked to give as much as receive, and her enjoyment of his body added to his.

After a kiss to show his approval, he ran a finger over her flushed cheek. "You've had time to adjust. I'm not going to be rough, sweetie, but I'm going to take you."

Her answer was to tilt her hips up.

She was a treat. His bed was precisely the right height, and he took full advantage, pumping into her heat, strong and steady, then taking time to rotate and tease her every nerve awake.

When her fingernails dug into his skin, he grinned.

His need to come started deep inside him, centered at the base of his spine, growing almost as fast as his desire to see her climax again.

Why the fuck not? He took her mouth again, invading, feeling like a conqueror, above and below. Leaving her lips, he straightened. The breeze from the window cooled his heated skin. The arm beside her shoulder bore his weight as he pushed her right knee away from her body, opening her further so he could reach her clit.

His first touch on the nub made her gasp, and the way she clenched around his erection made his balls contract with a force that almost sent him over.

He huffed a laugh—he loved when a woman had unmistakable signals—and sliding his finger over her clit, he drove her right back up to need.

"I can't," she whined, even as her inner thighs quivered and the flush rose in her cheeks. "Don't."

Ah, little submissives shouldn't try to give instructions—because the temptation was too much to prove them wrong. He held her gaze as he deliberately slowed his pumping and concentrated on her clit, watched her focus disappear, her eyes close.

Her back arched beautifully right before her cunt convulsed, battering at him. Her cry revealed as much surprise as it did fulfillment.

Jesus, she was beautiful. He ran his hands over her body, feeling her heart pounding, the softness of her breasts. And then he forced her knees up for still greater penetration and hammered into her.

Her little hands closed on his arms, holding him as firmly as did her cunt. Her hips tried to lift to help his strokes. A sweetie, all right.

At the base of his spine, the pressure increased. His own climax fisted his balls, and as he relaxed his control, jetted out his cock in a long, hot, mind-blowing release.

Jesus, she was liable to kill him.

He tucked her legs around his waist and dropped forward so he could nuzzle the hollow of her throat, taste the light sweat on her neck, kiss her. Her lips were soft and responsive and welcoming.

Her arms had wrapped around him, her legs scissored his waist, her cunt was snug and warm—and she kissed like an angel.

He might be in trouble here.

* * * *

Gin woke at dawn, disoriented. There was heat and movement along her back—the dog? But her head lay on something much firmer than her pillow. The warmth behind her wasn't Trigger, but Atticus who, to her surprise, had pulled her into his arms to cuddle her. Or, maybe not cuddle as much as claim. He was curled around her, his arm heavy over her waist, and his hand holding her breast.

Her mind might be awake, but her body didn't want to move. Not after he'd wakened her in the middle of the night, ignoring her half-awake protests, pinning her arms over her head as his mouth and teeth and fingers worked her into a frenzy of need. Until she was begging him to take her.

And he had, making sure she was satisfied first, and then enjoying himself, putting her into positions she hadn't thought real people even used. If he'd been thinking only of himself, she might feel less disconcerted, but he watched her during sex as carefully as he had when he'd roped her up. He knew before she did when an angle or position got to her, and he'd smile...and work her, right there until her fingernails would claw at the quilt...or him.

"Can't sleep?" she heard, his voice a dark rumble, his breath warm on her hair. The hand cupping her breast squeezed lightly, and his thumb stroked her still swollen nipple, sending tingles through her.

"What time is it?"

His head lifted. "Around seven. But it's Sunday. We don't have to be at the Lodge until around nine."

She stiffened. "The Lodge. But..." She'd heard the Hunts mention breakfast.

He moved her hair aside to nip at her nape. "You need to pick up your clothes, right?"

"Um. Yes." Walk into a roomful of people that had seen her leave with him? She turned in his arms to face him. "Atticus, I don't know anyone there very well. It would be awkward."

He propped himself up on one elbow, sending a flush of heat through her as he played with her as he'd done in the pavilion. Stroking her breasts, running a finger over her collarbone, her lips.

"Baby, it might be awkward, but most new situations are. I'm not exactly a lifetime resident of this place either; I've only known Logan and Jake for a year or so."

"I thought you'd been here for years. On a ranch. Sawyer mentioned it."

"The ranch is in Idaho."

"What in the world brought you to California?"

He ran a finger along the side of her face, moving the strands of hair away. In the faint dawn light, his face was carved of shadows, with darkness edging his jawline. "Sawyer. He was here visiting a buddy, got in that accident, and was sentenced here. Wasn't doing well in prison, so I moved close."

He'd left his home to provide emotional support to his brother. Her heart went all squishy. "Oh. And your family was good with you leaving?"

"My other brother was good. Mom died soon after Sawyer's discharge from the SEALS—part of why he was having trouble, I think."

"And your father?"

"He died when I was seven."

"I'm sorry." She stroked the softness of his beard, thinking of his mother. Thirty years alone? "Your mama never remarried?"

Under her fingers, his jaw turned to granite. "She did. A few years later, her husband got sent to prison for beating the crap out of her. He had a problem with anger."

And Atticus still had a problem with him. He was so protective. "I'm sorry. I guess neither of us had much luck with fathers. Mine took off when I was eleven."

"Found another woman?" His matter-of-fact tone made it easy to answer.

"Eventually, I'm sure. But mostly he wanted more than my mother and I could give him." Her mouth twisted. Her mother had done everything possible to keep him, and so had Gin. Fancy meals, a clean house, bringing him his drinks, his paper. He'd still walked away. *"Please, Daddy, I'll try harder."*

Atticus's eyes had softened as he studied her face. "Looks to me like—"

The phone rang, interrupting him, and he rolled away from her with a grunt of exasperation. After glancing at the display, he accepted the call. "Ware."

The caller talked for a minute.

"Got Gin here," Atticus said. "Once I return her to Serenity, I'll meet you at the trailhead."

He listened, and a wry grin appeared. "Hell yes, you owe me." His gaze ran over her, and a dimple appeared as he said clearly, "Sweetest ass I've had in my bed in a long, long time."

Gin's mouth fell open.

After tossing the phone to one side, he rolled, flattening her with his weight.

"Did you call me…?"

"A sweet piece of ass? Mmmhmm. And if I didn't have to leave, I'd tap this piece of ass."

His grin said he'd deliberately tried to get a rise out of her. She could read it on his face. For being a ruthless, cynical cop, he had a wicked sense of humor. A giggle escaped as she tried to think of a way to get revenge.

His kiss wiped out any thought she had left.

Eventually, he lifted his head, rubbing his bearded jaw against her cheek in a tender gesture. "You are so delightful." His voice had turned to a low, smoky rasp that melted her insides.

She wouldn't call him delightful. More like dominating…and dangerous.

"I fucking hate to leave you." His lips curved as he pressed his growing erection against her. "Especially now."

"Oh honey, what a shame you're going to miss out on morning sex." She tried to appear prim, but he undoubtedly heard the laughter in her voice.

"Sucks to be me. I'm gonna miss a lot. Morning sex. After-sex snuggling. Shower sex. Breakfast. After-breakfast sex." His lips curved. "Of course, after that, being as I'm an old man, I'd have a heart attack and be dead before lunch."

Old man. Right. He must be all of thirty-something. And not an ounce of fat on the man; he was solid muscle. "Oh my, we can't have you dying. I'll have the doctor put you on a low-fat, no-sugar, no-beer, and no-sex diet."

"When hell freezes over. Try it and I'll tan your ass…again." He nipped her neck and sent quivers straight to her pussy.

She ran her fingers through the springy hair on his chest. The feel of his rock-hard pectorals made her breathless. Heck, he probably had muscles on his toes. "Where are you headed off to?"

"Search and Rescue." He kissed her lightly and slid out of bed. "That was Jake. Some kid ran away from home and into the mountains. Dogs lost the scent with last night's rain. They were hoping I might spot something."

Her eyebrows rose. "That the dogs didn't?

"I'm a pretty good tracker." He put his hands under her arms and pulled her out of bed. "Found you, didn't I?"

Chapter Nine

Feeling a tad bit cranky, Gin sat on the floor in her living room and hugged her dog.

Three days had passed without any contact from Atticus. Why did it hurt so much when a guy didn't call soon afterward?

"So why hasn't he called? The sex was great."

Trigger whined in answer.

"I don't like it when you're logical." She scowled at him. "Fine. *I* thought the sex was great. Maybe Atticus didn't agree." Atticus was certainly a whole lot more experienced than she was. He hadn't acted as if he was just being nice, but maybe he'd found her inadequate, despite his compliments.

Trigger set a big paw on her thigh.

"No, I have only you for advice right now." She'd wanted to talk with someone who knew about Doms, but she didn't know Summer quite well enough to share. Kallie was guiding a wilderness tour off in the hinterlands somewhere.

Becca was lovely and would undoubtedly help, but her husband, Logan, was purely scary. Wouldn't it be awful if he stepped in to fix things?

"Really though, it's better if things die between me and Atticus."

Trigger gave her a disbelieving look.

"Seriously." The Department of Corrections and Rehabilitation had rules about interactions with a case's family members...and she'd broken them. If she saw Atticus again, she'd have to report it to admin.

Darn prison. She slumped back against the couch. If only the job had been more what she'd hoped for. The work was interesting, true. Although trying to get through all their defenses was difficult, she loved the challenge.

Her colleagues thought she was funny when she did a happy dance in her office when she succeeded in drawing one out, in helping one move toward health rather than sickness.

But the conditions were dismal. Although she'd suggested some easy changes, the mental health admin hadn't been very optimistic. The warden wasn't interested.

Well, she'd wait a bit and try again.

Meantime…she needed to get her butt out of the house. She was always telling her inmates to exercise off their bad moods.

Leaning forward, she smiled into the big brown eyes of her very own pet. Best listener in the world, even if he was too logical.

"C'mon, my friend. Let's have a stroll." She grinned when Trigger jumped up and woofed his delight. He didn't mind the backyard, but had let it be known that big dogs like to stretch their legs, especially in the forested area at the end of their street.

As she stepped out into the twilight, she pulled in a breath of bitingly cold air. Sunset-pink clouds drifted across the sky, but lower over the western mountains, thunderheads built their own dark range.

"Looks like we're getting a springtime shower soon. Don't go too far."

Ignoring her, the dog loped away and disappeared into the darkness of the well-canopied forest.

She smiled. Coming home to all his canine enthusiasm was so, so nice. Her evenings were less solitary with him sprawled over her legs while they watched television…although his conversational interests were a bit limited. And he totally didn't get how gorgeous Gregory Peck was in *The Big Country.*

Why couldn't she find herself a Gregory Peck?

Uh-uh. Not yet. No matter how lonely, she wasn't ready for a man—even a cowboy hero. Not until she'd worked through her small personal problem.

Following Trigger, she veered off the trail, making her way toward the water glinting through the trees.

Well, actually, her personal problem was maybe on the larger side.

How often had she attentively listened to Preston complain about his job. Yet, if she mentioned hers, he had changed the subject or turned on the television.

All of their interactions had been similar. She'd supported him mentally, emotionally, and physically without receiving anything back. Then, instead of dumping him, she'd tried harder to make it work. To please him.

Good thing Preston had cheated on her, or she'd still be with him. Dumb, right?

A master's degree sure didn't bestow *self*-understanding—although it did help somewhat after a person woke up.

She'd seen she formed the same pattern in all her relationships with men—with her father, a series of boyfriends, and finally her fiancé. With each, she'd worked her ass off to keep him, exactly as her mother had.

Like an alcoholic with no limits, she'd give and give until she lost all sense of herself. So until she was adjusted enough for healthy attachments, she needed to avoid relationships and serious ties with men.

Stick to friendly booty sex. That was the ticket.

A light patter above announced the first raindrops hitting the foliage…then her unprotected head. She shivered, turned, and headed for home.

Even before she could call, Trigger appeared, trailing her down the tiny animal path she'd been following. No matter how far he went, he never lost her.

"Typical male," she scolded as he gently mouthed her fingers in his favorite greeting. "Always running la—" Her voice trailed off as she realized she fed him, watered him, let him on the couch, walked him. Another demanding guy she'd let into her life.

Then again, he returned her efforts with a heart-warming outpouring of love. So, there really was a balance.

"Guess you're different from normal guys because you were neutered. Because you're not actually a male."

He gave her a reproachful look.

She grinned, imagining Atticus Ware's expression if she suggested that he get snipped.

Chapter Ten

Gin had conducted two awesome group sessions on Friday morning. Her case management paperwork was caught up. Her day had gone so well...until now.

She studied the inmate sitting across from her desk. He looked like a skinhead version of Frankenstein's monster. The swastika on the back of his shaved scalp summed up his politics. Holes from his piercings dotted his nostrils, ears, and lips. Yellowing around his left eye lingered from the fight he'd been in a month ago.

And, much to everyone's regret, he was out of administrative segregation and back in the general population.

His gaze roved over her body and increased her discomfort. "If you give me what I need, Slash can be very...generous," he said.

He often referred to himself in the third person. She'd heard some BDSM submissives would, but "Slash" used it for pure intimidation.

"I'm sorry, Mr. Cole. I can't get you an assignment working on the grounds." More like she wouldn't. After talking with him, she wouldn't trust him outside the building walls. From the aura of violence he gave off, she wondered how he'd ended up here in a lower security facility.

He shifted in the chair, his legs spread widely apart so his dark blue denim pants revealed a jutting erection. "Heard in the yard 'bout a counselor who likes the *beasts*. A lot." His gaze held hers as he stroked himself. "Maybe she's you? You wanna hear 'bout rape an' murder?"

"This session is over." Her stomach twisted. Surely there were no counselors attracted to murderers or sexual offenders. *Don't throw up.* Rising, she hit the desk intercom to summon the correctional officer.

The inmate jumped to his feet, leaned over the desk, and grabbed her right wrist. With his face far too close to hers, he snarled, "Made a mistake, cunt. You don't fuck with Slash."

"Let *go* of me," she yelled. Heart hammering, she struggled to free her wrist from the painful grip. Her other hand groped for a weapon. Anything. Her fingers bumped something, latched on—and she hit him across the face with her heavy ceramic coffee cup.

"Fuck!" He jerked back. "You *cunt*." He slammed her forearm down on the edge of the desk.

Pain exploded in her arm.

The CO burst into the room. "Hey!"

Gasping, she sank into her chair and cradled her arm to her chest. It *hurt*.

Slash turned to the guard with his hands up. "Sorry, boss. I shouldn't have yelled at Ms. Virginia. My bad."

The CO yanked him away from the desk. "Maggot, if you—"

"Didn't do nothin'," Slash protested. "And I want a new counselor. Fuck, I think this one pissed herself just lookin' at Slash."

"Ms. Virginia, what do you want me to do with him?" the officer asked.

Averting her face, Gin fought for control. A breath. Another. Her arm roared with pain. Another breath. "He gets a ticket for assault."

"You got it."

She noticed her coworkers in the doorway and said to the gray-haired receptionist, "Remove Mr. Cole from my caseload, please."

"Of course." As Mrs. Warner started back toward her desk, Penelope said in a too-loud voice. "You can put him on mine. I have room."

As the CO escorted the inmate away, Gin looked up.

Slash was laughing. He'd found the counselor who liked tales of rape and murder. Sickness clung to the back of Gin's throat.

"You weren't prepared for a creep like him, were you?" Mr. Slidell surveyed her from the doorway, his mud-colored eyes disapproving. "I warned you about trusting any of the bastards. Scum. They're all filth, and you girls don't have a clue."

Girls? Gin let her breath out. "It's a dangerous job. One big risk is thinking that all the inmates are alike. I'm afraid you *boys* often fall into that trap."

Color rose in his face, and anger compressed his thin lips. Without a word, he stomped into the hall.

Gin was shaking too violently to enjoy the victory.

* * * *

After visiting his brother, Atticus stopped to talk with two correctional officers before leaving the prison. Outside, heat waves shimmered off the concrete and sunlight glimmered on the razor-wired chain link fences. The place gave him a sense of being trapped; he couldn't imagine what it did to a man after months and years.

"Any recent problems?" he asked. Any rumors he picked up, he'd pass to Bear Flat's chief of police.

This facility reminded him of his high school. Most of the COs were good people, but the warden was an incompetent, venal dick, and laziness tended to slide downhill. The staff needed a good kick in the pants to up their game. From what Sawyer said, the amount of contraband smuggled into the prison was probably greater than marijuana across the Mexican border.

"We got more level IV convicts sent in again," one grumbled. "Bastards should be kept in the higher security facilities."

"No shit." Saldana was one of the better COs. "Dumping aggressive prisoners in here increases violence in the general population. Damn overcrowding."

"I can see why you'd be concerned," Atticus said diplomatically. Unfortunately, they hadn't stepped up security in response. This prison housed special needs inmates—kept here for their own safety—as well as the lower security inmates. The relaxed rules had caused the place to be called a vacation camp.

The prison staff rarely searched visitors—and it was amazing what a tangle of dreadlocks could conceal—let alone performed routine inmate strip searches. With the overcrowding, the COs were understaffed, outnumbered, and...if they weren't careful, they'd soon be outgunned.

Gin shouldn't be working here.

He glanced at his watch. Five p.m. She should be leaving about now...the main reason he'd hung around.

And there she was, across the room, turning in her body alarm and keys, taking back her chit, and signing out. So pretty. Not even her shapeless clothes could disguise her very feminine body beneath. The overhead lights glinted off the red-gold streaks in her auburn hair.

The sergeant was patting her shoulder, and Atticus smiled. She made friends easily, didn't she?

The two officers beside Atticus turned to see what he was looking at.

"Now there's one nice piece of ass." The new one massaged his crotch.

"She's a lady, dipshit." Atticus considered flattening the guy's balls, but controlled himself...although a growl escaped. "Watch your fucking mouth."

The man took a step back.

Good enough. Atticus nodded at Saldana, who was stifling a smile. "Catch you later."

"You bet. Take it easy." Saldana slapped his shoulder.

Atticus stopped on the pavement outside the building and sucked in the fresh air. A hint of frost. Clean without the stench of anger and violence, of sweat and fear and frustration.

To the right were the Level II yards, buildings, and pods. Watchtowers broke up the long line of double fencing. To the left was the lower security half. No watchtowers. The yard work inmates with their guard dog CO were raking the debris from the landscaped area. He had to be pleased that Sawyer had made it to that section.

Atticus watched the door for Gin. He hadn't wanted to greet her under the eyes of the staff. Most women in prisons tried to avoid being thought of in any sexual context at all, although—as the asshole CO had shown—a woman as pretty as Gin was still assigned the label *piece of meat.*

Jesus, he hated that she worked here.

Leaning a shoulder against the side of the building, he crossed his arms. His body was tired from thin rations, constant travel, and close to a week in the wilderness. Earlier, he'd turned Virgil down on his invitation for a beer at the ClaimJumper and had intended to head home and sack out.

But, somehow, his truck had turned up the road to the prison. Dammit, his craving for the little submissive wouldn't quit. Even if she didn't want to join him tonight, he'd be happy merely talking with her.

Then again...he did have a nice big bed.

There she was.

As she drew closer, he realized every freckle stood out on her pale face. Her arms were wrapped around her torso. Visibly shaking, she didn't even notice him.

"Gin," he called.

Her startled flinch looked close to panic.

"Easy." He kept his voice slow and even. "Easy, girl." He walked up to her at half-speed to allow her time to recognize him.

When she did, her shoulders sagged. "Atticus." She planted her face in his chest.

"Hey, hey, hey." He wrapped his arms around her trembling, fine-boned frame and rubbed his chin in her fragrant hair. Fury flooded his veins along with a craving to rip apart whoever had scared her.

But he'd learned, as a Dom and the son of an abused woman, that sometimes the best response was a willing shoulder.

And time.

After a couple of minutes, far sooner than he liked, she pulled back. Staring at the ground, she said almost inaudibly. "Thank you. I—"

He put a finger under her pointed chin and lifted, forcing her gaze up to his. "You can use my shoulder any time you'd like, Gin. It's not exactly a hardship to hold you, you know."

"You're...very kind." Brow crinkled, she pulled out of his reach. "I appreciate your time. It was nice seeing you again." With an obviously forced smile, she walked away.

What the hell? *Kind? Time?* Sounded a fuck of a lot like a brush-off to him. But why?

She'd forgiven him for being an asshole. Had liked being spanked. They'd made love, talked, cuddled. No fight, dammit. He'd walked her into Serenity Lodge before he left and...

Before he'd left *several days ago.*

He hadn't been in touch since, and she wouldn't be hooked into the police department's network to know he wasn't in reach.

Stretching his legs, he caught up to her. "Gin, I'm sorry I didn't call."

"It doesn't—"

"Yes, it does. C'mere." He pulled her closer, ignoring the way she stiffened. He couldn't blame her. *Hell.* Bet she thought he'd fucked her and kicked her to the curb. "My cell phone doesn't work in the mountains, and I just got back from Search and Rescue at lunchtime today. It didn't seem like a good plan to call you here."

She showed no reaction for a long minute. Finally, her gaze lifted. "You've been hiking since Sunday morning?"

"Yep. Lucky for you that I showered at the station."

After a second, she half-smiled. "You look like you've been camping. Your beard is longer. Scruffier."

Oddly enough, he hadn't trimmed it after his shower, thinking of giving her a new sensation in bed. Not that he'd mention it right now.

"Did you find the kid who got lost?" Her brow was wrinkled with concern.

He liked how she put aside her own problems for someone else's. "I did, sweetheart. And I'll give you the rundown later." Unfortunately, he needed to unsettle her again. "After you tell me what happened to upset you."

When she took a step back, he moved with her, curving an arm around her waist. "Let's find a place to talk."

The parking area stretched across the front of the facility. When he stopped at his truck and opened the passenger door, she pulled away.

"My car's over there." She pointed.

"You're too shook up to drive, pet. Come home with me."

"No." She shook her head, taking a step back.

"Hmm." Well, they were still new to each other, and she was obviously shaken. He'd have preferred quiet, but looked like he'd be joining Virgil after all. "Then we'll join a couple of friends. A cop from my station—Lieutenant Masterson—and his wife are at the ClaimJumper. I'll bring you back afterward."

As she stared at his truck, he could almost see the war going on in her head.

Too much thinking. With a grunt of amusement, he lifted her, set her inside, fastened her seatbelt, and closed the door.

When he swung into the driver's seat, he fully expected the narrow-eyed glare she gave him.

"I can make up my own mind, you know," she snapped.

"I know, Gin." He curled a hand around her nape and took himself a slow kiss. "But I didn't want you to think of reasons to say no. I've been looking forward to being with you."

Damned if he couldn't feel her anger seep away, and he smiled against her lips before enjoying another kiss. She was so fucking sweet.

* * * *

According to Atticus, the owner of the ClaimJumper Tavern loved old-time country-western music, but occasionally could be talked into the current century if a good-looking female asked…which was how

Gin ended up at the bar, asking for Keith Urban or Blake Shelton.

She waved her hands to show how much she liked the music.

After some grumbling in Swedish, Gustaf said, "For you, such a pretty girl, I put it on."

"*Pretty girl?*" *Love it.* Gin smiled. She wouldn't let Slidell get away with calling her a girl, but the old Swede used it in a way that was adorable. Maybe because he called the men *boys*.

As the music changed to *She Wouldn't Be Gone*, she did a victory dance step and wiggle.

A huge man seated on a barstool laughed. "Hey there. I haven't seen you here before."

"Ah, I don't come in here very often."

"Well, I'm glad you did. Get you a drink?" With a gap-toothed grin, he reached for her right hand.

Her chest seized up, and her skin went icy. She jolted backward. "*No.* I mean, no, thank you. I'm with friends."

"She's with me, Barney." When Atticus pulled her against him, the rush of relief was disconcerting.

Barney shrugged amiably. "Oh, well."

My stars, she was acting like an idiot. What had set her off like that? Pulling in a breath, she gave the man a nice smile. "Have a good evening."

"You too, missy."

Atticus jerked his chin up at the guy and guided her away toward their table in the back. To Gin's delight, Atticus's coworker, Lieutenant Masterson, had turned out to be Summer's husband.

At the table, Summer was pouring glasses of beer. The nurse's blonde hair was loose and shone brightly against her fluffy blue sweater.

Her husband sat in a chair next to her, one thickly muscled arm behind her back. His brown cowboy hat was a few shades darker than his sandy hair. He looked to be a smidge taller than Atticus and maybe an inch broader in the shoulders. Pretty darn big, really, and it was difficult to imagine petite Kallie as his cousin.

Even if Gin lived in Bear Flat for a decade, she doubted she'd get all the relationships worked out.

Politely, Virgil rose and pulled out a chair for her. "Good work with Gustaf and the music."

"Thanks. He's quite a tough sell."

"Sit here, baby." Unsmiling, Atticus helped her into the chair as if she were a ninety-year-old cripple. With a walker.

"Thank you." *I think.*

"Now hold still." He curled his fingers around her right hand and tugged her sweater sleeve up.

Red-black bruises at the wrist showed where Slash had grabbed her.

Mouth compressed, he bent her arm up. His firm grip on her hand prevented any attempt to pull away as he ran a finger over her swollen forearm.

She flinched. It still hurt, and no wonder. A thick purple-black line marked where the inmate had slammed her arm against the desk's edge.

"This what had you upset at the prison?" Although Atticus's face had darkened, his voice was even. Controlled.

"Um." Being among friends had let her escape the memory, but... She bit her lip, realizing why she'd almost panicked with the man sitting at the bar. Because he'd reached for her hand like Slash had. Atticus had noticed. "You're very observant."

"A-huh. Nice try at evasion. Now tell me what happened." The stern set of his jaw and continued hold on her arm made her bones feel like Jell-O.

Beside her, Virgil gripped her left hand and pulled up the sleeve. After a quick check, he told Atticus, "Nothing here." At her surprised look, he squeezed her fingers. "We're cops. Seeing marks on a woman tends to upset us. Now answer your Dom."

"He's not—" Her protest died when Atticus lifted a brow. Well, maybe he had been her Dom for one night—*okay, two.* But still... "Fine," she huffed. "An inmate came on to me sexually, so I summoned help. Before the guard arrived, the inmate lost his temper and slammed my arm on the desk."

"Jesus," Atticus growled and traced a finger over the black bruising. "He could have busted your arm."

Summer's face paled.

"I'm fine," Gin said hastily.

"The CO was slow getting to you," Atticus said with far too much comprehension. His gaze cleared, and he cupped her cheek. "I seriously don't like you working there."

His concern made her eyes pool with tears. Preston hadn't worried about her. If she'd been upset about a violent client, he'd never asked how it was going. If she were safe.

During a tropical storm, a tree had come down on her car. When she got home three frightening hours late, he'd been watching a movie.

When she was sick, he'd visit friends to ensure he didn't catch anything.

She'd never realized how...unloved...his indifference had made her feel.

With a wavery smile, she looked into Atticus's gunmetal blue eyes. "I'll be fine. And this inmate won't be back to see me again."

"Gang member?" Virgil frowned at her.

"One of the neo-Nazis who came in recently." According to the sergeant, their subculture tended toward irrational violence. She gave Virgil a wry look. "I was surprised that—at least in prison—a lot of established gangs require respect for female medical personnel. Apparently the skinheads go to the other extreme and hate women."

After a minute, Atticus took his chair beside her, still holding her fingers. He handed her a beer, took one for himself, and lifted it. "Here's to the southern magnolia moving to a better job." After the clicking of glasses and agreement, he brushed his lips over her cheek. "Although I'm grateful for the help you gave my brother."

He'd noticed the change in Sawyer. Happiness filled her.

As Virgil sat back, looking more like a cowboy than a cop, Gin glanced at Atticus. Black cowboy hat, battered boots, jeans belted with a rodeo buckle, and denim western shirt. Both guys looked as if they'd come in off the range. "Tell me, does the police station list horseback riding and roping as job skills?"

"Hell, they won't even let me wear my hat." Virgil grinned. "Tell you what, some of those skills come in handy, like the way Atticus tracked down the teenager."

"Will he be all right?" Summer asked.

"He'll be in the hospital overnight, but looks like mostly dehydration and frostbite," Virgil said. "I daresay he's pretty grateful to be alive."

"Might have found him sooner, but I got sidetracked following two of his friends." Atticus's eyes crinkled. "*They* weren't very grateful. Maybe because I caught them bare-ass naked and fornicating their fucking heads off."

Gin choked on her beer.

"I haven't been called names like that in years," Atticus said. "And that was the girl."

Summer was giggling. "The law enforcement career is a challenging one."

Atticus flicked a glance at Virgil. "Can see you don't get much sympathy from your woman."

"She makes it up to me in other ways," Virgil murmured, running the backs of his fingers over her cheek.

Summer flushed a dark red and turned to Gin. "Ah…so, I didn't get a chance to ask last time we met. You'd said the prison was very different. So what did you do in Louisiana? Not a prison?"

"Not even close. I worked in a mental health center that specialized in families and children. I loved it." Oh, she really had.

Atticus tilted his head, watching her silently.

"Then why didn't you pick something like that instead of a prison?" Summer asked.

"I should have." Gin pulled in a breath. "But I lost a client. He was only seventeen." So angry, so messed up. His mother and stepfather hadn't listened to her, hadn't instituted the precautions she'd recommended. Something had set him off. He'd taken every drug offered at a party, stolen a car…and driven straight into a semi.

Sometimes a person was simply too troubled to make wise choices. That was what had happened with Sawyer, after all. Her seventeen-year-old client had suffered from an alcoholic, abusive father. Sawyer had suffered through a war. Both were victims. At least Sawyer was alive to turn his life around.

"Didn't trust yourself because of that?" Virgil asked.

Gin nodded. "Losing someone under my care…"

"Leaves you wondering what you might have missed, might have done differently. And even if everyone says you did it all exactly right, you still feel guilty." The nurse's gaze held a matching pain.

When both Atticus and Virgil nodded, Gin realized a cop's type of protection and nurturing was different from a counselors…and yet very much the same.

"Doesn't seem like you to cut and run," Atticus said, surprising her.

"Well, I ran away because I broke up with my fiancé. But relocating gave me a chance to try something new." She smiled wryly. "Moving here was good. The career choice…perhaps not so much."

"Quit," Atticus said.

"Please. I can't walk out. Even if I could, I have a duty to my cases." *Like your brother.*

He watched her for a long moment before nodding. "So be it."

That was nice—that he could let a subject drop. Without arguing until he got his way.

Instead, he tilted his head, listening to the beginning of Tim McGraw's slow, sweet song *She's My Kind of Rain.*

"Come, baby. You got us good music from Gustaf—let's dance." He pulled her out of her chair and to the tiny space that only a blind person would consider a dance floor.

"I don't think there's enough room," she said.

With an arm around her waist, he pulled her close and set one muscular leg between her thighs. "Means we have to dance closer."

The feeling of being plastered against his hard, powerful body was divine.

When he cupped his hand over her rear end, she squirmed. "Atticus. Behave."

He chuckled. "Wiggle some more."

"You're impossible."

"And you're fucking soft." He rubbed his chin in her hair. "I'm sorry you got hurt, baby."

Darn it. How could she stay annoyed with him when he was so sympathetic? And made her so hot. His touch, his hold, made her remember everything he'd done to her in his bed. Made her...long...for more.

He felt the way she'd melted against him and growled in approval. And then just held her, swaying with the music.

With his warm embrace and his silence, the lingering tension from the attack drained out of her. Sighing, she contentedly rested her head on his shoulder.

All too soon, the music changed, turning to Kelly Clarkson's *Stronger (What Doesn't Kill You)*.

Darn. "That was wonderful. Thank you." When Atticus's embrace loosened, Gin stepped back and headed off the floor.

"Not so fast, darlin'. Don't southern girls know how to dance?" Moving smoothly to the beat, he grasped her right hand, frowned, and switched to her uninjured arm to swing her out. He spun her back and smoothly recaptured her again without losing a step. "Yep, you do."

He twirled her again and pulled her into a side-by-side turn.

Following his strong lead easily, she laughed in amazement, "You swing dance."

He grinned. "Amazing the skills a guy can acquire when riding rodeo. At the time, it was a good way to meet women."

She bet he'd scored a ton of buckle bunnies. "And now?"

He pulled her up against him, rocking her close enough she could feel he was half-erect. "Now it's a good way to hold just one."

Oh. Oh no. No. Not just one. She needed to nip this in the bud. "I like being held. And I'm enjoying being a friend with benefits," she said carefully. "This is very nice. Can we stick to just this?"

"And she draws a line in the sand," he murmured. His eyes held hers. Level. Unreadable. "I hear what you're saying."

* * * *

He'd heard what she'd said all right, Atticus thought. Hours later, in Gin's bed, he remained awake, savoring the lush body draped across him. She'd had a rough day; he'd made sure she had a gentle and thoroughly carnal night.

Although he'd planned to let her rest after the first round, she'd donned a golden nightie with dainty ruffles and lace, looking so innocently feminine that he couldn't resist. And he'd felt almost depraved when he'd tossed her on the bed, set her on hands and knees, pushed the nightie up, and taken her from behind. Then again, her shock at his unexpected actions hadn't kept her from coming long and hard.

Considering the amount of lingerie she owned, the woman was liable to be the death of him.

Well satiated, she slept deeply now. Her head rested on his chest, her fragrant hair spilling over his shoulder and arm. His hand curved over one bare ass cheek. Fuck, but he liked her round ass.

Friends with benefits, huh?

His mouth twisted with a silent laugh. After years of straightforwardly telling women that he wasn't interested in a relationship, he undoubtedly deserved getting the words back.

And he didn't like it.

Because this time, he wanted more. He'd never met anyone like Gin. Fuck, she was fun. Spirited. Independent. And yet he was thinking her need to give, to nurture, to submit, was equal to his need to protect, to tend, to dominate.

They matched, she liked him, the chemistry was amazing…but she was backing away.

What the hell had happened to make her put up all those barriers? Something to do with her ex-fiancé?

At the foot of the bed, her dog snuffled and resettled. His heavy head rested on Atticus's ankle, his body along Gin's legs.

How did Trigger manage to get under her defenses? Outdone by a skinny Labrador. *Way to go, Ware.*

But, dogs didn't push; Doms did.

Atticus smiled grimly. Once he found out what made her raise the barriers...then he'd help her tear them down.

Friends with benefits, my ass.

Chapter Eleven

On Mondays, the prison mental health department held their weekly staff meetings. Everywhere Gin had worked, meetings were an unavoidable chore. Unfortunately, this place held Howard Slidell and his prisoner-bashing rants.

And today would be worse.

The last to arrive, Gin dropped into a seat at the end of the long table. She leaned back as the counselors gave updates on their caseloads.

A few minutes before, she'd spoken with Sawyer, needing his...well, his permission. His forgiveness in a way because she couldn't continue as Sawyer's counselor after she'd been intimate with his brother. She might have been able to justify the BDSM scenes, but...no, even those had been inappropriate.

To her surprise, Sawyer had been understanding and even willing to discuss his preference in counselors. They'd talked about each of the staff, and she was darned well going to see he got his first choice.

More worrying, he'd said he'd terminate therapy if assigned to Slidell. His declaration had crystalized Gin's resolve. Tomorrow, she'd document her concerns about what her inmates had said about Slidell. She'd add what she'd observed. Then she and the administrator would have a chat.

Silence at the table brought her thoughts back, and she realized they were all looking at her.

"Gin," the administrator said, obviously repeating himself. "Do you have anything of concern?"

"Yes." She stood. "I'm dating the brother of one my cases, which means I need to turn the inmate over to someone else. His name is Sawyer Ware, and—"

"I saw him before." Slidell folded his hands over his paunch. "I'll take him back."

"That won't work," she said in a flat voice.

When Penelope lifted her hand, Gin ignored her. The woman would mess with his head. Thank goodness, the mental health department had only a couple of bad apples. The rest were highly competent and professional.

Gin turned to Jacob Wheeler. Around fifty with dark graying hair, ex-military, lean and fit, possessing a sardonic sense of humor. He was first choice. Unfortunately, he was also always overloaded.

"Jacob, Sawyer came back from Afghanistan with PTSD. He didn't get the treatment he needed—and he made a mess of his life. He's turning it around, but I don't want to let his progress stall. I do believe you'd be the best one to help him."

Slidell's face turned a dark red. "See here, you can't—"

Channeling Atticus's more intimidating mannerisms, Gin firmed her jaw and flattened her hands on the table surface, leaning into the opposition. "Yes. I can."

"Did you talk with Ware, Gin?" Jacob rubbed his lips, concealing a smile and talking right past Slidell, as if he weren't there.

"I did. He agreed to the change in counselors. And to you, if you'd have him."

"You covered your bases." Jacob tapped the screen of his tablet, checked the display, and looked up. His intent stare made her want to cringe. "Is this important enough to fuck up my entire schedule?"

"Yes." She lifted her chin. "Yes, it is. He's a good man."

Jacob's deep, focused gaze remained on her for a long moment before an approving smile softened his carved features. "Well fought, counselor. I'll free up time for him."

Gin resumed her seat, happiness filling her. *Success.* Sawyer would have someone who would truly understand him. Who'd speak his language.

And she could date Atticus with a guilt-free conscience.

* * * *

Midweek, Atticus swung by the prison.

From a distance, he could see his brother in the concrete yard with the basketball court. He watched for a minute, his heart lightened. Sawyer hadn't done anything active in the year he'd been imprisoned…not until the southern counselor had taken him in her soft little hand.

He felt damned guilty though, as though he'd stolen Gin from his brother. He wished she could remain as his therapist, but she'd assured him that the new social worker was an even better fit. God, he hoped so.

Sawyer sidestepped his opponent, made a basket—and laughed.

A bit later, after some extra rigmarole and calling in a favor, Atticus entered a reception room.

Sawyer was leaning against a wall, arms crossed over his chest. "Not visiting day, bro."

Fuck, how long had it been since Sawyer'd looked…whole? Not since his second tour of duty overseas.

Atticus held his hand out and used the grip to pull his brother close enough to bump shoulders. He cleared his throat, ordered his thoughts to business. "I wanted a word."

"Lookin' serious." Sawyer commented, positioning himself where he could see the door.

"We've got some increased crime in town—robberies, muggings. Any connection to the prison you know of?"

"Huh." Sawyer considered. "Always possible, but if so, my crew isn't in on the information." Prison populations tended to divide along color and gang lines, so independent prisoners could get badly hurt. And, although a SEAL could hold his own, it was good he'd found a few buddies.

"I wish you weren't in here." And he had another year to go. Each visit turned Atticus's muscles rigid as his instincts demanded he protect his little brother from danger. And he couldn't.

Sawyer's face darkened. "I screwed up." His pain-filled gaze met Atticus's. "Maybe my head wasn't screwed on good after coming back, but…I still don't feel like I deserve a free life."

"Maybe you could—"

"Bro, love you, man, but you're not raising me anymore."

"What?"

When Sawyer straightened, Atticus was surprised to see his little brother was an inch taller. Was packing on the muscle. Was an *adult*.

Jesus.

Sawyer's lips curved. "The light dawns."

"This must be how a parent feels," Atticus said ruefully. When their stepfather had gone to prison, Atticus had become the man of the house. And since their ill and overworked mother couldn't, he'd essentially raised Sawyer and Hector.

But Sawyer wasn't a child any longer. Not even close. "You were gone so long I forgot you grew up. Fuck, are you thirty-three?"

"Guess that makes you an old man, doesn't it?" Sawyer grinned, and then turned a level stare on Atticus. "Cut the apron strings, Att. It's my life, and I got this."

Hell. A Dom's temptation was to control everything, ensuring anyone more vulnerable or weaker was cared for. Letting go didn't come naturally. But there were times a Dom—or big brother—needed to step back.

Pride swept over him. His brother had hit rock bottom and was fighting his way back up with all the determination and courage he'd shown throughout his decorated military career.

"*I got this.*" "Damn straight you got this, bro."

Saldana appeared in the door. His marker had run out.

Atticus lifted his hand in acknowledgment.

"I'll keep an ear out for trouble here," Sawyer said. "And hey, congrats on the pretty new lady in your life."

Atticus jerked his chin up in acknowledgment, bit back a "Be careful," and headed for the door.

On the way out, he hesitated and kept going. No time to swing by and see how Gin was doing. And he was on call tonight, so he wouldn't be able to take her out.

He snorted. She wouldn't appreciate a visit anyway. Although the "benefits" had been rewarding for both of them on Friday, she was striving to hold him at arm's length. He'd backed off on the weekend to give her the illusion of control but had talked her into a meal tomorrow by playing the "I'm starving" card. The woman lived to feed people.

He liked that. Liked her need to make people happy. Liked everything about her. Maybe she wanted to keep a distance, but he damn well didn't. More and more, he was thinking he'd found the woman he wanted in his ropes, in his arms. In his life.

Chapter Twelve

"So, how is it going with Atticus?" Kallie asked through the phone's speaker.

In her kitchen, Gin used a fork to pattern the tops of the unbaked peanut butter cookies and thanked the stars her friend couldn't see her blush. "Atticus?" she asked casually, trying for a *who is Atticus* tone.

"Gin," Kallie said in reproach. "You do know you live in a small town now, right? And Summer, Becca, and I are all friends? And that Summer must have told us about how very, very concerned Atticus was with your getting hurt. And, perhaps, how he laid a good one on you in the ClaimJumper parking lot...before you got into his truck."

Oh, spit. "I forget you Yankees gossip as much as Southerners."

"After a long winter of being snowed in? We're far, far worse. Now, it's Wednesday, so spill. Is this getting serious?"

"*No.*" Gin looked at the poor cookie she'd flattened with a fork and winced. *Sorry, cookie.* She scooped it off the pan and turned. "*Psst.*"

Across the room, Trigger lifted his head. He caught the tossed treat with a snap of big jaws, and his tail swept the linoleum floor in appreciation.

"No, Snoopy-pants," Gin said to the speakerphone. "We're just having fun. Enjoying the moment. Nothing serious."

"Well, damn." A pause. "You know, all the submissives in the area think he's wonderful. Is he...um..."

Gin grinned. Kallie might try to present herself as one of the boys, but bless her heart, she was as curious as any girl. And the way she hoped Atticus and Gin were serious made Gin feel all warm and fuzzy.

But how to explain to her girlfriends the *friendly, booty-sex* clause? "He's definitely *um*. And more."

"Oh wow. I need to find a fan," Kallie muttered.

Gin heard a car door slam. "Got to go. I have company."

"Really? Your cowboy and his big ol' strumpet thumper showing up?"

Gin was still laughing when she opened the door for Atticus.

His eyes heated when he saw her. "You're all flushed, sweetheart." He moved in, inexorable as the tide, flattening her against the wall with his solid body.

When he kissed her, slow and deep, everything inside her melted like buttery cookies in a hot oven.

"You smell like sugar and vanilla," he muttered, nibbling her jaw and down her neck.

When he pressed his rapidly thickening...*strumpet thumper*...against her, she giggled.

He straightened, set his forearm on the wall above her head, and studied her face. The side of his mouth tilted up. "That's not a reaction I normally get," he said mildly.

She laughed harder, and even so, had to note that nothing shook his self-confidence. "Kallie called this piece of anatomy"—she tilted her pelvis against his rock-solid shaft—"a strumpet thumper."

"Ah." He grinned. "Lucky for me that I have a strumpet right here at hand." With merciless hands, he undid her pants and shoved her jeans to the floor.

He stepped back and opened his jeans. "And I have the equipment to deal with her too."

"My stars," she said faintly. He had a...*thumper*...to marvel at. Long and beautifully formed, perfectly straight. She traced a finger over the veins and velvety skin enclosing the iron shaft beneath.

She almost whined when he covered all that beauty with a condom.

"C'mere, strumpet." He lifted her in the air.

As her legs went around his waist, he placed her against the wall, impaled her on his cock, and thumped her so thoroughly, she'd walk bow-legged for a week.

Atticus had enjoyed his little strumpet, especially the way she broke into giggles every time her hips thudded on the wall. Damn, she was fun.

After a pause for a beer and fresh-baked cookies, he'd pulled her outside for a walk.

As they strolled, Trigger danced around them. Atticus picked up a stick and threw it. A typical Labrador, the dog loved to fetch.

In the coolness of the woods at the end of Gin's street, they chatted about work and the town, Sawyer and their friends. Quiet time, Atticus thought, much like his parents would enjoy after his father finished the ranch work.

Gin was fun to be with. She was knowledgeable about current events and could hold her own in political and sports discussions. She wasn't a pig-headed fanatic—except about the Saints football team—and was willing to concede a point.

When she scored on him, her gloating was cute.

"My turn to throw," she said, holding her hand out for the stick.

He handed it over without a word.

She let loose. The stick sailed over several stunted trees and landed in the tall-growing grass. Out of sight.

"You have quite an arm," Atticus said.

"I was the catcher on my softball team."

Her lopsided grin appeared, dimple in the corner—and told him everything. She'd loved playing. "Any other school sports?"

"Soccer now and then. Basketball until everyone got taller than me."

All team sports.

He regarded her until she lifted her eyebrows and said, "What?"

She was a bookworm though. "Did you belong to book clubs too?"

"Well, sure."

She liked people. In fact, she'd barely unpacked her boxes, and she'd surrounded herself with girlfriends.

He slowed, checking the brush.

"What are you looking for?" She drew closer. "Are there wild animals or something? Snakes?"

"No, baby." He couldn't quite smother his laugh. "I need a stick to replace the one you threw away."

"Oh, Trigger will find it. He always does."

Sure enough, Trigger was in the meadow, nose up, casting for the scent. A second later, he bounded across the field and pounced on the stick like he'd trapped a juicy rabbit.

Grinning, Atticus waited while the dog tore back to Gin and dropped the stick at her feet.

"Such a good boy. You're amazing," she exclaimed. And threw the stick again.

"He's got a better nose than some of the SAR dogs," Atticus said.

"He does?" Her gaze was on the Lab. "Jake's talked about Search and Rescue. But it sounds as if training the dogs takes a lot of time. And I'm not sure I'm cut out for running around the mountains." Her wry smile was adorable. "I'm very good on the flat, but not so hot on cliffs. Not like you. I saw the way you went up the climbing wall at the festival."

He felt his face tighten.

"What did I say?"

Hell. Looking away, he could feel her gaze on his face. The thought of explaining... "It's nothing."

"I think it is," she said lightly. "And I'd like to hear it if you can talk." She'd pulled on her damned counselor's hat.

"Not a chance." *Who the hell...* He groaned and rubbed his palm on his beard. Fuck, she *was* a counselor and a fine one. The hurt look in her eyes could rip his heart apart. "I'm sorry, sweetheart."

No, that wasn't enough.

He took her fingers. "Knee-jerk reaction. I don't like thinking about... Fuck. I guess I should explain." He slung an arm around her waist, pulling her closer, mostly so she couldn't see his face.

Her body was soft and warm and comforting flattened against his, reminding him that he was grateful to be alive. She didn't speak.

"A buddy and I got into free solo climbing."

Her expression said she wasn't following.

"Traditional climbing uses belay ropes and pitons and other people." He ran his finger down her cheek. "Traditional is what got me interested in bondage and suspension."

She rubbed her face against his hand in a sweetly submissive motion. "Does free and solo mean you aren't using some equipment?"

"No gear except chalk and shoes. No help."

"That's...scary." She bit her lip. "I've seen people climb boulders in the park with mattresses underneath."

"Mmmhmm. Similar. Bouldering usually is limited to twenty feet or under. With free solo, you climb as high as you want." He nodded toward Yosemite, where the tip of El Capitan could barely be seen.

"Mercy." Her eyes were wide. "A fall would kill you."

"Uh-huh." His mouth tightened. "Bryan and I were climbing different routes on a granite formation about a thousand feet high. We were close enough to see each other. We got hit with an unpredicted afternoon shower; it turned the rock wet." No quick way down or up since they were almost to the top. So fucking far up. He forced the words through a dry throat. "His hand slipped."

Bryan had clawed at the granite, unbalanced, his foot sliding. And he fell...

Shouting, completely helpless to assist, Atticus had slipped and barely recovered, but...couldn't do shit. The gut-wrenching thud of Bryan's landing had echoed off the surrounding rocks, like the fading beat of a heart.

"Oh, Atticus." Arms wrapped around him as Gin hugged him tightly, her cheek pressed to his chest.

After a second, he put his arms around her.

"He died?" she whispered.

"Yeah." Atticus had made it down. Called for help. Sat vigil by his friend's shattered, empty body.

"I'm so sorry." She squeezed him harder.

Finish it. "I lost a friend. And haven't climbed above a few feet since. I was on the wall at the festival trying to force myself higher." He shook his head. "Couldn't."

"I see." Gin tipped back and stroked his beard. And then she gave a quiet huff of amusement. "Honey, you've come to the right place. I've helped quite a few clients with this kind of problem. I'll give you some things to read and then we'll go through the exercises together."

He stared down at the top of her head. Sympathy was in her tone, but...also a matter-of-fact belief that he'd get past his fears.

And that she'd help. No wonder she'd performed miracles with Sawyer.

* * * *

Sunday morning, she carried her cup of tea and a blanket out to her back porch and settled into the secondhand patio chair. With a canine sigh of content, Trigger sprawled out on top of her feet.

Contentedly, she draped the blanket over her lap and sipped her tea.

The florescent orange California poppies were a splash of color against the weathered gray wooden fence. A lilac bush in full flower brought her the enticing fragrance.

The lawn...well, the lawn definitely needed mowing. Who knew grass could grow so fast?

On the porch, white verbena spilled out over the dark green planters she'd bought last week.

Gin tipped her head back to study the blue sky and enjoy the quiet.

Somewhere near dawn, Atticus had kissed her good-bye, tucked the covers around her, and let himself out. He was on call and his beeper had gone off.

Without any guilty feelings whatsoever, she'd fallen back to sleep. And slept late.

Gin grinned. She'd been pretty exhausted, after all, and even after a long hot shower this morning, she had some sore muscles. Atticus was a very inventive—and demanding—lover.

Although, he didn't seem to require much from her outside of the bedroom. Wasn't a Dominant supposed to want more?

But, he didn't, and they'd achieved a nice balance of give and take. Of course, a couple of times she'd had to remind herself that housecleaning and cooking weren't her job. Darn it, she liked doing things for him. She took a sip of her tea, feeling the warmth slipping down her throat.

However, since she'd been able to stem her need to serve, maybe her worries about turning herself inside out for a man were excessive. *Maybe.* Darn it, she still wanted some counseling, but aside from the prison staff, there were no mental health professionals in the area.

She gnawed on her lip for a minute.

I want to be with him. If she was doing all right, perhaps she might relax her self-imposed rules and enjoy what they were creating. Now that she was vigilant about her tendency to lose herself in a relationship, surely she could keep from turning into a doormat, from trying too hard to please him.

Because Atticus was worth fighting for, even if her opponent was herself.

Chapter Thirteen

Atticus rode his horse out of the forest and across the pasture. Festus's hooves thudded softly in the lush grass, and his ears were forward. He'd obviously enjoyed the winding mountain trail.

A shame the ride hadn't eased Atticus. His gut felt hollow. Hell, he couldn't even feel the warmth of the horse beneath him. Red splotches kept hazing his vision, obscuring the spring-green fields. Staring at the sun might cause lingering white circles; staring at a murder left bloody ones.

And there had been so fucking much blood...

The murderer hadn't gotten far, but shutting him behind bars wouldn't restore life to the young wife. *Dammit.* Hopped-up on meth and steroids, the bastard had become enraged with his woman's worrying about their finances—and silenced her with a knife.

She couldn't have been over twenty-one.

Atticus realized he'd brought Festus to a stop and was blindly staring at the mountains. Deep breaths didn't erase the stench of released bowels and blood, of hate and violence. With a sigh, he stroked the horse's neck. "Sorry, buddy, I'm—"

"Are you all right, Atticus?"

He clapped his hand to his sidearm before recognizing the voice.

In a soft blue sweater and tan jeans, Gin stood on the Masterson side of the wooden rail fence.

"Hey." His voice came out like gravel.

Her brows drew together. "What's wrong?"

"Nothing."

She sniffed in exasperation and climbed up to sit on the top of the fence. She lowered her voice to an imitation of his. "'*First lesson for tonight: be honest.*'"

His lips refused to curve in a smile. "You got me, darlin'." He guided Festus closer and plopped Gin sideways onto the horse's bare back in front of him.

Nice squeak. She grabbed his shirt.

As he pulled her soft, wonderfully warm body closer, he kissed her shoulder and inhaled the fragrance of lavender and vanilla. The world did still hold sweet and clean. Jesus, he'd needed to know that. "Gin, I—"

To his surprise, she twisted and hugged him tightly. "*Shhh.* Whatever happened, we can fix it. *Shhh.*"

His mouth flattened. There was no fix for what had happened to the victim. Yet Gin's sympathy and determination to help loosened the knot in his gut. His next breath was deeper. The tendrils of blackness receded. He could hear the horses in the next pasture, the wind rippling through the conifers, snippets of the Masterson men arguing in their stable.

Life surrounded him. Was in his arms. He lifted his head, kissed her curved cheek, then her lips.

Her fingers curled around his nape. She prolonged the kiss, giving him everything, like an unexpectedly generous harvest.

Lifting his head, he looked down at her, seeing concern etched in the tiny line between her brows. She cared. "Thank you, Gin."

Her smile transformed her from lovely to a heart-stopping beauty. "My pleasure, I'd say. Are you going to tell me what's wrong?"

"Noth—" Almost blurting out the same lie, he caught himself and gave her a rueful glance. "A murder. In town. It was bad."

She winced. "Aren't they all?"

"Truth." To his own surprise, he added, "The victim was a young woman. Her man lost his temper." *The goddamn bastard.* "We apprehended him, but she was…" The clipped words stopped as his jaw turned rigid. *The hell with talking.*

Leaning forward, he grabbed Gin's left leg and swung it over the horse's neck so she straddled Festus. As he loosened the reins and nudged the horse into a walk, she made a faint worried noise. City girl hadn't ridden bareback before.

After a moment, she cleared her throat. "Didn't you say your stepfather was an angry man?" Her question was as on target as if she'd shot an arrow into the bull's-eye.

His hands must have pulled back since Festus halted, and, after a second, lipped at the new grass.

My goddamned stepfather. Atticus stared over Gin's head at the thick evergreens climbing the valley slopes. There had been blood on his mother too often. Every day after school, he'd been terrified at what he'd find.

With an effort, he cleared his throat and gave the counselor the truth. "Yeah, maybe that's why this homicide got to me." He clicked and eased Festus into a slow walk toward his house.

"Um, Atticus?" Gin waved her hand toward the Mastersons' spread. "I came down with Kallie to feed the horses and visit Summer, and then we're going back to Serenity Lodge to finish our visit."

"Guess you're visiting me instead." At her disgruntled look, he found an unexpected smile. "Call her when we get to my house."

"Listen..." She scowled over her shoulder at him, hesitated, and said gently, "All right. If you'll eat what I make for you."

"I don't need a cook. I want—"

She crossed her arms over her beautiful, full breasts. "This is the only deal you're offered, Ware."

"Aren't you a tough one?" And fucking cute too. With his free hand, he slid his palm under her arms to cup one of her breasts. Maybe he could work out a better deal.

Atticus Ware was a stubborn man, Gin thought. She'd called Summer and Kallie to tell them she'd been kidnapped. Summer's voice held a wealth of satisfaction when she'd told Gin to have fun. Her girlfriends approved of Atticus.

For a man who'd only lived in this town a year, he'd made awfully good friends.

She turned back to her job. The pork chops had been browned, and cream of mushroom soup bubbled around them at a low simmer. The oiled and salted baking potatoes went into an oven turned high enough to make crispy skins.

When Atticus had tried to help, she'd noticed he was still in his work clothes, which were stained with... No, she didn't want to think about such things. She'd sent him to take a shower.

The water upstairs was still running. Had removing his bloody clothing reminded him of the crime? Twisted him up again?

Her heart ached. Did all strong men have the misconception they should be able to protect everyone under their care?

Maybe so, since she felt the same way about people she allowed close. They were hers to nurture. She wanted to give them peace, and if possible—joy.

At the thought, she ran up the stairs to Atticus's bedroom. She pulled off her sweater, tossed it on the bed, and then stripped off her pants and underwear.

His bedside table held condoms.

With a hand on the bathroom door, she hesitated. If he didn't want her, the knowledge would hurt. Nonetheless... Shoulders back, she stepped in. Clear glass doors showed the black marble shower was filled with fog—no, he had a steam shower.

Fingers crossed that she was doing the right thing, she pulled open the door and entered. Blurring the air, steam curled over her bare skin in a sensuous brush of heat.

A wooden shower bench took up space to her right. The far end held a U-shaped marble shower bench where Atticus reclined with his back against the wall. His face was drawn, mouth compressed in a thin line.

He saw her. Frowned. He saw what she held and a sensuous hunger darkened his features. "I get an appetizer?"

She blinked. "Well, no, I didn't bring—"

His growling laugh ran along her nerve endings. "Sweetness, you definitely brought my appetizer." He rose to loom over her, smelling of clean, wet male. After plucking the condom from her hand, he tore the wrapper open and sheathed his very erect dick.

"Stand right there, sweetling." He pumped a handful of suds from one of the dispensers and stroked over her shoulders, massaging lightly, before moving to the front of her neck. Her collarbone.

The scent of pine wafted into the air. She'd smell like him; it was disconcerting how much she liked the idea. "Aren't you a nice man to help me get all clean," she said in a teasing voice.

And then that nice man reached her breasts and rolled her nipples mercilessly.

Her knees buckled with the sudden arousal.

He anchored her with a steely arm around her waist, her back against his rock-hard chest, before reaching around to soap—thoroughly—her pussy. She had a moment to be grateful she'd shaved…down there… before his clever fingers drove every thought from her head.

"Oh my lord," she whispered, gripping his forearm. "Atticus."

"Shh." Ruthlessly, he teased her.

Her clit swelled, tingled. The pressure grew. She was close…

Before she could come, he stopped.

"Noooo…"

"Patience, little subbie. Now give me your wrist." The look in his eyes, the set of his jaw, sent an anxious thrill through her as she placed her hand in his big palm.

Turning toward the wall, he lifted her arm to a white peg, head height. Using the Velcro wristband dangling from it, he secured her to the peg. When he fastened her other wrist to another peg, her arms were outstretched slightly wider than her shoulders, and she was leaning forward. He drew a wooden bench across the shower stall and set her left foot on top of it and secured her ankle there, forcing her to stand with her weight on her right leg.

"I cannot believe I'm letting you do this to me." Her mind was coming up with all sorts of dreadful scenarios.

He chuckled. "I think I mentioned what happens if your mind wanders from the here and now?"

"I don't rem—"

"I do something to drag it back." His callused hand hit her butt, and the smack of bare flesh on flesh echoed in the steamy shower.

"Ow!" Her body jerked and tried to move away. Arms restrained. One leg. She wasn't going anywhere. The knowledge was terrifying—hot—terrifying.

He spanked her, over and over, five more times, hard stinging slaps. Wet skin hurt worse.

Her body was shaking but somehow the pain in her skin was sending sizzling currents of heat to her pussy until she couldn't tell which was throbbing worse.

"I think your mind is focused now," he murmured and pressed against her back. Her bottom burned when his cock rubbed against the abused area, and she inhaled sharply at the surge of arousal.

His powerful hand curled over her hip, securing her as he set his shaft at her slick entrance and slowly, determinedly penetrated her. As she stretched around the solid, thick intrusion, her body shook with shivers of need.

"Fuck, you feel good," he growled.

Her head was spinning. He was rougher this time—securing her where he wanted her—taking her as he wanted. And the sensation filled her soul as thoroughly as his cock was filling her body. This—this was what she wanted. Her hands closed into fists as he thrust in harder.

His chest slid against her back as he reached to one side and flipped on the controls. Body sprays came on. One upper spray hit her in her chest, another her low stomach. He leaned forward, his shaft surging in deeper as he shut down the upper spray and adjusted the lower to a fine fierce spray...and pointed it downward right at her widely spread pussy. When it struck her exposed clit, she jerked.

His chuckle was a subterranean rumble in her ear. "There's a good spot."

"Atticus, no." She struggled to free her hands, to cover herself. The water pounded at her flesh, tingling and biting in a hundred droplets, and then he gripped her hips, withdrew his cock, and slammed into her.

"Oh. *God.*" Sensations assailed her, inside and outside.

"And she does swear, after all." He was laughing as he hammered her hard and fast, and the water teased her clit unmercifully. Her body gathered, pressure building. And then unstoppable as the ocean, the orgasm rolled through her, incredible spasm after spasm, shaking her violently. Too, too much pleasure. Her leg buckled; Atticus tightened the arm around her waist.

"Very nice, darlin'," he said in her ear in his deep, sexy voice. "You almost sent me over with that one."

But she hadn't, and he was still long and thick inside her as he slowed to a gentle thrusting. His hand curved over her clit, protecting her from the spray.

Why hadn't he turned the water off?

But he unhurriedly slid in and out, nibbled on her neck, using one hand to play with her breasts. Taking his time and openly enjoying her.

She loved it, both that he'd taken the time to make her come, but to know that he'd use her for his own enjoyment was so, so satisfying.

As he played and as his dick made slow circular motions, her arousal kicked in again. Her nipples puckered; her insides clenched around him. As the exquisite torment continued, she whined in protest.

He nipped her neck in warning.

When she didn't speak, he murmured, "There's a good girl." Holding her steady, he reached forward to rotate the spray head to a brutal pounding pulse...and removed his hand from her clit.

The thrumming jets hit right on the spot, sending her to her tiptoes. "Nooo."

He gripped her hips and held her right there. Holding her implacably, he started thrusting harder, deeper, not slowing as she tightened, as her clit engorged, as she hovered on the precipice.

"No, no, no—" Her neck arched back as her muscles drew taut, driving her over the crest. Her whole body spasmed with the relentless pleasure. On and on…

His powerful hands squeezed her hips, and he growled his pleasure as he came. The pulsing sensation so deep inside her was devastatingly intimate, as if they had been joined in every level possible.

As her heart rate slowed, her muscles seemed to be melting. She sagged in his grip.

"Easy, sweetling." He nuzzled her cheek, anchoring her with an arm around her waist. She could feel the thud of his heart against her back, the heat of his body against hers as he ripped open the Velcro to free her restraints.

Pulling free, he turned her and wrapped her in his arms. As he ran his hands over her ever so gently, he kissed her, deep and long. "Now that was what I call an appetizer."

An hour later, at his wide kitchen table, Atticus smiled over at Gin. The little submissive had dressed again after their…shower…but her long hair still lay in tangles, the red glints reappearing as it dried. The dazed expression she'd worn through most of the meal had given him an inordinate sense of gratification.

Damn, he loved the way she reacted to bondage. To him. His dick gave a twitch of agreement.

"What are you looking at?" She gave him a quizzical glance.

You. "This was great," Atticus said as he set his plate to one side. He'd somehow plowed his way through the chops, baked potato, salad, as well as a glass of wine. And he felt back to normal. "Thank you for cooking."

"My pleasure."

When he picked up his dishes, he realized she'd also emptied the sink, done the dishes, and scoured the kitchen to a gleaming brightness. "And for cleaning. You must have worked your ass off."

"You're welcome." Her lips turned up in her quirky smile. "You may call me a full-service guest."

"Cleaning and fucking and cooking? I'd say so."

"I hadn't realized I'd done so much." A line creased her forehead, and she looked around the clean kitchen as if she didn't recognize it. Her expression turned almost frightened before becoming unreadable. "I should get home."

"Why?" Now what had set her off? He hated to admit he didn't totally understand her yet. Hadn't had the chance to get to know her past, and she wasn't exactly spilling all her deets to him. Wary woman. He rotated the wine glass in his hand and considered her. "Does it bother you that we fucked?"

She looked startled. Then again, the little Southerner didn't throw the *fuck* word around a lot. Or talk about the act itself.

"Um. No. Actually, no."

"Well, then." She couldn't possibly think he was using her for sex. Surely he'd made clear he wanted more.

He watched as her gaze flitted over the table, the room, anywhere but him. Something contracted in his gut. "Gin, I'd like you to spend the night. Is that a problem?"

"I... No. Yes." She gave him a frustrated look and buried her face in her hands with a muffled, "Ack."

Well, damn, wasn't she a mess of contradictions? He walked around the table.

Before he reached her, she rose. "I think it's time I got back."

"I think it's time we talked." He held his hand out to her, but she backed away as if he'd threatened her. What the hell? "Gin..."

"I'm so sorry, Atticus. I need to go home." She wrapped her arms around herself.

Maybe if he knew her better, if she was *his* submissive, he'd be justified in pressing her. Unfortunately, she'd made her position clear. They were friends with benefits. Nothing more. He paused, giving her a chance to change her mind, then shook his head in defeat. "Get your things. I'll fire up the truck."

A few minutes later, he slowed for the turn into the Mastersons' spread.

"Not here. My car is at the lodge." At his lifted brows, she added, "I was visiting Kallie. She took me with her when she went to feed the horses."

Although Kallie helped out with chores when the other Mastersons were off in the mountains, she lived at Serenity Lodge with her husband, Jake. "Got it."

Stepping on the gas, he continued up the mountain. The gray of the road darkened with his mood; the silence was a weight all its own.

He pulled into the Serenity Lodge parking area and got out.

Gin didn't wait for him to open her door, but jumped out on her own. "I'm sorry, Atticus. You had a horrible day, and I'm... Instead I dragged you back out. I'm sorry." Her gaze searched his face. "I hope you sleep all right and... Well. Good night."

She headed for her ride.

Eager to get away from him? His mouth tightened. This was bullshit. He caught up, opened her car door, and gripped her arm carefully, but firmly. "Talk to me, Gin. I'm missing something here."

Her gaze dropped to the beaten-down earth and the flattened weeds.

He let her think. He'd wait for fucking ever if need be. What the hell was going on inside her?

After a minute, she straightened her shoulders. Her face was pale and strained as she stared at the trees. Not him. Not a good sign. "Okay, it's like this," she said. "I moved away from Louisiana to get away from...myself. No, to get away from the man I was seeing. He was... No, I was..." She bit her lip. "The problem is how I let him—all men— use me. It's something wrong in me, and I left because it was the only way I could think of to stop the way things were."

Atticus bit down on his molars until he could hear them grind in protest. Be a pleasure to meet the asshole who could make this gentle woman look so torn and lost. "So you moved here."

"Exactly." Her gaze finally met his. "I love it here, but I don't want to get into...a relationship...with you. I don't trust... No, I mean, I try too hard to... I'd do anything to—"

"What?" She didn't trust him? The insult snapped his spine straight. *Jesus Christ.* "You think I'd use you?" His stepfather had used his mother. Abused her. "I didn't ask you to cook or clean for me."

"You don't understand." She shook her head. "I just don't want to be the one giving all the time and—"

Coldness filled him. He opened his hand and released her arm. "We sure as hell wouldn't want that to happen. Guess it's best you cut this off now."

Her hand rose as if she wanted to touch his face.

He stepped back. Too late. Jesus, he hadn't even wanted her to cook, hadn't invited her into his shower. And now she accused him of taking.

Gin felt despair filling her as the hurt expression in Atticus's eyes changed to a bitter icy color. As if he saw a stranger. One he didn't like.

He turned on his heel and strode back to his truck.

She stared after him, feeling the words battering at her closed throat, the memories swirling in her head. *"I'm sorry, Daddy. Don't leave. I'll make everything pretty in the house."* But he'd walked away without looking back.

"I'm sorry I didn't get the dry cleaning, Preston. I'll pick it up tomorrow."

Just don't look at me as if I let you down.

Love me, please. Don't leave me.

And here she was again, wanting to do anything, say anything, to persuade a man to stay. She swallowed the nausea, swallowed the words.

The truck door slammed. With a dull roar, the pickup exited the lot.

She stood, paralyzed, listening to the sound fade.

Gone.

A sob shuddered through her, and she gulped it down too. This was for the best, for both of them. She'd gotten too close to him and relapsed into her old patterns. It certainly wasn't his fault—this was all on her. She knew better than to get involved with a man. Any man. Because what happened? She turned into a doormat. She couldn't let herself fall into those patterns again.

But, she'd hurt him. Made him angry. Oh, she'd never meant to do that.

Everything in her told her to follow. To apologize. Atticus wasn't Preston, wasn't her father. In fact, he was so, so special. Which made her want even more to give him everything. Anything he wanted.

She mustn't. She knew better.

"I'm not going to slave for a man," she said aloud. Firmly. But she kept seeing the unhappy look in his eyes. The *hurt.* What had she done?

She took a step forward. She needed to explain.

No. She'd go right back to him and give up her entire being—that's what would happen. What always happened.

But loving him would be worth it.

No. Her thinking was wrong. *Girl, you are so screwed up.* "No man is worth—"

"That what you think?" The harsh masculine voice snapped her head up. Becca and Logan stood beside Becca's car.

Becca looked dismayed.

But her husband... Logan's deadly expression rivaled the granite mountains behind him. His condemning gaze held Gin's long enough to shrivel something inside her, and then he jerked his chin. "Beat it."

The rest of his words remained unspoken, but clear. "You're *not worth it.*"

Her breathing hitched painfully. Without looking at them again, she got into her car. Turned the key. Stepped on the gas pedal.

Branches scraped the passenger door.

Oh Atticus, I'm sorry. I hate this. Hate what I've done. Blinking the tears from her eyes, she found the gray concrete road, cold and barren, leading her back down the mountain.

Chapter Fourteen

Shouting came from outside Atticus's office. One of the uniforms must have brought in a noisy drunk.

Atticus rubbed his beard. Needed a trim. One of these days. He tried to concentrate on the report he was filling out. Items stolen from a hotel room. Platinum earrings. A diamond necklace.

He'd never given Gin any jewelry. Why did he feel as if he'd let her down? She'd be beautiful with—

No. They'd been friends with benefits. Right? Not jewelry-bestowing lovers.

But if they were only buddies, why did he feel as if he'd lost something...essential? As if he'd been gutted and left to die?

Since she'd fled his house, the days had run into each other, dark and gloomy in the drizzling spring rains. It'd been over a week, maybe a week and a half. The others in the police station avoided him. Not that he'd punched anyone out, but maybe he wasn't as...polite...as normal.

Atticus backspaced on his shit-excuse for a computer. Necklace and bracelet and earrings. Another robbery. Four this month. And a rape. An assault. Felt like he was living in a goddamned city, even though tourist season wasn't even in full flood.

Virgil walked into the office, kicked the door shut with his boot, and set a coffee on Atticus's desk.

Atticus eyed it. "What's the occasion?"

"Just being a good subbie." As Atticus stiffened, Virgil dropped into a battered chair, ignoring the wood's complaint at his heavy frame.

He nodded at the coffee. "What, you don't like service?"

"If you're not here about police business, then how about you head out," Atticus said in a carefully level voice.

"How about you tell me what happened?"

Atticus's lethal stare bounced right off the bastard. Like Atticus, Virgil had two obnoxious brothers and had undoubtedly developed excellent shields. Unfortunately, beating the shit out of the lieutenant might be considered unacceptable in a police station.

"Atticus, Summer's upset." Virgil ran his hand through his hair. "She likes Gin."

"Not a problem." Atticus heard the strain in his voice. "I wouldn't step between her and Gin."

"First, Gin's not taking calls from her friends. Second, Summer happens to love you." Virgil clarified, "Like a brother, mind you, but she's worried about you as well as Gin."

The warmth of friendship didn't melt the ice residing in his gut, but helped. He cleared his throat. "Thanks."

"I'd like to know what happened."

Persistent bastard. "Fuck if I know. It was after the Bowers homicide. Think she felt sorry for me. She told me she'd come over if I ate what she cooked. She offered—and gave—shower sex. She cleaned my kitchen while I was upstairs." He yanked at his lengthening beard. "Then she tells me how men use her and she won't have anything to do with them. Or me."

"Women have screwed-up logic, but that takes the cake."

Atticus growled. "Tell me about it. Thing is, she looked happy right up to that point. She's a service sub, for God's sake."

"Appears to me like she needs help getting her head on straight." Virgil propped his big boots on Atticus's desk. "What you going to do about that, boy?"

"This." Half rising, Atticus smacked Virgil's feet off the desk so forcefully that Virgil almost tipped out of the chair. He watched Masterson resettle—feet on the floor—and added, "Oh, you meant about Gin?"

"You got a nasty temper there. Yes, about the subbie." Virgil gave him a level look. "Any chance your past is interfering with your thinking?"

"Get real." As if he'd let... *His past.* He saw his mother's battered face. Saw her frantically cooking something before her asshole of a husband got home from work. Saw her scrubbing the already spotless table as if it would keep her from being slapped around.

Gin had said, "*I'd do anything to—*" But she hadn't completed her sentence. He had, in the way his mother would have—*I'd do anything to keep from being hurt.*

Only, he'd never hurt Gin. She knew that.

He frowned. The stubborn little counselor didn't react as a physically abused woman would. So, what exactly *had* she meant? "I might need to talk to her again," Atticus said slowly.

"Might be." Virgil rose. "Let me know what happens. If she gives you too much grief, I'll send Summer over to read to her from the good book."

"The good book? Jesus, you've got to stop reading old Westerns." Atticus shook his head, then when Virgil reached the door, he added quietly, "Thanks."

"What friends are for. And hey, next week, all us ladies are goin' for pedicures. Wanna come? Jake said to invite you 'specially so we can share our feelings."

Virg was quicker than he looked. He had the door closed before the stapler hit it.

* * * *

Preston had called from a Bear Flat restaurant. The phone call had made Gin so angry, she'd thought her head would explode, but within minutes, her mood had fallen back into darkness.

She parked her car in the gathering twilight, feeling as if she were dragging herself through the motions of living. She needed to get over this. Get over Atticus.

Yesterday, the grocery store guy had glanced at her face and hadn't even joked with her as he usually did. People in small towns knew everything. Like when a woman spent her evenings feeling forlorn and cuddling with her dog.

Get Over It. Furiously, she thumped her head against the neck rest of the seat—which only made her head hurt.

Honestly though, this was pitiful. After years of college and grad school, years of telling other people how to manage their lives, somehow she kept screwing up her own. The adage was true—plumbers didn't fix their own faucets; counselors couldn't figure out their own emotions.

But she had. Kind of. She'd managed to figure out that her reactions to men were wrong. That she went overboard trying to please them and be needed. Surely it was sensible to avoid relationships until she got her head on straight, wasn't it?

Only hurting someone in the process was unforgivable. And she had.

"I wish I could tell you how sorry I am for being such a mess, Atticus." She shook her head. Why couldn't she have met him in another five years, when she could love him the way he deserved to be loved? And without tripping over her own issues.

But life wasn't so easy, was it?

And now, lucky her, she had to deal with her ex-fiancé. She slid out of the car and slammed the door. At least being grumpy had put her in the mood to kick some ass. Her footsteps thudded on the boardwalk like an angry metronome.

Scowling, she shoved open the black oak door to the Mother Lode. Although still early, the restaurant had started to fill with people celebrating the arrival of the weekend.

A second of nostalgia made her pause. Summer and Kallie had joined her for lunch once, for stories and laughter. Now, along with Atticus, she'd lost her new friends. They hadn't given her up and had called constantly, but she didn't answer. Their husbands were buddies with Atticus and worked with him. Better that she kept a distance.

The loss of their companionship created an aching sadness. Becca, so pulled-together and bossy. Summer, with her kindness. Kallie, competent and funny. She'd always had a girl gang, but these…these women had become what she thought sisters might be.

And wasn't it perverse how much she wanted Atticus to hold her while she cried over her lost friends.

With an effort, she set her problems aside and turned into the bar area with its high-topped tables.

A simmering anger blossomed as she looked around the darkly paneled room for Preston. Several tables were pushed together for a TGIF group of women. A flannel-shirted logger near the entrance whistled at her, looking as if he'd started happy hour early. At the bar, men were intent on the televised basketball game.

And there he was at a table, a tall man with sandy hair in his usual tailored suit. He rose with a pleased smile.

She wove through the tables to join him. "Preston."

Unfortunately, she got too close. Really, after working in a prison, she should have better instincts.

Taking her hand, he pulled her into his arms. "There you are. I missed you, Ginny." He burrowed his face in the corner of her shoulder and neck.

Her irritation rose with each whiff of musk and balsam aftershave. How she'd loved his scent. Once. Before he'd flattened her love like a sleet storm in a garden.

"Let go," she muttered, then gave him a strong shove. "Let *go*."

With marked reluctance, he did, and like the gentleman he was, held her chair. "I'm sorry, darling. I'm just pleased to see you again."

"What *are* you doing here?" Her chest cramped. He looked exactly the same. Clean-cut, well groomed, the image of a successful executive. "How did you find me?"

"The receptionist at your old job gave me your address." With a smug smile, he took her hand.

She tugged.

He didn't let go.

"Hey, Gin, how are you?" Barbara walked up to the table, pulling her pad from her spotless apron. "What can I get you?"

Preston squeezed her hand. "My fiancée will have a Jack Daniels."

"No, I won't. Nothing, thanks, Barbara." Gin glared across the table. "Fiancée? Seriously?"

"We might have had a little misun—"

"Do you see a ring on my hand?" Gin yanked her hand free and held it up. "No. Because I threw it at you when I found you screwing your 'associate.'"

His well-groomed brows drew together. "Ginny, please. Annalise and I were only talking. I told you what happened."

She glanced at Barbara, who hadn't moved. "It's good *he* explained. She couldn't get a word out—not with his dick halfway down her throat."

Barbara made a stifled sound and hurried away. Her laughter was drowned out by the basketball viewers cheering a basket.

"Ginny, was it necessary to share our problems with a waitress?"

"I like honesty." Not a term in his vocabulary, unfortunately.

"Well. Fine." Obviously forcing himself to remain calm, he smiled at her. "At least we're together now. I want to apologize for my...mistake."

"Mistake?"

"Yes, I had a lapse in judgment. But it didn't mean anything."

"So you thought it was all right to screw someone else because your feelings weren't involved?"

He cleared his throat and stayed silent.

How about that—he was listening to her. *Too little, too late* said her weary heart. No fiery passion or heated emotions remained. "You're forgiven. Now, go home."

"Ginny. I can assure you it will never happen again. In a way, it's good because I came to realize how much I love you. How much I need you."

She shook her head. She'd known their relationship was dying. Yet, despite her nagging misgivings, she'd written her vows for the wedding and planned to go off birth control.

And then she'd come home early. Seen them. She'd stood there... *Her knees almost buckling, tears blurring the room, holding her chest to keep her heart from tearing apart. He'd been the one who was supposed to love her. The man who she could love with all her being.* Only he wasn't.

She'd thrown his ring at him. And as her dreams shredded into tatters, she'd cried.

Now, thinking back to the indescribable pain of that moment, she knew her response had been inadequate.

She should have thrown a cast-iron frying pan.

Staring at him, she had to wonder what had happened to the man she'd thought she'd known. As her friends bucked her up, she'd realized his cheating was one more indication he hadn't cared. And still, she'd fought the desperation to crawl back. To be loved. Needed.

Yes, being needed was a drug to her, and like any addict, she'd had to go cold turkey. Needed to continue to avoid the drug and the triggers.

And now...now came the apology she longed for. "Too late, Preston."

"Nonsense, darling. I love you; you love me, and—"

"Actually, I don't."

"Nope. Doesn't look to me like she loves you." The rough voice came from directly behind her, and a powerful hand closed on her shoulder.

She jumped and looked up and up to meet Atticus's gray-blue eyes. The relaxed impression from his cowboy hat and denim jacket was contradicted by the danger in his stance. "Sweetheart," he murmured.

The feeling of his hard hand on her shoulder made her world tilt sideways.

He took advantage of her paralysis to plant a firm kiss on her lips. *Oh. Oh, oh, oh.*

"What..." Preston rose, shock on his face. "Who the hell is this,

Ginny?"

"I'd be the man in her life now," Atticus said.

His pissed-off growl wasn't lost on Gin—and didn't matter at all. His voice sank into her like a spring shower on a drought-stricken plant.

"I doubt that seriously. You need to leave." Preston gave her an earnest look. "Ginny, send him away so we can talk. But don't worry, honey, I understand what happens to a woman on the rebound."

"You don't know much about women, do you?" Atticus said.

Preston gave him an annoyed glance. "Ginny, I don't hold this lapse against you. We'll still get married as we planned." Preston curled his hand back around hers. "Yes, I want to marry you even if you had a fling. We'll call it even and start over."

Oh my stars. What kind of messed-up karma was this? "No, we're not even, and we're not starting over. We're done." She yanked her hand away and realized Atticus was still right behind her. His powerful hand still gripped her shoulder.

Never let go. Please.

She closed her eyes. And her reaction to his touch was one more reason she couldn't be with him.

"Preston, go home." She rose, turned her back on him, and gave Atticus a level look. The words this time came much, much harder. She made her tone forceful. "I'm sorry, Atticus. But I do believe we are not together."

How could each word feel as if it were drawing blood?

His cowboy hat shaded his eyes as he studied her thoughtfully. Then he nodded and made a motion toward the door for Preston, deliberately letting his jacket fall open to show off his giant sidearm.

Men.

After a second of hesitation, Preston took a few steps. He turned and cast her a hopeful look. "Call me, darling."

"No. Never."

Hurt filled his eyes.

Oh. Oh no. No, she couldn't hurt him. Not him; not anyone. "Oh, honey, I'm not the woman for you. Really I'm not. But you *will* find one who suits you better. Don't give up."

After a second, he nodded and wove his way through the room and out the door.

Atticus, after another unreadable gaze, followed—taking her heart with him. When he'd said, *"I'd be the man in her life now,"* she'd felt only warmth. Happiness.

But...for heaven's sake, he wasn't in her life. They'd split up, hadn't they? Whatever relationship they'd had was over.

So why had he said that?

* * * *

When she left the diner, she found Atticus leaning against his mud-spattered pickup, which was parked in front of her car. His long legs were extended, his arms crossed over his chest. Under the glow of the streetlight, the black hat shaded his features, increasing the ominous look of his dark beard.

"Why are you still here?" She wanted to smack herself for the inane question. "In fact, what were you doing in the restaurant right then?"

"I saw you drive past the station, looking upset. Wanted to make sure you were all right." He leaned forward, hooked his fingers in her belt, and tugged her between his legs. His hands settled on her hips. "You still look a mite shaken."

Why did it feel so good to be the target of his concern?

"I'm fine. He was my ex-fiancé."

"Got that."

"It's long over."

"Got that too. But a woman like you cares deeply. Losing someone would be like hauling a tree out by the roots. You'd hurt...for a long time."

Her eyes prickled with his quiet understanding. "I did." She forced a smile. "But I'm all better now."

He snorted and drew her into his arms. "Liar."

His masculine mountain scent held a hint of gun oil and leather, and nothing was as comforting. For a moment, maybe two, she nestled against him, soaking up his strength.

And then she moved back. Her heart couldn't handle being torn apart again, and this man could do far, far more damage than Preston. "Thanks for the hug."

"My pleasure." He studied her. "Looks like your evening is free now. This would be a good time to talk." He opened the pickup's passenger door.

"Talk? No."

Ignoring her protest, he hoisted her up into the seat. "Stay put. Let's get this done, Virginia." The angle of his jaw displayed an intimidating sternness.

Her throat dried up around her protest. Her fingers started doing a wringing thing. Maybe this was good. Surely, she could explain better. She'd hurt him last time, and she'd never have done that for anything. "Where are you taking me?"

His satisfied smile showed he knew he'd gotten his way. "My place."

Once at his house, Atticus didn't want her to have a chance to change her mind. He pulled her straight into the bedroom. This time, she'd listen and so would he.

"Hey." She tugged against his grip. "You can't—"

He took her hands between his. "I want to say I'm sorry."

Her brows drew together. "For what?"

"When you told me how you felt that day in the parking lot, I reacted badly." He still felt the burn of the insult and shook his head. "You're a counselor. You know how people process events through their own filters, right?"

Her struggle stopped. "Well, yes. What filter were you using, Atticus?"

"My stepfather beat my mother."

"I remember you said that."

"He also 'used' her. She slaved to be perfect so he wouldn't have a reason to hit her." His mouth twisted. "Of course, violence doesn't need reasons. But when you said you tried too hard, it felt as if you meant you thought I'd hurt you if you didn't."

Dismay filled her face. "No. Oh, no, honey, I didn't mean that at all."

He brushed her lips with his. "Took a while, but I figured it out. I'm sorry I reacted instead of listening as I should." Holding her face between his palms, he looked into her unhappy eyes. "Can you forgive me, Gin?"

"There is absolutely nothing to forgive. This is all related to my problems. You did nothing wrong."

This kiss was long and gentle; her lips were as soft as her heart. She hadn't even thought twice about forgiving him. He sank deeper into the kiss, his tongue stroking hers, before he pulled back. They had issues to resolve first.

"I want you out of the clothes." Without letting her protest, he quickly stripped her down, pushing aside her half-hearted attempts to hinder him. Shoes, pants, sweater, shirt. Pretty yellow underwear.

"We're not going to...this isn't the time, Atticus."

Her gaze focused on his face as she tried to read his expression. With luck, she wouldn't be able to.

In contrast, she was an open book. Dark circles under her eyes told him she hadn't been sleeping. Her skin had lost its glow. Those changes were on him, he knew. His inability to get his head on straight had meant a rough two weeks for her.

Him as well. Seeing her in the restaurant with the asshole had strained his control. He'd never felt the full force of jealousy before—or wanted to beat the crap out of another man. But he'd touched her. Had made her unhappy.

Of course, his softhearted woman had forgiven the bastard. Told him to have hope. Gin really was something. He touched her cheek gently.

The confusion in her gaze, the rigidity of her shoulders, the trembling of her fingers—he figured the mixture of ex-fiancé and unsettled relationship with her new man had put those there.

He didn't like knowing he'd have her shaking much harder before the evening was over. Since he finally had an idea of the problem, he'd push ahead, even if they'd both be miserable while he did.

Oddly enough, even with her naked in front of him, he wasn't aroused. The heaviness in his gut said this wouldn't be an easy "session" even though he wouldn't put her through a complete scene. If they'd been together longer, she might have trusted him to tie her up and dig out the traumatic details of her past. Yet—catch-22—if she had confided her story, she'd be able to trust him for more in-depth scenes.

Instead, tonight he'd be operating handicapped. But even without bondage, he could demolish some of the barriers to intimacy and truth.

"Atticus."

He was dressed; she was naked, reinforcing the dynamic. "Shhh, little counselor. Although I love having my hands on you, sex isn't happening tonight." Remembering her guilt earlier, he pressed the remorse button. "But I really think you owe me a bit of a talk, don't you?"

Her forest-green eyes were unhappy, but she wouldn't back away. She had more strength than she gave herself credit for—and she'd far rather hurt herself than someone else. "All right. But after, you'll take me back to my car."

"I will." He stroked her soft cheek. "There's a terrycloth bathrobe in the closet. Put it on and wait on the back deck."

"I..."

"Shhh." When she didn't move, he nudged her forward.

Her obedience showed in her silence. As he walked out of the room, he heard the closet door open.

After pulling out a couple of glasses and a bottle of whiskey—and a hair tie—he went outside.

Dark had fallen completely and a breeze carried a hint of snow from the snow-topped mountains. Gin stood in the center of the cedar deck. The bathrobe sleeves hung over her hands so far she looked like a child playing dress-up. Damn, she was cute.

He set the tray on the deck and uncovered the hot tub. Steam rose into the night air.

"You have a lovely place." She motioned to the lantern-shaped solar lights edging the wide cedar deck. "But, I don't think—"

"Exactly." He pulled her robe off. Gathering her hair up, he fastened it on top of her head with a scrunchie. "Tonight, you're too tired to think. You simply do what I tell you to do."

"*What?*" Her back went straight.

Enjoying the stunned reaction of an independent woman, he kissed her nose. "Hop in."

Despite her exasperated expression, she didn't argue further. The sag of her shoulders and her pale drawn face showed the altercation with her ex had used up her fight-back stores.

The hot tub was level with the surface of the deck. Bending, she sampled the water with a toe, and her hiss made him chuckle.

He kept the temperature toasty, and she had beautifully delicate skin. "Go in as slow as you want as long as you get there eventually."

And there was her spunk. Her chin came up. "Why did I have the misconception that you were a gentleman?"

Difficult to get offended by an insult delivered in her melting southern drawl. "I've got no idea, baby. Maybe because when the gentleman meets the Dom, the Dom wins?"

At his level stare, her gaze fell.

As she worked her way in, he stripped, flipped on the jets, and stepped into the heat. As bubbles hissed on the water's surface, he poured drinks.

Gin took her time getting in. When she finally settled and leaned back on the side, he handed her a glass. "Feels good, doesn't it?"

Her low hum agreed, despite her snippy, "If a person likes feeling like a roast in a crock pot."

With his right arm on the side, he could play with the silky tendrils on her nape. As he enjoyed his whiskey, he let the heat work on his— and she was damn well his—submissive.

The bourbon wasn't Jack Daniels. She swirled the amber liquid and sampled again. The taste of caramel and brown sugar, full and balanced, ended with a hint of leather. The alcohol was warm, so very warm on the tongue and going down. Far too soon, she realized she'd finished.

"Like it?" His penetrating gaze was on her as he refilled her drink. He was studying her, as he was wont to do.

"It's not Jack Daniels." Despite the sense of disloyalty, she gave him the truth. "It's quite wonderful, actually. What is it?"

"Pappy Van Winkle's Family Reserve. Still southern-made, li'l magnolia." He leaned back, arms outstretched along the edge. The soft glow of the lights shadowed the strong muscular planes of his chest. On his right deltoid, a "Semper fi" tattoo spanned a colorful eagle, globe, and anchor. She ran a finger over it. "You were a Marine?"

"Yep."

His other arm had a butt-ugly bulldog with a Marine Corps cap and a cigar between its teeth. So ferocious. "He's rather adorable, isn't he?"

Atticus looked affronted. "He's not adorable."

Yes, he was, but *oops*. Tough guys were awfully endearing when defending their sacred masculinity. Unable to resist, she ran her free hand down his chest, slowing at several jagged, raised scars over his ribs. "What are these from?"

"Caught some frag in Baghdad," he said lazily. "Lucky I wasn't closer."

She shivered at the thought and took a gulp of the whiskey. He could have died; she'd never have met him. "Atticus…"

His arm curved around her, pulling her against him. "The past is over. We're here and alive. Let's concentrate on that, yeah?"

"Yes." Even as the jets massaged her tense muscles, the alcohol was lighting a small fire inside her. If she kept drinking, she'd end up a puddle of jelly. She turned to set the glass down.

He poured another shot in it.

Politeness said she should drink. With no lunch or supper, she could feel the alcohol spinning her thoughts, like a slow motion tilt-a-whirl. She should get out, put her clothes on, and get home. Instead, her mouth took on its own independence. "Why are you doing this, Atticus? Ah thought—" Oh spit, her drawl was thickening.

"There we go," he murmured.

She gave him a confused look, then continued voicing her concern. "*I* thought we'd…um, broken everything off between us."

"Got a few things I need to know first, baby, that've bothered me. You said men use you. But, from what I saw, you're stronger than your ex is. Can you tell me what happened?"

His fingers kneaded her knotted neck, the jets massaged her taut back, and she felt so, so warm, inside and out.

"Gin?"

He'd asked her a question. Her body tried to tense, but all her muscles had turned into overcooked noodles. With an arm around her shoulders, he pulled her close enough to rest her cheek against his chest.

She gave in. "I somehow ended up doing everything—whether he asked or not—and the more I did, the less he helped. The less he listened. The less he listened, the more I worried about our relationship, so I worked harder."

Atticus made a sound of encouragement.

She motioned with her hand, realized it held a glass, and finished the pretty amber liquid. "I was spiraling down, like a whirlpool. I knew if I didn't do enough, he'd walk away. Leave me because I…"

"Because you what?" Atticus's deep rumble compelled an answer, whether she had one or not.

"Because I wasn't enough to make him happy."

"Preston told you that?"

"No. He never did." Up the nearby slope, trees rustled in a pleasant accompaniment to the bubbling water. Tipping her head back, she saw the stars in the black sky had grown from mere pinpoints to wide discs of light.

A hand closed over hers, drawing her back to earth. "If the bast—if Preston never said that, who did? Who said you weren't enough to make him happy?"

"No one."

At his grunt of disbelief, she frowned. The glass was plucked from her hand and returned with more liquid. "Who, baby?"

Even alcohol couldn't blur that memory. The sharp-edged words had been carved into her heart with a rusty knife. "Daddy."

"Ah." The tone held satisfaction. "He was displeased with you?"

"With us." *Why, Daddy?* How could she possibly explain? She set her palm on Atticus's broad chest. Beneath the springy hair were his rock-hard pectorals. He was so strong in both body and character. How could a man like this understand weakness? "Mama constantly tried to please him, always cleaning and cooking and soft-spoken."

"What did he do?"

"He was a sales rep for an international firm. And he loved it. He'd take a position overseas for months at a time."

Atticus's eyes narrowed. "Leaving you over and over."

The memory hurt. "Mama didn't function well alone. It was like she needed a man to affirm her existence." Gin chewed on her lip. "Really, she should have had a career or cause to balance her."

"Baby." Atticus's touch on her cheek brought her attention back. "What happened to your father?"

She shrugged. "Eventually he couldn't take it anymore and told Mama she didn't make him happy. *We* didn't make him happy. When the divorce papers came in the mail, Mama fell apart. I think she cried for months."

"And you?"

"Oh, I had school—and Mama—to keep me busy." Definitely Mama. Cooking meals and coaxing her mother to eat, figuring out the bills and prodding her mother into telling her how to write checks, doing the laundry and manipulating her mother to get her to socialize again.

"So you took on caring for your mother." His smile was slow and understanding. "When you told me about becoming an adult before my 'childhood peer group did,' you knew personally what you were talking about, didn't you?"

"We're a pair, aren't we?" To escape the subject of her ugly past, she picked up the whiskey bottle and looked for his glass. "Refill?"

He set his drink out of reach and took the bottle from her as well. "Do you ever see your parents?"

"You are one stubborn man." She pouted for a second. "Daddy never came back. Mama married again about three years ago; I visit now and then." Her lips twisted down. Hopefully Mama's relationship would last this time. "They're in Florida."

Atticus's gaze was on her mouth, then her eyes. "She repeat her crying performance with other men?"

The insightful question knocked her off-kilter. "I don't like mind readers." Gin tried to edge away.

He laughed and pulled her against him. "Baby, you have an

excellent poker face unless you're drunk. Then you're an open book." After kissing the pout off her lips, he said firmly, "Now answer my question, counselor."

He was so stubborn. She glanced at the stairs leading from the hot tub.

His arm tightened around her.

"She…had trouble. I coaxed her back each time." From crying fits, from depression.

"Jesus. Did you get *any* care *at all* from your parents?

"Of course I had care," Gin said indignantly. "She was a wonderful mother. Loving and fun and…" Her voice trailed off. And then, after the divorce, she hadn't been. Gin hardly existed to her…except when Mama had hysterics. Clinging and sobbing and repeating over and over, "*I don't know what I'd do without you.*"

"And?" He was frowning.

After her father abandoned them, her mother had been…gone. Ignoring the school papers Gin brought home to be signed, never showing up for any extracurricular activities, not asking about her daughter's day or troubles or anything. Their roles had reversed. "I grew up at eleven," she whispered. "They weren't the best relationship role models, were they?"

"Not hardly." Atticus's hard face showed his understanding.

Gin puckered her brow. Her glass was empty again. "You know, I tell my clients how knowledge is the first step on the road to change. Pretty easy to say to someone else. Not so easy to do."

"We'll work on that, pet."

After pulling Gin out of the tub and into the living room, Atticus settled her on the fur-covered pad in front of the fireplace. Feeling as if he'd run a marathon, he waited for his second wind to kick in.

But he had an answer or two. Her father—actually both screwed-up parents—had taught Gin that she had to "do" to be seen. To be loved.

But, although he was finally getting answers, he couldn't keep the little sub in a hot tub, especially the way she'd reacted to the alcohol. "What did you have for supper?" he asked as he lit the kindling under the logs.

The firelight picked up the red sparks in her hair and the fading color in her face. "Supper?" Her brow wrinkled. "I didn't—"

"Right. Did you happen to eat lunch?" She'd mentioned her job wiped out her appetite.

The shrug answered his question. "I'll get us some cheese, then." When she started to rise, he stopped her with a stern stare. "Stay right there or there will be consequences."

She wilted.

In the kitchen, he smiled. Considering her spirit, he could foresee a future where a threat would result in even brattier behavior, especially if she came to like "consequences."

When he returned with a plate of cheese and crackers, she was staring into the fire.

Down on one knee, he set a glass of water to her lips. "Drink it all, babe."

Unusually obedient—or exhausted—she complied. Then he hand-fed her until pink returned to her cheeks.

Good enough. He needed to continue before the alcohol wore off. Ignoring her protest, he pulled her robe off, then dropped down onto the pad and arranged her on top of him. When her softness covered him, his body untensed, as if something lost had been restored.

Her irritation already forgotten, she propped her arms up on his chest and smiled down at him. Her gaze was still unfocused. "Did I ever mention how much I love your living room?"

And he loved seeing her drunk. Next time, though, they'd drink for fun and not shit like this. "Thanks, sweetheart." With his robe open in the front, they had hot-tub-heated skin against skin.

Despite her disapproving frown, he felt her hips wiggle. Yeah, chemistry was something they'd never lacked.

But he had a few remaining facts to get straight. "The breakup with Preston made you realize you were doing the same thing as your mother?"

"Mmmhmm." Her lips turned down. "I'm just like her—trying to please a man past the bounds of reasonable. It's like a sickness. This is why I can't be with you."

"You can't be with me?" he asked carefully.

"Don't you see? When I came over and tried to help you feel better, I got carried away. I'd have done anything for you. I still want to."

Finally. Now he knew what had triggered her flight. In fact, he'd set her off himself by teasing her. *"You must have worked your ass off." "Cleaning and fucking and cooking?"*

She'd seen her kindness as an indication she was losing herself.

He'd been an idiot. She'd tried to explain her reasoning in the parking lot, but he hadn't listened. Had let his past lead him down a false track.

He rolled her over, pinned her beneath him, and saw the unhappiness in her eyes. "Baby, do you hear what you're saying? Do you really believe you have to work your ass off for a guy to sustain a relationship?

"I—" She bit her lip. "That doesn't sound right...does it?"

But she'd nodded before her brain had kicked in. Yep, that was her belief. "Don't you think you're lovable just because you're you?"

Her baffled gaze made him smile.

Looks like he had his task cut out for him. But he had a feeling he'd enjoy teaching her this one.

"Atticus." Some of her reasoning ability was returning, and she shook her head. "You're a Dom; you expect to be served. And I'm more like a drug addict who can't have a taste of her drug—serving you—or I go too far. This thing between us won't work."

"Li'l magnolia." He twined his fingers with hers to pin her hands over her head. Her pupils dilated as her body responded to the vulnerable position. "I think your service has two opposing mindsets. One—you're afraid a man won't love you if you don't. You with me, so far?"

She nodded. "Exactly. This is what I'm—"

"The second frame of mind is different. If you're submissive, you serve because you love to meet someone's needs. Especially your Dom's."

Her expression went blank.

He allowed her a minute, then asked gently, "When you were cooking for me, I saw no anxiety. I saw only pleasure that you could give something beautiful." He remembered all too clearly, the happiness shining in her eyes as she offered herself in the shower, as she set food on the table and watched him eat. Nothing based in fear could have brought the Dom in him such contentment. "What were you feeling that day, Gin?"

As she understood what he was saying, her eyes filled with tears, turning the color of a tree-shaded pond. "Joy. I felt joy."

Chapter Fifteen

Happy Saturday. Hand on the cart, Gin did a quick dance step down the aisle of the grocery store. This morning with Atticus had been…fun. Light-hearted all the way, starting with shower sex and finishing with cooking breakfast together before he took her back to her car.

And during the night, as if he'd known how shattered she'd felt, he'd loved her so gently and generously that he'd reduced her to tears a couple of times.

Tonight, she'd said she wanted to be alone. After an unhappy moment of consideration, he'd agreed.

She totally needed some time to process everything. How he'd treated her, how exposed she felt when he dug for answers—and the revelations he'd brought forth.

No wonder she'd been confused by her own behavior—submissive service and neurotic service together made for a challenge. She shook her head. It would take time to get it all straight, but she darned well would. Hey, she was a counselor.

Since he was giving her "me" time, Atticus said he'd see her on Sunday—and refusal was not an option.

She smiled. Refusing hadn't even crossed her mind.

Humming a tune and pushing her cart, Gin rounded a corner in the grocery store and stopped in surprise.

Atticus stood near the bin of oranges.

Her hand on his chest, a tall, slender brunette stared up into his eyes. "So, what are you doing next weekend, Atticus?"

Gin's jaw clamped shut. *Don't touch my man.*

But he wasn't. Not in any official terms. Not that there'd been any time to discuss it. Were they *together* together?

She was afraid to ask.

To Gin's relief, Atticus said to the woman, "Sorry, babe. I have plans." He moved sideways and noticed Gin. "Gin."

The woman glanced over her shoulder and gave a sniff. Turning back, she stroked her palm down Atticus's chest. "You give me a call if you get freed up, darling." With a blatant swing of her hips, she picked up an orange and sauntered away.

His gaze didn't follow her. Instead, Atticus walked over to Gin. "Are you getting something wonderful to cook for me tomorrow?"

Why didn't he kiss her? "Of course," she said in a strained voice. No hug. Nothing.

Had the woman tempted him? Maybe. They hadn't agreed to being monogamous or even a relationship. And...her stomach sank. Doms didn't always follow the same rules that they enforced on their submissives, right?

"Looks like everyone is shopping for the weekend," he said. "I saw the Serenity crowd near the meats."

"Oh." With a smothered flinch, Gin resolved to avoid the meat section of the store, even if she needed hamburger and chicken. She hadn't seen Becca since the scene in the lodge's parking lot. After getting only a brief nod from Jake when they'd passed on the street, she'd avoided Kallie and Summer and had refused their calls.

"Something I should know?" Atticus asked softly. She could swear his regard had actual weight.

"Of course not." She turned away and hesitated. "Are you... I mean, are we—" She was acting like a teenager. "Would you like to come over tonight? I can cook. Make you a... Would you like steak?" She could pick out a couple of steaks, once the Serenity people were gone, and—

"Stop." Mouth tight, he moved forward until she had to tilt her head back to see his face. "Take a deep breath."

"What?"

"What, indeed?" he said gravely. "Gin, did you offer a meal because you love cooking for me or because you're scared about losing what we have together?"

"I...I do love cooking for you." But not tonight. She'd been looking forward to alone time, to doing girly, indulgent stuff and writing in her journal.

Why had she asked Atticus to come over?

For pity's sake, she was an idiot. She closed her eyes, feeling the apprehensive place in her belly, the one that said he didn't even like her, that he wouldn't want her unless she filled all his needs.

And now she was going to burst into tears in the middle of a grocery store. She blinked hard; her breathing turned all wonky.

"Easy, li'l magnolia." With firm hands, he pulled her close and wrapped her in determination and warmth. His breath was warm against her ear. "Tell me, baby."

"I got scared," she admitted into his flannel shirt. "That woman was awfully pretty, and you didn't even touch me, and I thought maybe you didn't want...me."

He made an acknowledging noise, giving her a squeeze. "Got it." He nuzzled her cheek. "I didn't know whether a counselor would be comfortable with public displays of affection. After all, you work in the prison here."

"Oh." She sagged against him. Truly, she tended to be fairly reserved, but this was Atticus. "I like when you touch me. Even around other people."

"So noted. As for other women, I'm not interested. You take up all my time; I like it that way."

A ribbon of happiness swirled through her. "Me too."

"Good." He pulled back. "Little counselor, do you think you can remember how you felt here and recognize it next time?"

"Yes. Probably... You know, you'd be a very good *shrink*, Atticus," she added.

His growl made her giggle. "Keep it up, baby, and we'll try some avoidance therapy. A good paddling or—"

Blushing, she put her hand over his mouth. "Sorry. Sorry. I didn't say a thing."

Under her palm, his lips quirked. When she took her hand away, he said, "As long as I'm in therapy mode, your homework is to list ways to deal with the anxiety—without resorting to cooking me meals you don't want to cook."

A laugh escaped her. "You talked to Sawyer."

"Yep. He mentioned your penchant for list-making exercises. His new counselor has had him continue the practice." His smile increased. "He shared his last one—the list of what he wants to do when he's released." Atticus bent and kissed her tenderly. "Thank you for helping him heal, Gin."

She couldn't speak through the thickness in her throat.

"However, since you gave me homework as well, consider this revenge." When he grinned, she remembered how she'd assigned him reading—and list making—to work through his height phobia.

"Have you been...?"

His short nod said he was finished with the subject. Instead, he stepped back and swatted her ass. "Now finish shopping. I'll see you tomorrow the way we'd planned."

"Agreed."

Smiling, she continued through the store, checking off items. The extra was the package of double-stuffed Oreos, because she darned well deserved chocolate after having a meltdown in a grocery store.

Two seconds later, she reached the end of the aisle, turned, and ran over a boot. "Oops. Sorry..."

Her voice trailed off as she stared at Logan. His brother stood behind him.

Logan nodded briefly.

Jake said, "Gin." They stepped out of her way.

Her head bowed as her heart shriveled two sizes, leaving her chest a mass of emptiness and pain. She wanted to protest that she'd been angry that day in the parking lot. She hadn't meant she wouldn't serve Atticus. But at Logan's dismissive glance, the words wouldn't come.

They hated her.

Before the betraying tears spilled over, she turned her head away and veered to the right. Then stopped.

No. They might not know she and Atticus had made up. And they were misjudging her; she had a right—a duty—to correct them.

Her big girl panties were going to give her a wedgie at this rate.

She turned and put her hands on her hips. "You're wrong about me, Logan Hunt. You judged me unfairly."

Logan turned. After regarding her for a long moment, he closed in on her.

She barely suppressed a squeak when he settled a hard hand on her shoulder. "Did I?" he asked, his voice flat.

She pulled in a shaky breath and tried to yank away.

"Easy, pet. Let's get this out," Logan said in a rough voice. "Jake, grab Atticus. I want to talk."

"There's a change," Jake said. A second later, she heard him call, "Ware. Here."

Footsteps heralded Atticus's approach as she searched for composure. If he saw her upset, he'd get all riled up.

An arm came around her, yanking her from Logan's hold. Atticus took her chin in a careful but unyielding grip and lifted her face. His eyes darkened. "What the hell, Hunt?" He pulled her behind his back as if readying for a fight. "What'd you say to her?"

Her attempt to shake his arm was as futile as moving a granite mountain. "No, Atticus. It was me. I did—"

"A tiny thing like you couldn't do anything to give these two assholes grief." His voice was uncompromising as he stared at the two Hunts.

Oh, heavens. Where was a testosterone drain when she needed one? "Logan saw our fight in the Serenity parking lot. After you left, I was talking to myself and said *no* man was worth serving. He heard me."

Atticus's eyes lit with amusement. "I always did like subbies with tempers." But when he turned to the Hunts, his expression turned black.

Gin tugged on his arm to recall his attention. "They're just unhappy with me on your part."

"I don't need big fucking brothers."

"You're together again?" Logan was studying her. "That mouthing off was because you were pissed-off?"

Atticus shot him a glare. "Like your redhead never says anything she doesn't mean?"

"He's got you there, bro." Jake turned to Gin, then glanced at Atticus. "Permission?"

To her dismay, Atticus moved away.

Jake curled his fingers around her upper arms. His level gaze met hers. "We messed up, Gin. Overreacted. Atticus kept hooking up with selfish submissives, so we goaded him to be with you. When it sounded as if you'd scraped him off because you didn't want to serve, we figured we steered him wrong." A corner of his mouth kicked up ruefully. "And blamed you, of course."

Oh. Of course they did. The bands of tension around her chest released. "I understand," she said softly.

"Not sure I do," Atticus grumbled.

She elbowed him in the ribs. Hard. "Oh, you get it. You were much nastier when you were defending your brother."

"Shit," he said under his breath. "Got me there, magnolia." He glanced at the Hunts. "I appreciate the way you got my back"—he smirked—"against a half-pint."

Logan winced, then took Jake's place. The sincere regret in his face eased her heart. "I'm sorry, sugar, for putting those tears in your eyes."

"Forgiven." At his obvious relief, she could only smile. Atticus was lucky to have such loyal friends.

"I'll tell Becca," Logan said. "Be the first time I have gossip before she does."

As the Hunts moved away, Gin glanced up at Atticus. He was watching her gravely.

"I think we're done here." Rising on tiptoes, she kissed his cheek.

Before she could step back, he put an arm behind her back, yanked her fully against him, and planted a long, long wet kiss on her.

When he finally released her, his hand was squeezing her ass, and she was dizzy and hot.

She might have to rethink her stance on those public displays. Sex education for children shouldn't occur in grocery stores.

"Now you can go. And I'll see you tomorrow." Atticus's gaze roamed over her face, and his lips quirked. With a final caress of her cheek, he headed down the aisle, leaving her staring after him.

Men—walking, talking proof that God is a sadist.

Distracted as all get out, she took twice as long as normal to finish shopping. As she went through checkout, hope was rising in her heart. Maybe Logan or Jake would talk to the women. Would say Gin wasn't a total bitch.

Before she even made it out of the store, her cell rang. "Hello?"

"About time you answered your phone," Becca said huffily. "How about a girls' night out, and you can tell us everything."

Gin gave a shimmy of delight. "How about a girls' night in? Can you come to my place? I have two gallons of chocolate chip ice cream I got...before."

"Oh. My. You're certainly in sore need of help. I'll gather the others—and bring hot fudge syrup."

* * * *

That *man.* On Thursday, Gin finished vacuuming the carpet in Atticus's bedroom and rolled her eyes, laughing at herself. The correct word was that *Dom.*

For the past week, since her hot tub "interrogation," Atticus was in her life, either spending the night at her place or taking her—and Trigger—home with him. He constantly asked what she was feeling, why she was doing something, prompting her to search her emotions.

The man was like a therapist on steroids.

"What are you up to, babe?" As if her wayward thoughts had summoned him, he appeared in the doorway. He studied her, the vacuum, the cleaned carpet, and shook his head. "No, let me rephrase, why are you cleaning my carpet?"

"Oh honestly. No, I'm not doing housework because I'm worried you'll dump me." She set the vacuum away with a scowl. "Or for the joy of it either. It's because this morning, I stepped on a piece of some unidentifiable *stinky* substance." She wrinkled her nose. "I do believe it came from the floor of the stables."

He stared at her a second and burst out laughing.

Heavens, she loved that. Open, hearty laughter wasn't heard nearly often enough in the prison—and Atticus had a deep, wonderful, infectious laugh.

"As the homeowner, I should inspect to make sure you did a thorough job."

What? The floor was spotless. "Oh, really. And how exactly are you planning to do that?"

"Piece of cake." He unbuttoned her shirt. "I'll put you on your back on the carpet and apply some…weight. When we're through, I'll check your skin, and if you have any dents from dirt, I'll spank you and let you vacuum it again."

"Spank me. Oh, you best not even try—"

His mouth silenced her, and then he pulled her shirt up to tie it over her head, blindfolding her.

An hour later, she tried to tell him the "dent" on her bottom was from his teeth, but he spanked her anyway…using his fingers every few swats so effectively that she came twice before he finished with her "punishment."

Chapter Sixteen

Her mama would have had a fit to see Gin rest her forearms on the restaurant table and lean forward. But Friday nights at the Mother Lode tended to be noisy, and Becca was telling how their dog Thor had almost given a lodger a heart attack when the man approached the baby.

It was good to be with friends—especially her three besties with their husbands—or maybe she should say their *Doms,* cuz boy, when the men were together, the testosterone was thicker than the perfume at a churchwomen's social.

Beside Gin was Atticus. To her right were Virgil and Summer; across the table were Logan, Becca, and the baby, as well as Jake and Kallie.

"You're right, babe. This is great." As Atticus signed the check, he used his free hand to steal the last bite of her strudel.

"Thief," she said without rancor, far too full to be upset.

He rubbed his shoulder affectionately against hers. "Like being back with your girlfriends, don't you."

It wasn't a question. "Yes. I missed them."

His smile faded. "Magnolia, no matter what fights we get into, I won't ask your buddies to choose between us. That'd be a fucking cowardly thing to do." He tugged her hair. "If I'd known you were avoiding them, we'd have talked sooner. I see I need to watch you more closely."

She made a disparaging noise in the back of her throat even as her inner girl wiggled in happiness. "I don't see how you possibly could."

In the dim restaurant, his grin was bright. "I'll figure out a way. Speaking of which, we need to talk about you starting a journal."

"I have one—and it's for me, not you."

His lips twitched. "'Fraid not, babe. D/s journals are what a submissive shares with her Dom. Because sometimes writing is easier than talking. You know all about not sharing, right, little counselor?"

Trapped. "Listen, you're not—"

"Next time, I want to know you're feeling insecure before I find it out in a grocery store," he said softly.

When he talked like that, she wanted to burrow right into him. As his gaze held hers, every smidgen of her resistance dissolved.

She should learn his technique. The skill would be most useful with her caseload of hardened convicts.

"Atticus," Jake said from across the table. "You going on the Search and Rescue climbing day? We could use someone familiar with the rigging."

"Sure."

Gin stiffened. "You're climbing?" she whispered.

"SAR needs everyone it can get. And those exercises you gave me are helping." He touched a finger to her cheek. "Don't worry, darlin'. Even if—when—I can climb without needing to puke, I'll use gear."

Thank you, little baby Jesus.

A flash of pain showed in his eyes. "You know, I'd planned to quit free soloing, but Bryan was still into it." He shook his head. "I should have stuck to my guns. Maybe he'd…"

"Oh, honey. Over the years, I've learned that decent people are walking storehouses of regrets." She tipped her cheek into his palm. "If you'd died and Bryan was the survivor, would you forgive him?"

"Well, yeah."

"If Bryan's ghost could talk, would it blame you?"

The corner of Atticus's mouth edged up. "He'd get a kick out of being a ghost—and he never held a grudge in his life."

"Well, then."

"You have a tender heart, counselor." He bent down, slanted his mouth over hers, and ran his tongue over her bottom lip, before giving her a leisurely intoxicating kiss. He tasted of dessert, making her think of other treats a woman might have if she tried.

A baby crying and chairs moving broke them apart.

"Easy, buddy," Logan was saying. Ansel's face was red, fat tears on his cheeks.

Rebecca plopped a pacifier in Ansel's mouth. Silence. "Sorry, everyone, but we need to go before the youngest Hunt gets cranky. He takes after his father, you know." As laughter ran around the table, she bent to pick up the diaper bag from the floor.

Logan shifted Ansel to his other shoulder and took advantage of her position to run a finger along the top edge of her chemise. "Nice breasts, little rebel. Good thing they keep me—and Ansel—from getting too cranky."

Becca rolled her eyes. "You're the reason those breasts are so big, thank you very much."

"And it was my very great pleasure."

Gin grinned as she shoved back her chair. In her usual country-urban style, Becca wore faded jeans, fancy stiletto boots, and a flannel shirt unbuttoned far enough to show off her lacy chemise. She'd complained her breasts had increased two sizes with pregnancy, but no man around seemed to mind.

As Logan stood with Ansel in his arms, the baby was chuckling and kicking his little feet inside the onesie.

Becca was a lucky, lucky woman.

Atticus picked up Gin's coat and saw her watching the baby with a longing expression.

She wanted children. The knowledge kindled a kindred desire inside him. But one that might take a while to materialize.

Although she was slowly coming to rely on him, she didn't yet trust him not to vamoose. Eventually, she'd learn he wasn't like her previous lovers—or asshole father, for that matter. Time would show her he was honorable and wouldn't walk away from the woman he loved.

Loved?

He froze in place for a moment—and then shook his head ruefully. Snuck right up on him, hadn't it? But, there it was—the woman he *loved.*

Now he had to figure out how to share how he felt without her fleeing the state. Smiling, he helped her into her coat and helped himself to a long hug. His woman gave good hugs.

Outside, the rain was still pouring down, and after a quick good-bye, Logan and Becca and Ansel, Jake and Kallie headed for their vehicles.

Under the overhang, Gin was talking to Summer about a proposed shopping trip when Atticus caught her attention. He jerked his chin toward the convenience store across the street. "Didn't you say you needed dog food for Trigger?"

"Oh, spit. Yes, I do."

Summer eyed the wet street. "I have to make a run too. The bottomless pits called the Masterson men are out of milk and—horror of horrors—chips. You wouldn't believe the way they go through junk food."

"I can't believe you *cook* for them." Gin pulled up her hood.

"Everyone takes a turn, and each of the guys has a specialty—like Morgan does all the Asian foods. But the cleaning? Oh, God, you should see the messes they make."

"Nurse, meet pigs, right?" Gin giggled. "But you shouldn't have to put up with that."

Atticus grinned as he and Virgil followed the women.

And, yep, as the women entered the store, Gin was giving Summer ideas on how to effect a change in the brothers' slovenly behavior.

Dumping all their scattered stuff in the stable? Possibly effective, although the horses might get offended by the stench.

Upping any offender's share of household expenses to hire a maid for their scheduled cleaning days? Now that was plain evil.

Virgil rubbed his chin. "My brothers might be in for a shock."

"I take it you're not on the shit list?"

"Nope." Virgil smirked. "If I do my part, then my submissive has enough energy to last through what I want to do to her. Win:win."

"Smart man." After shaking the water from his hat, Atticus followed Virgil into the store.

"Hey, Lieutenant. Detective." The grizzled owner, Mark Greaves, stepped from behind the counter. "Any chance you two could help me out? I have dry rot under a fridge in back. Didn't notice it until today when it started sagging. I can't budge it, and I'm afraid it'll go through the floor before I get Harve's crew out here tomorrow."

"That'd suck," Atticus muttered.

"Not a problem," Virgil said. He raised his voice. "We'll be in the back, Sunshine."

The women were perusing a potato chip bag label, discussing health and fat grams.

Jesus, seriously? Shaking his head, Atticus followed the men. If Gin brought home "healthy" chips, he'd warm her ass.

Over the next few minutes, he soon regretted the hearty meal he consumed. The fucking industrial refrigerator weighed a ton.

Greased by an ample amount of swearing, they eventually managed to shove the damn thing to a stable section of floor.

Leaving Greaves to plug his machine back in, Atticus led the way out of the backroom, rotating his strained shoulders. Hot tub tonight.

He froze at the smack of flesh on flesh. A woman cried out in pain.

Gin. Atticus broke for the front. Virgil veered off, taking another aisle.

The front was deserted.

"Leave her alone!" Gin's raised voice came from the right. "Get out of here before our men return."

Atticus leaned over the counter to check Greaves's store monitor.

Third aisle. Two men. Gin and Summer. Someone lay on the floor.

"Hey, looky-looky, the cunt wants to play." The man's voice held an ugly note.

"I don't see no men, do you?" Another spoke. "Bitch is lying."

Atticus sped toward aisle three, glancing down each row as he passed. *No one. No one. There.*

At the far end of the row was his woman, back to him. United against two men in leather jackets, she and Summer stood side-by-side, protecting the black woman sprawled on the floor behind them.

Gin held a bag of dog food in her hands. The men had no weapons out, and his fear receded a notch.

Even as Atticus yelled, "Police," the men attacked the women.

Gin threw the dog food at the biggest bastard's legs.

He tripped and fell to his hands and knees.

Screaming bloody murder—*good girl*—Gin backpedaled.

Summer shrieked, "Virgil, help!" With a sweep of her arm, she knocked an entire display of cereal boxes at the other man.

He stumbled, doing fancy footwork to keep his feet.

Snatching cans from the shelves, Gin bombarded her target, and Summer followed suit.

"Fuck. Shit." Cursing accompanied the thud of metal against flesh.

Charging up behind the men, Virgil dodged a thrown can, skidded to a halt—and roared with laughter.

Despite his fury, Atticus was already laughing. He reached over Gin's shoulder and grabbed her next missile. "Okay, slugger. We got this."

She glared at him. "I do believe you were dawdling."

Hell of an accusation in that slow drawl of hers.

She stepped around to join the injured woman. "Are you all right, ma'am?"

"*Police*, motherfucker. Stay down." Virgil kicked the feet out from under one assailant. The crash and yelp of pain was pleasing. "Summer, can you help Mrs. Ganning?"

Atticus shoved the other asshole face down in the cans. Both bastards had racist tats on their shaved heads and necks. "We got an infestation of skinheads around here, Virg." He tossed Virgil a zip tie, secured his perp, and called the station for pickup.

"My day off and now I have paperwork," Virgil muttered. "I got these assholes. You want to check the women?"

"Will do."

Summer had disappeared.

Sitting on the floor, Gin had an arm around the waist of the elderly woman. "Don't try to stand up yet, ma'am."

"Mrs. Ganning." Atticus knelt on one knee. He gently touched at the swelling on the side of her face. "They got you good, huh?" Bastards. The old librarian might weigh a hundred pounds on a good day.

"Detective." She reached out and patted his leg with a shaky hand. "You have a very brave woman here."

Damn straight. "I would have to agree with you there." His smile brought pink to Gin's cheeks. "Are you hurt anywhere else, ma'am?"

"Oh, I'll have some bruises, I fear. Those two followed me from the street, making"—her expression sickened—"filthy comments."

"This would be the one time I'm not in the front." Greaves appeared, jaw clenched with anger. "I'm sorry, Maud."

"No need to fret. I was rescued quite nicely by these young women—and our law enforcement."

Summer trotted around the corner. Gently, she applied a towel-wrapped ice pack to Mrs. Ganning's cheek.

"It's good we were here, Greaves," Atticus said. "I doubt the assholes would have backed off for one man." They'd have flattened him and robbed the place as well.

The thump of boots heralded the arrival of the uniformed officers along with Fire and Rescue for Mrs. Ganning. As they bore off their various charges, Atticus guided Gin out to the street.

"You…" He could only shake his head. "That was one of the bravest, most ballsy things I've ever seen. And you scared a goddamned decade off my life." He opened his arms.

When she hugged him without a single hesitation, his chest

tightened.

Jesus, he was still scared. "What the hell were you thinking?" he growled, pulling her completely against him.

"Well, there wasn't much choice. I could hardly let them beat her up."

Far, far too many people would have. And she hadn't even considered walking away an option. Truth: he loved this woman.

And she thought on her feet. He kissed the top of her head and smiled into her silky hair. The story would be all over town tomorrow: *Skinheads downed by Campbell's soup.* The heroes—two terminally cute women.

Gin lifted onto tiptoes to say quietly in his ear, "By the way..."

"Mmmhmm?"

"Thanks for coming to my rescue."

His arms tightened around her. She hadn't had enough rescues in her life. Not enough backup. Too many people had abandoned her. With a good mom and two brothers, he'd been the lucky one. "Of course I rescued you."

She was his now to care for and protect—and she needed to know that. He lifted her face up and met her eyes. "Virginia, I'll always come after you. I keep what's mine."

He could see the declaration strike home. See the gleam of tears in her eyes. See her love.

Oh yeah, it was there, even if she hadn't said the words.

* * * *

"Virginia, I'll always come after you. I keep what's mine." For the last few days, Atticus's words had played a continuous loop in Gin's head.

She set her journal on the coffee table and pulled her feet up on her small couch, jostling Trigger. He set his head back on her thigh and fell back asleep.

"Always." Such a wonderfully reassuring—yet frightening word. Atticus was implying they had a...a future. Which meant she'd have to invest herself.

And—darn *Shrink Atticus*—as she'd journaled, a theme emerged. She not only thought she had sacrificed herself in a relationship, but she also believed that any man would leave her eventually.

Not a good revelation. She scowled. She should have realized this before. Then again, how often had her clients been blind to the cause of their problems? The mind tended to avoid thinking about past pains. And without sharing its reasoning, the subconscious would try to prevent any re-creation of traumatic events.

She had been making choices based on avoidance. That time was over.

She scrubbed her hands over her face. At her movement, Trigger set a paw on her thigh.

"Thanks, my friend." She stroked his big head, grateful for his presence. "You know, you're far, far better company than Preston ever was."

Trigger whined his agreement. He thought he was superb company.

"You do realize Atticus is wonderful too, don't you?"

Trigger's tail slapped the couch. He adored Atticus.

So did Gin.

Her lips curved as she considered the man. Such a *whoa, honey* all-man sort of guy.

The kind who didn't think twice about risking his life to help others. The ease with which he'd subdued the creep had been intimidating and, later, when she'd stopped shaking, extremely hot.

She grinned. Being all man, he'd enjoyed the way she'd shown her gratitude for her rescue.

He was also the type of guy who'd automatically clicked to whatever sport was on television. At least, he enjoyed snuggling on TV nights. And, he loved classic Westerns. In turn, she enjoyed his contemporary modern-day police and detective thrillers. They'd found common ground.

Mostly. Getting him to watch a chick flick had required a bribe of chocolate cake.

His "family room" was a testosterone-laden rec room. And awfully fun. She couldn't yet beat him in pool, but she'd slaughtered him in Ping Pong.

Yesterday, he'd made her trim his roses, insisting all Southerners knew how to tend flowers. *The idiot.* Even worse, she did know how…

She'd paid him back by making him dig her an herb garden, saying digging wasn't ladylike and pitchforks fell squarely into the guy arena. He'd not only dug the bed, but also helped plant the basil, oregano, and chives.

Sunday morning, he'd found the spot on her ribs that sent her into incontrollable laughter. In turn, she'd discovered his feet were ticklish. The ensuing wrestling match was amazing, although she'd lost. Rather than demanding a blowjob for his prize, he'd insisted she learn to ride Molly, the mare he'd brought with Festus from Idaho.

After her lesson with the horse, Atticus had dumped her in the hay...and taught her how to ride a human. "Cowgirl position." But she sure hadn't mastered "posting a trot," as he called it.

On the walk back to the house, her legs had wobbled so badly he'd had to hold her up. Riding was tiring. Climaxing a kazillion times? Totally exhausting.

And then he'd helped her cook supper since he'd worn her out.

She frowned. The man did too much for her.

In household work, they ran about even. True, he did more yard work, if given a choice. But inside the house, he always picked up after himself. His socks hit the laundry basket, not outside. Unlike some of her lovers, he put his dirty dishes in the dishwasher. So they balanced in that area.

But in sex? Was it stupid to want him to ask...more...from her during sex? And maybe other times too. Actually, not to ask, but to *demand.*

Okay, yes, he was in charge in the bedroom, but it was all about mutual satisfaction. If anything, she came out ahead, since she'd get off more than once.

But there were times she just wanted him to use her, to be a little selfish and take his own pleasure without thinking of hers.

She wanted to...serve...him. How weird was that?

Chapter Seventeen

In the middle of the following week, Gin walked into her house, smiling in happiness. The last inmate of the day had shown he was getting somewhere.

"*I could see it last night, Miss Virginia—my future. Going to work. Getting a real paycheck and putting money in the bank.*" Braden was one of her youngest cases, convicted of car theft. He had so much potential and yet couldn't visualize a future other than more crimes and more prison. But she'd broken through finally. Now that he'd seen other possibilities, they could work on achieving them. Her sense of satisfaction bubbled inside her like champagne.

She needed to plan out the next session. Her fingers itched for a pencil as she set her purse on a chair.

She heard Trigger's woof from the backyard and hurried through the house for her favorite day-brightening canine greeting. "Hold on, boy."

Wait. The deadbolt on the back door wasn't latched.

Hand at her throat, she spun in place. A beer stood on the counter. Someone was in her house. She grabbed her phone and punched in 9-1—

"Gin, let the dog in before he busts your door down." The voice came from outside. *Atticus.*

She threw the door open and landed on her butt from Trigger's enthusiastic greeting. "Ouch!"

The wiggling Labrador shoved his head against her shoulder,

squirming around until she'd had a chance to pet all of his wet fur.

"Honeybunches, you are a very bad guard dog."

Not repentant in the least, he snuck a quick lick to her chin.

How had the silly beast come to mean so much to her? She planted a kiss on his furry nose. "Let me up, baby. I need to smack some sense into your human friend out there."

She walked onto the back steps and set her hands on her hips.

Crouched down beside a bush, her target was barely visible. But he undoubtedly could hear her.

"Atticus Ware, what were you thinking? You almost gave me a heart attack when I saw the door unlocked. I thought I had a burglar."

He rose to his feet.

Her mouth went dry.

The drizzling rain sprinkled onto bare shoulders that could have graced a Viking warrior, a muscular chest that was streaked with sweat and dirt, and ridged abs that defined the term six-pack.

Oh, my stars. Her body flashed from fury to arousal.

Laughing, he hadn't even noticed the way she was staring. "Gin, my pickup is parked right there on the street."

She hadn't seen it. "Oh." The heat roaring through her scorched away any retort.

Climbing the steps, he tipped his cowboy hat back. The pale cloud-covered sunlight lit his rodeo belt buckle, pulling her gaze down.

Low-slung jeans were God's gift to women, all right. Her fingers itched to follow the happy trail—or to detour to the sexy oblique crease just above his hip.

She swallowed. "What are you doing in my backyard? In the rain?"

"Building you a doghouse—rather, I'm making a house for your bony-ass mutt."

A snort escaped her. He constantly insulted Trigger, yet was always slipping tidbits of food to the Labrador. Stopping to pet and talk to him.

Trigger adored him.

"A dog house would be wonderful. Thanks." Stars above, look at the man. Atticus didn't shave on his days off so stubble darkened his neck below his beard. He looked dangerous. Predatory. Unable to help herself, she stepped forward and ran her hands over the strong, muscular planes of his chest, over the brown dusting of hair to search out the flat male nipples. His skin was overheated and slick with sweat and rain.

He caught her wrists. "Gin, I'm filthy and—"

"I know," she breathed and whipped her sweater up and over her head, then opened the front of her bra.

The look in his eyes changed instantly—yes, he was all man—and his hands, gritty with dirt, palmed her breasts.

"Yesss," she hissed softly. She moved forward, close enough to undo his belt and zipper. With the eight-foot wooden fence around her backyard, no one could see in.

His hands closed on hers. "Gin," he warned.

A proper submissive asked permission, she knew, and yet she wanted him in her mouth more than she wanted her next breath. "Atticus," she responded teasingly.

Dropping to her knees, she pulled his cock all the way out, inhaling the intensely masculine musky scent. He was hardening, and she slid him into her mouth to enjoy how the baby-soft skin turned taut over the iron beneath. "Mmmmm."

"Jesus." His hand flattened on the wall behind her as he gave it his weight.

She lifted her head long enough to grin up at him. "I didn't ask permission, oh Dom. You'll have to punish me later."

"Don't think I won't," he muttered, sending a thrill through her. Because he would. As a Dom, he enforced his rules consistently, fairly— and with a hard hand. She loved that about him.

What she didn't love was how he never asked her for anything. That wasn't right. He was always doing things for her, and the balance was unfair. Now that she knew a desire to serve wasn't unbalanced, that it made her happy, she wanted to give him more.

Wanted him to *demand* more.

Swirling her tongue around the head, she sucked lightly and took him in.

His next breath was harsh.

She bobbed her head, applying light suction. His testicles were round and heavy in the palm of her hand, and she fondled them as she circled his cock with her tongue. *So good...*

She stopped and sat back. "Well, we should move this inside." Smiling inwardly, she started to stand.

"Don't even think about it." The hand on her shoulder forced her back to her knees. He tilted her head up to study her face. "Yeah, you enjoy giving head."

He had no idea. She smiled at him.

He ran a finger around her wet lips. "You're also topping from the bottom, little girl. Manipulating me to"—his eyes narrowed—"to ask more from you."

She swallowed. True, she'd wanted him to push her, but he'd figured her out within minutes and called her on it. *Uh-oh.*

"We're going to talk about this, but first, I'll take what you so kindly offered." His fingers closed, trapping her hair.

When her mouth dropped open, he fed his cock between her lips, and, carefully, but mercilessly, facefucked her. His grip in her hair kept her totally under his control, and *he* was the one to regulate the pace and depth as his hips rocked forward and back.

Bracing her hands on his thighs, she closed her eyes and...surrendered. He'd drive her—his shaft hit the back of her throat, making her almost gag, shutting off her breath—but never too much, because this was Atticus, and he knew her. Cared for her.

She relaxed into the pace, the knowledge she could trust him to control her and take what he wanted, the glory of giving it to him.

When he came, she swallowed and swallowed, then cleaned him with her tongue before slipping him out.

As she blinked back to reality, she wrapped her arms around his hips and rested her cheek on his bare stomach. The feeling inside her was big, overwhelming, as if her heart had expanded past what her ribs could contain. Not love, *please, not love,* but—gratitude, joy, and the devastating sense of being where she belonged.

She kissed his stomach and said, almost inaudibly, "Thank you." As his hand smoothed her hair, her scalp stung from his tugging. Her knees hurt from the wood of the porch—and her panties were damp with her arousal.

He chuckled. "You're very welcome."

For one breath, two, she savored contentment.

Then, with a grunt, he yanked her to her feet. "Go in the kitchen and strip. Kneel there and wait for me."

Heaven help her, she was in trouble.

A long while later, Atticus sat on the living room floor with his back against the couch, listening to the rain drumming on the roof.

One well-punished, well-satiated little submissive reclined between his legs, her head against his shoulder.

During her punishment, he'd tried to explain that—while he'd enjoyed the hell out of the blowjob—she wasn't allowed to manipulate him into something. She understood, although she hadn't liked learning the difference between a fun spanking and one for discipline.

But after he finished disciplining her, well, holding a squirming little subbie—especially when the subbie was Gin—had turned him on.

So even while the tears were drying on her cheeks, and she was struggling not to call him names, he'd held her down, sucked her clit into his mouth, and spurred her to a quick orgasm before taking her hard and fast. It wasn't often his dick rose to the occasion twice in an hour, but damn, she was fun to spank.

The blowjob, spanking, and fucking had worn her out though. She was half-asleep.

Comfortable and content, Atticus considered getting up to cook supper. Would Gin be able to sit in a chair at the table? He grinned. Tomorrow—Friday—was his day off, but she'd have a long day of sitting as she counseled inmates.

His smile faded. Goddamned prison. He hated her working there. And what if the increase in local crime was tied to the prison? The skinheads arrested last week had no reason to visit Bear Flat—and their hotel room held a wealth of firearms and cell phones.

The call to the warden had been unproductive. The idiot's head was up his ass and not emerging any time soon.

A sound came from the kitchen. Atticus tensed before recognizing the clicking of Trigger's claws on the hardwood floor.

The chair in the corner creaked.

"Trigger, are you allowed on the furniture?" Atticus asked quietly.

The dog jumped down with a thump. Heaving a disgruntled sigh, he settled into his dog bed against the wall.

Gin stirred and pushed up to look over Atticus's shoulder. "Your back is to the room. How'd you know what he was doing?"

Since she was awake, he could move. Atticus scooped her up and resettled them on the couch. "I recognize the sound of a sneaky dog. Odysseus would sleep on the furniture when I wasn't looking."

She propped herself up, forearms on his chest. "You named a dog Odysseus? Seriously?"

"Mom did. She majored in classical fiction and taught high school English."

"An English teacher. No wonder you Wares have unusual names. Atticus is for Atticus Finch; Sawyer for Tom?"

"Yep. And my youngest brother is Hector from the Iliad. His dog is Andromache; Andy for short, since Hector can't stand Greek mythology."

"Is he still in Idaho?"

"Mmmhmm. Kept the ranch, although he sold off a corner so I could buy acreage here."

Gin studied him. "Was he making you a gift or did he sell your own portion of the property?"

"Part of mine." He resettled her, tangling his fingers in her hair. The firelight danced over the fine strands, bringing out different shades of red, making her fair skin glow, deepening her green eyes. He doubted Helen of Troy could have been lovelier. And no one had a more generous heart than this woman in his arms. "Now, let's talk about what you were up to this afternoon."

She huffed. "You certainly have a violent reaction to getting a blowjob."

"Violent? Let's go for honesty here, pet. Considering where you work, you've seen real aggression."

"I—" Her gaze took in his serious expression. "Okay, fine. You walloped me, but you weren't angry."

His lips quirked. "Difficult to be, since I got a blowjob. Which you're incredibly good at, by the way."

Her smile held the delight of a submissive who'd been complimented by her Dom. Damn, he loved that look on her face.

Then shame filled her gaze. "I'm sorry, Atticus. I think I've been working in the prison too long. The inmates excel at manipulative behavior, and I tried the very same thing on you."

"Yep. Tell me why."

Emotions chased across her face like clouds in a brisk wind. "It's odd. I love doing things for you—especially now that I realize I serve you because I like to. But you never ask for anything. And I wanted you to...to use me sometimes. Even if I know I'm being weird."

Hell, he'd figured it correctly. She needed to know she wasn't asking more than she should, which meant he had to explain his own behavior. But, talking about the past? He'd rather shoot himself in the head.

With one hand tangled in her hair, he rubbed his thumb over her cheek. "You're not weird at all. You're submissive, Virginia, and one kind of submissive delights in giving. Making people happy. Filling their needs. It's probably why you chose counseling for a career. You'd be even more driven to offer your talents to your Dom. It's normal, babe."

"Normal." She relaxed with a wry comment, "Feminists would burn you at the stake for your stance."

"Nah. See, submission and giving are true with male submissives too. Equal opportunity service, got it?"

She had an adorable smile. "Yes."

"As for me..." Explaining his behavior wasn't simple. "My stepfather's treatment of my mother makes me...hesitant...to do anything where I feel I'm taking advantage of a woman."

"I had a feeling your past might be affecting you." She frowned. "Your stepfather ended up in jail. Did your mother finally turn him in?"

The memory was foul. "Once. But he didn't hit her where it showed and she didn't see a doctor. So he was assigned anger management therapy and behaved himself until his therapy was over. Then he strangled Sawyer almost to death. Said he'd kill us if Mom had him arrested again."

"And that right there is one more reason you don't—didn't—trust counselors. No wonder," Gin muttered. "So, what happened to get him in prison?"

Her understanding created a warm glow in his belly—that didn't erase the chill of having to talk about his past. "He came home shit-faced one night when I was twelve." Stumbled into the kitchen, gunning for a fight. Any excuse would have sent him over. Atticus could still feel the dread infusing the house. "He decided he didn't want fried chicken and started to throw the pan at her."

Gin stared. "Hot grease?"

"She'd have been burned. Blinded. I charged him, knocked it out of his hand." They'd both been splashed with the grease. A punch sent Atticus to the floor. A kick curled him up like a pill bug. "He was...enraged. Sawyer—being a bright lad—called the cops before jumping in. He got thrown into the wood stove. I thought the bastard had killed him."

"Oh heavens." She touched his cheek and drew him back from seeing his brother's body on the floor.

"He was drunk." Atticus had staggered to his feet. Dizzy, sick. Didn't matter. He'd put his head down and charged. "I was fast. Mom and Hector threw things. We kept him going." For a while.

She must have seen the expression in his face. Her question was right on target. "You were only twelve. Did he get his hands on you?"

"When the cops came, he was whipping me with his belt—buckle and all. They heard my mother's screams and busted in the door." Sawyer had been unconscious. Broken. His mother unable to rise. Hector curled in a pain-ridden ball. Atticus covered in blood. "Got my fondness for law enforcement right then, I think. Even more, when he got shipped to prison."

Her brows drew together. "First conviction. He wouldn't get too long."

"He was out before I enlisted. Moved back to town and behaved while on probation."

"And when he got off probation?"

"I was in the service when Mom reported he'd visited her and was aggressive." Atticus eyed Gin. She should know the truth about him because, if needed, he'd do the same thing all over again. "I took leave and paid him a...persuasive...visit."

Her eyes widened and then she gave him her quirky smile. "Good for you. And?"

"He decided the weather was nicer in Arizona. Never returned."

She patted Atticus on the chest as she might one of her clients. "For some reason, I have a very primitive delight in knowing how protective you can be."

"Jesus, you're something."

"*We're* something. I worry about giving too much. You're concerned that asking might be abuse. Can this relationship be saved?"

"You finally admit we have a relationship?"

"I—*no*. I mean, that's the title of a column in a women's magazine." Her face had turned the delightful color of a summer-ripe tomato.

Unable to resist, he said, "But, sweetheart, if we don't have a relationship, then why are we talking like this? Fuck-buddies don't need to talk, do they?"

"We're more than..." She glared. "You're baiting me."

"Hell, yeah." He tugged on her hair. "Babe. Haven't you noticed we're in a serious relationship—a monogamous, *we're-dumping-the-condoms* relationship?"

Her face paled.

Stubborn female. Any other woman would be badgering him for a declaration.

After a second, he ordered his thoughts. "Back to the subject." He manned up, though this was like stepping into a firefight without body armor. "As your Dom, I'll up my demands. In turn, I expect you to tell me if you need more. Or if I ask for something you're unwilling to give."

"Huh, I should have complained this afternoon," she grumbled. "I had an entirely different kind of blowjob planned for you."

"Don't bullshit me, pet. You loved it." He'd been a Dom a hell of a long time, ever since his Captain had taken him to a BDSM party and then mentored him in the lifestyle as well. Atticus ran his knuckles down her cheek. Yeah, he knew when a submissive hit her happy space from being controlled, being taken, being pushed into serving.

Her attempt at a pout was spoiled by her smile. "I did." And then she showed the courage he adored and took the next step. "We're in a relationship. Yes. Dump the condoms."

He kissed her soft lips, tucked her head against his shoulder, and relaxed. They really were a pair. Both of them scarred up from the past, wary as jackrabbits when the coyotes were yapping.

But it didn't matter what battles they'd run into in the future. For now, all he needed was right here in his arms. *Mine.*

Chapter Eighteen

The rain had finally eased off, and the flowerbeds were bright with colorful blooms. As Sawyer walked beside his new shrink outside the admin building, he savored the feeling of sunlight on his skin.

Under a CO's watchful eye, an inmate crew was raking the grass of the debris that had blown in. Pit with his colorless eyes, tall and skinny Crack, short and wide Stub, Lick—into perversions, and Bomb, ex-military. The leader, Slash, was a power-lifter and the biggest at six-two, about two-thirty pounds. A swastika tat decorated his scalp.

They were all nasty, fanatical bastards. How the hell had they received work assignments outside the building walls, let alone together?

Closer to the chain link fence, Ms. Virginia and another counselor sat at a picnic table. Most prison staff on break avoided areas with inmate workers, but Ms. Karen was surreptitiously smoking a cigarette—not something she'd get away with in normal staff areas.

Ms. Virginia had smiled at Sawyer but left him and his counselor to their privacy. He had to say, despite her loose fitting, unfeminine clothing and pulled-back hair, she was a pretty woman—and he'd recovered enough to notice.

It was interesting how different counselors could be. Where Ms. Virginia tried to look unattractive, the therapist named Penelope acted more like a mare in heat. The woman had an obsession with inmates, the more violent the better, and from rumors floating through the cells, she liked to fuck to stories of murder.

But Ms. Virginia was a good woman—and she belonged to Atticus. Competition for her attention wasn't on the books, even if he'd been interested…which he wasn't. He didn't want a woman who'd examined his soul the way a pathologist might examine a man's guts.

"Time we were heading in," Wheeler said. So far, Jacob Wheeler seemed like a damn good counselor, even being the one to suggest an outside session.

Felt damn good to be outside a building and the enclosed yard spaces, even if still inside the perimeter fence.

Sawyer was getting better. No nightmares for a week, aside from the normal ones experienced by most prisoners. His depression— fucking pansy word—had lifted. Frustration still remained. The way each day disappeared with nothing to show for it could make a man crazy.

And he still felt as if he didn't deserve any better.

"By the way, I have some exercises I want you to do this week," Wheeler said. "I'll print them off for you."

"What kind of ex—"

A high-pitched sound interrupted him. Screams? He tilted his head. Although the minimum-security "park" was at the back corner of the prison grounds, noise always made its way through the heavy walls. This didn't sound like the normal mass movement rumble of prisoners during mess times.

"Is there a fight?" Virginia called, rising from the table where she'd been sitting.

Sawyer exchanged glances with Wheeler.

"Sounds more like a riot in Yard A," Wheeler said.

Sawyer frowned at the women. "Ms. Virginia, you should—"

"Karen, stay put," Wheeler said at the same time. Even as the lockdown alarm clanged, a dull noise came from outside the fence.

What the fuck?

A H1 Hummer topped a small hill and roared down the grassy slope, full-tilt toward the fence. *Jesus.* No one was in the driver's seat.

A grunt, then ugly hoots made Sawyer turn. The yard workers were cheering. The CO lay on the ground, neck obviously broken. A moment's inattention had turned deadly. One inmate brought his rake handle down on the CO again—although the guy was already dead.

A montage of gory images swam through Sawyer's mind, blood everywhere, turned over vehicles, body parts of his teammates. He shook his head hard, forcing himself to stay in the present. Bitterness coated his tongue.

The heavy all-terrain vehicle hit the fence with a ground-shaking crash, uprooting a cemented-in post. Links snapped, another post tilted and toppled. Wrapped in chain link and razor wire, motor roaring, the vehicle fought the fence.

A gap appeared. More cheers came from the inmates. They tossed down their rakes.

Shit. The women were between the inmates and the fence. Sawyer backed toward them, Wheeler at his shoulder.

The inmates trotted closer.

Bomb spotted the women. "We got pussy here!" The inmate veered toward the women.

Rage seared Sawyer's veins. He stepped into the bastard's path. No way would Sawyer let Att's woman be hurt. No *fucking* way. "Bomb, you got no time for women—or fighting. Just move on."

Bomb lunged.

Sawyer threw a punch to his jaw and then blocked Stub's incoming fist from the side. With the adrenaline rush, time slowed—but not enough. Six to one. Sucked.

Wheeler put a hard kick into Pit's breadbasket. Good man—but it was still six to two.

The leader was hanging back, letting his boys do the fighting.

Oh, no. Punching her body alarm button over and over, Gin backed away, even as the inmates surrounded the table where she and Karen were.

The first one Sawyer had punched, Bomb, dodged past him. His jaw was bleeding profusely. "C'mon, cunt." He seized her arm.

She slapped his hand away, kicked his shin, tried to kick higher to his privates. He blocked her with his thigh.

"*Bitch.*" He backhanded her so hard she fell to her knees. Pain shot through her cheek.

Grabbing her hair, Bomb yanked her to her feet, and she bit down on a scream. Tears blurred her vision.

"Prime pussy, eh, Slash," he yelled.

Slash. Gin's heart sank even as she continued to fight. That was the inmate who'd slammed her arm into the desk. She hadn't noticed he was with the group. *No. Please no.*

His lips turned up, the effect ugly in a face scarred with tattoos and holes from piercings. His eyes were cruel as he stared at her. "The redheaded bitch is mine to rip up, Bomb. Bring her. For me."

The words hit Gin like blows. *No.* Her heart felt as if it would explode inside her chest.

"Selfish bastard," Gin's captor muttered, then yelled, "Stub, grab the other one for us."

The skinny, shortest inmate with broken-off teeth circled where Wheeler and Sawyer were fighting with the rest. He grabbed Karen as she tried to escape past him—and hit her over and over, battering her to the ground.

Gin tried to go help. Bomb kicked her legs out from under her. As she struggled to her hands and knees, grunts and shouts came from close. Farther away, the noise of the riot in Yard A was muffled but filled with fury, out of control. Alarms were going off…finally. So long. She got to her feet.

Holding his ribs, Wheeler was on one knee. A convict kicked him in the head, felling him. Sawyer was fighting with the inmate who had tats covering every inch of his skin.

"Move it, assholes," Slash yelled and pointed to the fence. "Through the hole."

Bomb grabbed Gin's hair, dragging her after the group.

No. If the prisoners took her with them, she'd die. Die horribly. As they passed the still running Hummer, Gin grabbed the hand in her hair, spun, and kicked his testicles.

"Aaagh!" He fell to his knees, wheezing horribly.

She turned to run.

From the side, the tallest one shoved her straight into the Hummer. The impact stunned her, and she sagged, trying not to fall, blinking away blackness.

"Cunt." Bomb was up. Enraged, he pinned her against the vehicle, hand around her throat, gripping, cutting off her air. She couldn't *breathe.* Her fingernails scratched at his hand; her pulse roared in her ears.

Suddenly he was gone. She fell to her knees, gasping for oxygen, her hands to her throat.

She heard a sound like the snapping of sticks. Bomb's body landed at her feet. Eyes open. Dead.

For a second, she couldn't—couldn't move.

"Run, girl!" Sawyer's shout snapped through her, and she shoved off the Hummer. Another body—the heavily tattooed inmate—lay on the ground.

Sawyer was between two more, fighting for all he was worth. One staggered back. Then the leader lunged at Sawyer—and he had a long shank in his hand.

"No!" She ran at Slash, kicking at his legs, trying to scratch his eyes with her fingernails. Someone ripped her off and landed on top of her so hard her breath exploded from her lungs. Her ribcage bent painfully as he rested his weight on her. He ground his groin into her. "Slash's got plans for you."

He yanked her up, punched her in the gut, and dragged her to the fence.

Past Sawyer, who was on the ground, head turned toward her. Blood was pooling around him, red against the green grass. His eyes were open. Unblinking.

No. Grief hitched her breathing, despair filling her, as they dragged her through the gap in the fence.

* * * *

"Who's a pretty lady?" Atticus crooned to the mare, stroking her pregnant belly. "Won't be long now, will it?"

In the next stall over, Wyatt Masterson was grooming a bay gelding. "I figure a couple of weeks. Appreciate you taking a look at her hoof."

"No problem. Vets are always overloaded in the spring." Once the snow melted, every domestic and farm animal was either in heat or dropping babies. Atticus had to wonder if the warmth affected human females the same way. He'd have to tell Gin, so he could enjoy her cute giggle again.

Wyatt bent to check the gelding's hooves. "I'm glad we have you to call on now and then. Your folks must miss your know-how back in Idaho."

Families were strange things, weren't they? Wyatt was an inch shorter and an inch narrower in the shoulders than his oversized brother Virgil was. He, his brother Morgan, and Kallie had inherited and now ran the Masterson Wilderness Guides. And they teased Virgil about abandoning the family business to be a cop.

Sounded familiar. "My parents are dead." He nodded at Wyatt's muttered "Sorry, man," and added, "My youngest brother took over the ranch. He's even better with animals than I am. Got a gift."

"Your other brother comes up for parole next year, right. You figure on staying in Bear Flat after he's out?" Wyatt opened the door to the back corral and shooed the horse out.

"Not sure." The mountain town had become home. The sense of community was strong, and the townspeople were a tad more liberal than his Idaho hometown. Trouble was, he hated seeing Gin at that damned prison. But options around here were limited for a counselor. They might need a city.

A door slammed before the grating sound of boots on gravel. Morgan appeared in the door moving so fast he almost skidded into Trigger.

The dog scrambled out of the way.

"Got a bug up your ass, bro?" Wyatt asked.

Morgan shoved his brown hair out of his eyes. "Virg called. There's a prison riot in Yard A. But while that happened, a Hummer took out the fence in the minimum-security section. Several racist gang members—skinheads—were on yard work. Four grabbed a couple of the female staff and escaped."

When Atticus's hand stopped in midstroke, the mare nudged him chidingly. "What about Gin? Is she all right? Has anyone seen her?"

"Buddy," Morgan's gaze was stark. "She was kidnapped."

"*No.*" The word came from his gut. Then he moved. Left the stall. Shut in the mare. "Lend me a car." He could—

Morgan grabbed his shoulder and ducked the reflexive punch. "Hold, man. They had a Jeep. Abandoned it up around Banner Mountain. The trailhead there breaks into a shitload of small paths. Virgil wants us to mount up, take the Flint trail, and see if we can cut their tracks."

Smelling trouble, Trigger came to sit at Atticus's feet.

Despite the fear for Gin tearing through him, Atticus forced himself to pause. *Think.* Hummer for the fence. Must have had the Jeep waiting. All on yard work. That shouldn't have been allowed. Had they planned the riot as a diversion? They probably had gun or drug money to blow on bribes. Everything pointed to a coordinated plan.

Well thought out. So they'd know roadblocks would be set up. "They'll have gear from the car. And maps. Are probably making for a point where they can be picked up by car."

Wyatt had swung into action. When home, the Mastersons assisted Search and Rescue; they kept packs ready to go.

"Ware, catch." Saddlebags flew through the air.

Atticus caught the load. *Yard A.* Sawyer wasn't in that one. Still... "Any word on my brother?"

"Virgil didn't say anything." Morgan was saddling his horse.

Stay safe, bro. Keep your head down. Atticus saddled Festus and turned his mind to the task. The fucking inmates were canny enough to set up a prison break. They had hostages. And they'd react like cornered rats if found.

Gin, hold on, sweetling.

Atticus only had his service weapon. *We need more firepower.* "Wyatt, we're going to need rifles. Accurate ones."

"On it, buddy." Morgan ran for the house.

Time to go hunting.

* * * *

The sun went behind a cloud, dimming the forest to a twilight green. In the center of the trail, Gin bent with both hands on one knee and attempted to regain her strength. Sweat stung her branch-scraped face. Her limbs trembled incessantly from exhaustion—and fear. Her wrists were lashed together in front of her, and Crack held the other end of the rope. He'd finally tired of yanking her off-balance after Slash yelled he was slowing them down.

Unused to the wilderness, the four convicts had stopped to argue. With each new branching of the trail, they checked a map. Someone had obviously preplanned the route. What would happen when they reached the end?

A steep cliff lay to the right of the trail. *Yank the rope from Crack and dive down it?* She grimaced. She'd smash her head or fracture her back when she slammed into something. Or the inmates would open fire and kill her.

Because they were now armed.

Hours ago, they'd abandoned the Jeep and changed into regular clothing. Whoever had left the car had stocked it with light packs, a rifle, pistols, and enough ammunition to slaughter an army.

Despair had filled Gin. She'd seen the same understanding in Karen's gaze. Their chance of escape had diminished to almost nothing.

Rescue was the last hope.

Surely the prison riot had been stopped. Surely they'd discovered inmates had escaped. And Karen and Gin had been taken.

Her eyes stung with tears. Had they found Sawyer?

He'd fought so hard, using the murderous skills he'd spoken of in their sessions. The inmate today wasn't the first man he'd slain in hand-to-hand combat. He'd never wanted to kill again, had been glad to be out of the military, but he had killed for her, trying to save her. And he'd died. *Oh, Sawyer.*

Atticus, I'm so sorry.

Lordy, she hurt, inside and out. Blood trickled from her skinned, gashed knees. How often had she fallen? Her hands were scraped raw. Branches had torn at her face and arms. Her shirt was ripped open; Pit had wanted access to her breasts. Her lower lip was split, her cheek bruised, one eye swollen partly shut.

Could be worse, she tried to tell herself. Only...the future didn't hold much hope.

The convicts were hurrying to reach their pickup location before dark, which meant they hadn't had time to do more than grope her, but tonight...would be bad.

She glanced at Karen. The other woman was in a fugue state, eyes dull and hopeless. She'd given up.

The light brightened for a moment, and Gin looked up. Above the western mountains, the sun was setting, taking her hopes with it.

* * * *

Wyatt had led them up the trail at a pace not healthy for man or beast, although the horses were holding up well. Atticus wiped sweat from his face and muttered apologies to Festus. He heard Morgan doing the same with his mount.

Trigger trotted at the rear. *Fucking dog.* They'd left him tied up at the Mastersons', and he'd slipped his collar and appeared on the trail half an hour later. Now they were stuck with him.

Atticus couldn't slow down.

A prison riot. *Sawyer, my brother, keep your head down. Stay safe.*

He stared out at the conifer-covered mountains. Valleys formed dark green stripes; granite glinted in the sunlight. Gin was out in that damned wilderness. Being roughed up. Hurt. Possibly raped.

Pray God the convicts hadn't taken the time to stop, but fuck... His hand clenched on the reins as he drove the thought away. *Be alive, counselor. Anything else we can work through.*

Urgency coiled in his gut.

After the inmates met up with their ride, there'd be no need to handicap themselves with hostages. Once on their own turf, they could get anything they wanted.

We need to move faster.

But the Mastersons and Atticus were covering ground at an incredible pace. The Mastersons had grown up in these mountains. They'd hiked, fished, hunted, and led wilderness groups all over this area. But they couldn't work miracles and the sun was setting.

Off and on, helicopters buzzed past, their effectiveness limited by the forest canopy and the huge amount of area to cover.

At the summit where the trail forked, Wyatt pulled his horse to a stop and shoved his Stetson up to give Atticus a look. "Need a decision here. Left or right?"

Atticus moved the buckskin beside him. "Give me a rundown."

Pointing to the left, Wyatt said, "All forest. Small trails. A couple paths come out on Argyll Road; more emerge on to Bent Hill Road." He nodded toward Banner Mountain on the right, then scowled. "Atticus, could the bastards manage to set up a copter pickup? Prisoners can't communicate easily, can they?"

"Anything can be organized with a smuggled-in cell phone. They've had everything else arranged like clockwork." Atticus scowled.

"A copter could fly under radar through the valleys," Wyatt said.

"If they hike through the Green Creek area, they'll reach the backside of Banner Mountain. There are wide, flat clearings where a copter can land." Morgan tossed Atticus a piece of beef jerky and added, "Search and Rescue used one last year for an emergency pickup."

"True that." Wyatt pulled on his thick mustache. "They'd have to traverse the Green Creek ravine. Got an old cable and plank footbridge but the wood rotted. It's blocked off to hikers, but that wouldn't stop fugitives. Might slow the cops since no dogs or ATVs could use it."

The thought of the two terrified women being forced across a chasm... *God, Gin.* His mouth tasted of despair as Atticus stared at the two trails. Choosing was a crapshoot. If he was wrong... "We're already close to Banner Mountain past the Green Creek ravine, correct? This trail to the right intersects the route?"

"You nailed it." Wyatt lifted his chin. "Your woman, Ware. Your call."

If they finished this, she was damn well *going* to be his woman. The vow didn't ease the constriction in his chest. He checked the sky. Sunset was in about an hour. Would the assholes risk a night copter landing?

They would.

"Virgil should have enough men to cover the other trails, especially if dogs keep him straight." Maybe. There were a hell of a lot of mountain paths terminating on the small county roads. Atticus pulled off his hat and swiped his arm over his forehead. "Let's take the area where the dogs can't go. But if we're wrong..."

Gin and the other woman would pay the price.

"Pa always said—if not overused—an honest prayer would be heard in heaven." Morgan glanced up at the sky. "So put in a word for us, old man."

Atticus nodded, motioned to Wyatt to lead off, and nudged Festus. At a fast walk, they started down the backside of the mountain and into the growing shadows.

* * * *

After the bridge incident, the convicts had chosen a terrifying trail down steep switchbacks into a mountain valley. Gin's short-heeled pumps weren't anything close to hiking boots. From the slick feel, blisters on her toes and heels had broken open and were bleeding.

"Here. This is the place." Slash led the way out of the trees and stopped.

In the gray twilight, a mountain valley opened up, treeless, wide, and flat. Gin's hopes slid down further into hell. The prisoners had said a helicopter would pick them up. This must be the site. As freezing wind whipped at her clothes and hair, she shivered from the cold. From the fear.

The rest of the inmates and Karen stopped next to Slash.

"Viper called it right—shouldn't be any problem landing here." The scar across Slash's upper lip pulled his smile into a snarl. "Now we wait."

"Let's get our asses out of the wind. And out of sight." Crack turned in a circle, stopping to slap Karen. "Don't eyeball me, cunt."

Flinching at her coworker's low cry and hopeless weeping, Gin forced herself to stay put. She'd tried to help Karen when the woman had refused to step onto the horrible broken bridge. Crack and Stub had taken turns punching and kicking until both women were curled up and sobbing. Then they'd shoved them onto the bridge, taking bets whether one would fall when they got to the parts with only cable and no planks.

She'd hated them so much right then.

She wanted them dead. Wanted Atticus to come and kill them for her. Wanted him to save her. Just...just wanted him. *Where are you?*

As a detective, he'd have been notified of the riot and escape by now, surely. He'd come after the escapees—and her. He wouldn't stop. Would never give up on finding her.

No matter what the inmates did to her, even if they killed her, Atticus would find her. The certainty was a tiny trickle of warmth within her.

"There's shelter over there." Stub pointed.

A line of granite rocks looked like fifteen-foot fingers extending out of the ground. The curved tops were pink with the last of the setting sun.

"Let's go." Slash led the way.

Crack jerked the rope, and Gin staggered after him.

By the time they reached the edge of the meadow, Gin was shaking with the cold. The massive boulders, scattered here and there as if a giant had been playing marbles, loomed over them as the inmates dragged her and Karen deeper into their shelter.

When Crash dropped the rope attached to her wrists, Gin sagged against a huge boulder, grateful for the way it blocked the wind.

As the men tossed their packs onto the ground, Pit appeared with a load of branches from the trees.

"No fire," Slash stated. The scant moonlight pooled in areas not shadowed by the boulders. "Pigs might continue with the helicopters." He tossed his pack on the ground and pulled out a protein bar and water bottle. Whoever had prepared their backpacks had been a savvy camper.

Still shivering from both cold and fear, Gin watched. Her mouth was so parched she could hardly swallow. Everything on her body hurt from the blows and kicks, from falling, from branches tearing at her.

Slash turned and Gin tried—tried—not to cringe. But the expression on his face told her what was coming next.

"No one's there," Atticus said in a low murmur as he crouched inside the tree line to survey the dark clearing. *Empty.* His gut clenched.

He set his hand on the dog's neck. When they'd intersected the Green Creek ravine trail, Trigger had caught Gin's scent and taken off, almost out of sight before Atticus could call him back. He and the dog had worked together, playing to their strengths. When Trigger lost the scent in streams and rocky areas, Atticus had picked up the track in other ways.

As the sunlight dimmed, they'd relied more on Trigger. What if the dog had led them wrong?

Atticus scowled at the meadow. They'd tied the horses a quarter mile back to avoid the noise of saddle gear and hooves. But nothing was here. He'd been so certain...

Wyatt tugged on his mustache as he squinted at the dark landscape. "Crap," he growled. "Should have gone the—"

"That's a nasty wind." Morgan's voice was almost drowned out by the rustling trees. "They're not stupid. They wouldn't stand in a clearing and freeze their asses off."

Jesus, Masterson was right. "Where would they go?" He eyed the increasing silver glow in the east. Hidden behind a high bank of clouds, the moon would be exposed in a few minutes. Once free of the clouds, it would shine down directly into the meadow.

Wyatt pointed left. "Weren't there boulders over there, Morgan?"

"Quite a few. Good-sized ones."

Squinting, Atticus edged out of the trees far enough to spot the tall shapes, like crouching ogres. "Let's check it out. Quietly—they might be canny enough to post a guard." He made his way through the forest, grateful he'd worn dark clothing.

A few minutes later, they reached their goal—several ten- to fifteen-foot "stones" at the base of a cliff. The closest was a massive boulder as high as a house.

Morgan's hand closed on his arm. The man tilted his head. Below the howling of the wind, men's voices could be heard.

They were in there. But was Gin still alive?

Trigger whined and pulled on the rope leash Atticus had constructed.

"Easy, boy," Atticus whispered. Fuck, no way of telling where in the boulders the convicts had holed up. His team couldn't sneak up on the bastards—not if they'd posted a guard. A straightforward assault would likely get the women killed.

Doing nothing wasn't an option.

"Morgan, stay on the right flank and set up to cover the meadow." Wyatt's younger brother—by a year—had a wall covered in blue ribbons from shooting competitions. And the rifle he'd brought would make any sniper proud. "If we don't get the women out, it'll be up to you. Take out the copter if you need to."

"Aye," he muttered and faded into the forest.

Unusually enough for him, Wyatt waited quietly.

Atticus pointed to an angle off to the left. "Morgan covers the exit. You move in from the west. Give me about"—he eyed the house-sized boulder he'd chosen—"ten minutes."

Wyatt followed his gaze. "You climbing that bastard?"

God, he didn't want to do this. A sick feeling unfolded in his gut. "Not like you're going to." Neither Masterson was into rock climbing.

"You up to it?" Wyatt's gaze was assessing before he nodded. "Yep, you can do this."

Masterson wasn't a bullshitter and his confidence was bracing.

"I can." He had to. Because the biggest boulder was the one that would measurably block the wind—and that was the one they'd probably be camped behind. If he could manage to scale the goddamn thing, he'd come out above them. He handed Wyatt his rifle. "I can't carry anything more than my automatic."

"Got it." Wyatt hesitated. "You going to hold off if..."

If the women were getting raped? The knot in Atticus's gut twisted. "We can't move without a chance of taking them down before they can kill the women. Even if..." *Gin, I'm sorry.*

But she was a strong woman; stronger than any he'd known. Smart. She wouldn't give up. He had to trust her to survive. Did she know he'd be coming for her?

At the foot of the boulder, he studied the rock for a long, long moment. Half of climbing was setting out a mental map. Fingers here, toes there, shift... The hardest spot would be the almost-smooth dome, which gleamed in the brightening moonlight. It had less holds than the area where Bryan had slipped. Had fallen. Had died.

No. No flashbacks. He removed his boots. His socks. Adjusted his belt so the pistol holster and knife sheath lay against the hollow of his back. No chalk to dry his sweating palms. He exhaled, inhaled. Relaxed his abdomen. Repeated the sequence. *Easy.*

His gut stuck halfway to his heart as he started to climb. Moved up. Up. Up.

And then, a piece of splintered rock broke off. His foot slipped.

Jesus. His fingers went rigid, taking his weight as he struggled to find a foothold. Far, far below, the rock hit with a dull thump too much like the sound of Bryan's landing and the hollow thud of his skull cracking on stone.

That sound... Death was different, more shocking, off the battlefield. Bryan was laughing one minute, screaming the next.

Stop it.

Gin needed him; he couldn't think of anything except the mission. He remembered the homework exercises she'd assigned him, and he took a breath to center himself. *I can do this. Got to rescue my counselor.*

Sweat beaded on his forehead, stinging his eyes. His toes curled into a tiny crack—barely enough support to relieve the pressure in his fingers. He ran his free hand over the rock, searching for his next hold.

A glance upward showed the silvery moon, the infinite stars in a black sky. *"Pa always said—if not overused—an honest prayer would be heard in heaven."*

Well then... Shoving his face against the abrasive granite, he growled, "Listen up, you fucking angels. Yeah, I mean you, Bryan. Could use a little help here, you know."

"Jesus, it's still winter in this shithole area," Crack said.

It was, Gin thought. The mixed granite and gravel under her hip was icy. But she wasn't about to try to stand again—not after Pit had smacked her down the last time. Instead, she watched as Slash dug through his pack and found a down vest.

"A small fire wouldn't be seen," Crack continued. His tats formed full sleeves up his arms, turning them dark as he searched in another pack.

"No." Slash pulled on his vest. He motioned to where Karen lay. Moonlight shone down into the rocks, highlighting her bruised and bloody face. "Go fuck your bitch; you'll warm up quick enough."

"Now you're talkin'."

Karen whimpered, trying to scramble away.

Crack grabbed her leg. With her hands still tied in front of her, her struggles were useless.

Gin couldn't save her. As frustrated tears prickled her eyes, she looked away...and saw Slash moving toward her.

Her stomach turned over.

"What about me an' Pit?" Stub blocked his way. "You got to fuck that counselor already."

Gin frowned. What counselor?

"That was work, you dumb fuck. Penny, the pussy, needed to be *motee-vated*, and you don't got the equipment—or brains—to do it."

"Like you do," Pit sneered.

"Got her to arrange the yard work assignment—and us all together, didn't I?" Slash's grin was ugly. "Told her a story 'bout the family we butchered. She got all excited."

"Fuck, you didn't." Pit's expression was shocked.

"Made Slash laugh. Clueless bitch." Slash ripped the wrapper of the protein bar.

"Yeah, well, you had pussy already." Stub pointed to Gin. "We want a turn with that one afore you ruin her."

Hand on his crotch, Pit nodded.

"Dream on, asshole. She's mine." Slash stopped, his gaze still on Gin. "Gonna ream that cunt while I cut pieces off the rest of her."

Terror blasted Gin so violently she almost heaved. *Run.*

How? Even if she managed to run, they'd catch her before she made it out of the rocks.

Or they'd shoot her down like a rabbit.

"Fine, I'll wait for the other bitch," Pit snarled. He glared at Crack. "Be done before I come back from taking a piss, asshole." His boots crunched on the loose rock.

"Keep watch," Slash told Stubb. "Slash got shit to do…"

"Fuck that. Pit can watch." As Stub's voice rose in protest, Gin stared out at the darkness.

A bullet would hurt. *I don't want to die.* Her belly tightened. But… No matter what, there would be pain and death. Through burning tears, she watched her fingers tremble. She wanted to live. To stay in this little town. To be with Atticus.

Because she loved him. Oh, so, so much—more than words could express. And she'd never told him.

A tear slid down her cheek, hot against her chilled skin. *I just found him. This isn't fair.*

Heaven didn't answer her protest.

She bit her lip and pushed her despair back. There were only two choices here. Should she wait like a victim to be put through horrors and murdered? Or take a bullet trying to escape? Either way, Slash wouldn't let her live.

Atticus…he was coming. She knew it. *"Virginia, I'll always come after you. I keep what's mine."* Like an old-fashioned cowboy, he wrote his own code, and he'd never give up. But he couldn't arrive in time to save her.

She breathed out slowly. Her man had borne enough in his life; he didn't need to see what Slash would do, see her brutalized body. No, she couldn't do that to him.

The sound of ripping fabric brought Gin's head up. Karen's voice was muffled, but she was crying. Trying to scream.

Karen. No. Gin pulled in a sobbing breath.

If I run, they'll chase me. All of them. She'd win a few minutes reprieve for Karen.

There was her goal. A positive goal. *Save Karen.* Even if only briefly.

Which way then? Run to the right, toward Slash and Stub and Pit, wherever he'd gone.

Or to the left, toward the clearing. No cover there, though.

Or straight out from the huge boulder at her back toward the forest. Crack and Karen lay right across that escape route.

But...but... She gave a huff of bitter laughter. *Heh.* No one expected a victim to run directly at him.

Curling her hands around a softball-sized rock, she shifted from a half-sprawl and stood, hiding her bound hands in the wreckage of her dangling shirt.

Stub and Slash stopped arguing. Slash took a threatening step toward her.

Taking her cue from Pit, she blurted out, "I-I have to pee. Please...?" She motioned to her right.

"Stupid cunt." Slash drew his knife. "Playtime."

Before he could move, she darted forward, straight toward Crack.

Straddling Karen, Crack had his attention on the struggling woman.

Gin skidded to a halt and brought the rough piece of granite down on Crack's head with all her strength. The impact hurt her half-numb hands. The stone dropped.

She ran.

Shouts of fury came from behind her.

Son-of-a-bitch. Hearing furious shouts, Atticus abandoned restraint and frantically heaved himself upward. Almost... Fingernails ripped as he slid back.

One toe found a crack.

With another surge, he scrambled up and over the smooth dome face—and almost slipped off the other side.

The moon shone down on the frantic activity below.

Gin! She was sprinting directly away from his boulder.

"Cunt!" One con grabbed a pistol from a pack. He aimed at her back.

Fuck, no. Atticus dove straight off the top. Freefall. He hit the bastard in the spine—bones snapped like dry spaghetti—and they slammed into the ground with the convict on the bottom.

Breath knocked out of him, Atticus rolled free, trying to inhale. A bullet spit dirt into his face, and he kept rolling. The next shot would—

A rifle blast echoed off the rocks.

Someone groaned and gave a rasping gurgle. Atticus turned enough to see a body crumple to the ground. But who?

Atticus fought to move, to sit up. Couldn't. His vision was blurry. Still gasping for breath, he struggled to reach the holster at his back and finally managed to pull his weapon.

A shape blocked the moonlight. A friendly.

"You dumbass, son-of-a-bitch, you almost got yourself killed." Rifle in one hand, Wyatt kicked a weapon away from a body sprawled on the ground. "You dove headfirst off the fucking rock. Are you fucking insane?"

A pistol snapped.

Wyatt staggered back, blood blossoming on his shirt.

A shadowy figure emerged from between two rocks. A convict.

Shit. Arm still half-paralyzed, Atticus struggled to lift his pistol.

A black shape coalesced out of the shadows to attack the inmate. Trigger's furious snarls filled the air. The convict's pistol dropped as he fought to keep the dog from ripping out his throat.

Morgan trotted into the clearing, reversed his rifle, and butt-stroked the inmate. As the man fell, Morgan grabbed the dog's ruff and pulled him back. "Good job, mutt. Now settle."

Straightening, he surveyed the area. "You all right, bro?"

"Hell, no." Wyatt lurched forward, holding his bloody upper arm. "You're late."

"Looked to me like I was right on time."

"Bullshit, you—"

"Check the area. Stay on guard," Atticus ordered. "And find Gin and the other woman." He could hear a woman sobbing nearby. As the brothers split up, he struggled to sit.

The sound of running made him turn to look. "Shit," he hissed as pain spasmed his muscles. But then relief swept through him.

Gin, emerging from the darkness between two boulders, was heading straight for him. "It *is* you. I heard your voice..." Eyes widening in distress, she dropped to her knees. "Oh honey, look at you."

Before she could move, Trigger tore across the space and bowled her right over.

As she patted the frantic Labrador with her restrained hands,

Atticus felt the knot inside him relax. *Alive.* She was alive.

All right then. He twisted his belt around and holstered his pistol—and just that amount of movement hurt like hell.

With the dog calmed, Gin moved closer.

"Hold still a second, sweetling." Atticus pulled his knife from the belt sheath and cut the ropes around her wrists. Scraped raw, goddammit. "That's better."

"Where are you hurt?" Her freed hands trembled as she yanked his ripped-up shirt open. Her concern bordered on hysteria so he let her look.

He glanced down at the bloody scrapes covering his chest. Fucking granite. "Not as bad as it looks, baby." His voice tore his throat like gravel.

After a quick, reassuring hug, he moved her back so he could do his own assessment.

She was moving without obvious injury. In the thin moonlight, he could see scrapes, bruises, gashes. Shirt ripped to shreds. Slacks still on. They hadn't had time to…

His next breath came easier. "Are you hurt, sweetling?"

"Am *I* hurt?" Her voice rose. "Me?" She looked like she was ready to punch him. "*I* didn't jump off a *mountain.*"

"Not much more than a big rock." He eyed it, surprised he'd survived even with the crash pad of a convict. "I'm fine." Although standing up was going to feel like hell.

"Sure you are, you…you idiot man." Tears gleamed in her eyes. "You c-came. Oh, G-God, you're really here." Shaking so hard he could almost hear her bones rattle, she dropped her head to his shoulder

God, she was adorable. Touching her bruised cheek, he took himself a gentle kiss. "Guess if you can yell at me, you're not too badly injured."

"I'm fine."

Bullshit. "Sure you are." He squeezed her shoulder lightly. "Now focus, Gin. We heard four inmates. Is that correct?"

Her hands fisted as she fought for control. God, she made him proud. Then even though her breath was hitching, she sat back on her knees. "Four. Yes." As she looked around the clearing, her face whitened further.

The eerie, pale moonlight illuminated bodies in motionless heaps. Hell, this was no sight for her. He pulled her closer and kissed the top of her head before raising his voice. "Morgan, report, please."

"No one else around. Wyatt's tending the other woman." Morgan yanked a final knot on the dog-savaged inmate and rose. "This asshole's alive. The one you landed on is dead. Broken neck."

Atticus breathed out and put the hit to his soul aside. He'd deal with the emotions later.

"The asshole with his dick hanging out might—or might not—make it." Morgan jerked his chin to the right. "Looks like his skull got busted. Which of you did that?"

"Ware's little bit helped us out," Wyatt said from the left. Heedless of the blood soaking his shirtsleeve, he was trying to untie the weeping older counselor. "She smashed a rock over his head."

"Seriously?" Morgan sounded as if he wanted to laugh. Well, adrenaline took some men that way. "Go, Gin."

"And the last inmate?" Atticus asked.

Wyatt's shoulders turned rigid. "My shot took out the other one. He's dead." The very lack of emotion in his voice shouted pain.

Damn me. The Mastersons were civilians. "Wyatt..."

Masterson didn't lift his head as he helped the counselor sit up.

"*Wyatt.*"

The man looked over.

"You saved my life, Masterson. He almost shot me."

Even as Wyatt's expression eased slightly, Gin burst into tears, holding Atticus so tightly he couldn't breathe. *Hell.* Shouldn't have said that about almost dying. She hadn't cried when saving herself or when being rescued. Not until now.

He wouldn't have loosened her embrace for the world. This was where she belonged. As he rubbed his chin in her hair, the words escaped him in a whisper, "God, I love you."

Chapter Nineteen

Gin sat in a wheelchair in Atticus's hospital room and waited. Patiently. Or maybe not so patiently.

Having driven to Sonora to lend her help, Summer sat on a chair in the corner.

Virgil stood in front of Gin. "You're exhausted. Let Summer take you home." He crossed his arms over his chest in an intimidating way. "Atticus might be in x-ray for a while; after, he'll be debriefing."

"No. I'm not leaving until I see him." *And you can't make me.* Gin rose, waited a second for her head to stop spinning, and then shoved him back. Hard.

The stinging pain from her bruised, scraped palms helped clear her thoughts. But, *ow.*

Virgil's brows drew together as he studied her in the way Atticus did—like a Dom. "Means that much, does it?"

She managed a nod.

"All right then—"

"Gin." Atticus's voice came from the doorway. Hoarse, but strong.

Abandoning the wheelchair, she tried to run to the door and achieved a speed at least as fast as a tortoise. "Are you all right? What's hurt?" She stopped, afraid to touch him. "Is anything broken?"

"C'mere, pet." He gripped her forearm above the wrist dressings and tugged her into his lap.

She couldn't miss his wince when her weight landed on his thighs. "Atticus, no." She wanted to jump up, but sat perfectly still, afraid to hurt him further.

"Fuck, yes." As she put her arm around his shoulder, he pulled her closer.

Her entire body hurt, and still she'd never felt anything as wonderful as being in his arms. She could feel him breathing, feel the warmth of his body.

"Thank you for staying," he murmured. "I needed to hold you. Know you're all right. Alive."

"Me, too." Ignoring the pain in her swollen lip, she kissed his cheek, his beard, finally his mouth—very gently—and felt him smile.

"You look like a boxer who lost a round or two, sweetling."

"No doubt." The pain in her body slid into her soul as she brought up the subject she'd been dreading. But the news should come from her. "Atticus, your brother…was there when the inmates broke out. He—"

"I heard," he said.

The tears she'd kept at bay spilled over. "I'm sorry. I'm so sorry. He died trying to save me…"

"Died?" He stiffened. "Gin. Whoa, baby, Sawyer's not dead."

She buried her face in the curve of his neck. "I saw him, honey. Slash stabbed him. He—"

Firm hands on her upper arms set her back. His gaze moved over her face. "I got a report from the surgeon. He made it through and is up on the surgical floor. Gonna be all right, although he lost a shitload of blood."

"Alive?" Her question rasped out even as relief and gratitude bubbled up inside her. "Really?"

"The Wares are hard to kill," Atticus said with a slight smile, using his fingers to wipe the tears from her face.

Alive. Her head felt so heavy, she rested it on his shoulder. *Alive.* Sawyer was alive. Her rage and sorrow and guilt began to melt away.

And Atticus was alive too, smiling at her. Nothing in her life was more important.

She heard him talking to Virgil and Summer and was content to sit on his lap, savor his deep voice, feel his hand stroking up and down her back.

"Still don't know why the fuck the skinheads tried to escape," Atticus was saying. "Their sentences didn't have that long to run. They were in for auto theft, right?"

"Right. But we downed their escape helicopter. The pilot talked. L.A. had an unsolved murder of a black family. New evidence turned up pointing to Slash and his gang. Slash and crew wanted out of prison before someone talked."

"No wonder," Atticus said.

Someone tapped on the door and said, "Detective Ware?"

"Yeah. I'll be there in a minute," Atticus said.

When Gin sat up, she felt Atticus's arm tighten as if he was as reluctant to be separated as she was. "I have to let you go."

He grunted agreement. "Duty sucks."

She took his face between her hands and looked into his eyes. "You're truly all right? The X-rays didn't show anything?"

"Nothing busted. They're keeping me overnight just in case. More for liability issues than anything else."

"Okay then." After stealing one last kiss, she carefully slid off his lap and stood, her legs shaking. She staggered.

Her arm was grabbed.

"No!" Panicking, she struck out—and hit Virgil.

He released her immediately. "Easy, little bit." His voice was soft, careful.

"Oh heavens." Her heart was pounding; her mouth tasted of ashes. "I'm so sorry." She glanced at Atticus.

His jaw was like granite as he held his hand out. She set hers in his big warm palm and realized she was freezing.

"You had a rough day today." Gently, Atticus massaged the coldness from her skin. His concern showed in his gaze. "Baby, you're going to have more bad days for a while."

She could see how much he wanted to stay with her. His frustration emanated from him in almost visible waves. "I'll be fine." She almost managed a smile. "I need to tell Trigger he's a hero."

"There is that."

She took a step and heard an admonishing *tsk tsk* from Summer, who stood by the wheelchair. With a mock scowl, Gin sat in it, knowing far too well she needed the ride.

"Dammit," Atticus was saying as Summer wheeled her into the hallway.

Yes, dammit. Gin stared down at her hands, feeling the quivers still going inside her.

"By the way," Summer said quietly. "You have three choices— you're spending the night with me or Kallie or Becca. No other options offered."

Gin closed her eyes as relief slid over her. "Have I mentioned how much I love you guys?"

"We know." Summer stopped the wheelchair in the foyer and walked around to sit on a couch in front of her. "There's something else you should consider though."

"What?" Why did she get a bad feeling about this?

Summer took her hands. "You weren't raped, but you were sexually abused—handled, poked, tormented."

"I'm fine." Her mouth compressed. Her insides knotted. This was the last thing she wanted to discuss.

"Mmmhmm. I know you've counseled others who've been through the same thing. What would you tell them they needed now? If Karen comes into my clinic, how should I advise her?"

The trap stood open, and Gin gave the nurse a respectful glare. Then sighed. Denying what had happened wouldn't help. "You're right. But how? I can't use the prison staff, and there isn't anyone in town."

Summer frowned. "Hmm."

Gin felt her shoulders relax. "So, there isn't really any way." No counseling, no need to talk about the horrible, horrible day. She'd rather rip out her fingernails…and her stomach turned over as she remembered Atticus's hands. Bleeding, ripped. Two nails torn off.

He'd pressed on past his fear and risked his life to climb a mountain. For her. Then dived off and almost killed himself. For her.

She closed her eyes at the wave of guilt. She'd almost broken up with him because of her old neuroses. Now she had a whole new set.

Well, this time she would darned well face up to her fears. She bit her lip, knowing how many resources she could call upon. They just weren't in the area.

She looked at Summer. "I know counselors in San Diego. Can y'all drive me to the airport and babysit Trigger?"

And would Atticus understand she was doing something for them both?

Chapter Twenty

Look at him. On Sunday, Gin stood in the hospital room doorway. As her eyes filled and spilled over with tears, the man in the bed blurred. Sobs rose, fast and hard, and Gin covered her mouth, trying to muffle the ugly sounds.

Sawyer heard and looked up. "Ms. Virginia." He took a second look and his brow creased. "Aw, now don't do that. No crying." He made a helpless gesture. "Listen, this is a no-crying zone, woman."

She giggled through her hiccupping and wiped her face. "Bless your heart; you're more scared of a woman crying than rioting inmates."

"Isn't everyone?" he said under his breath. "What are you doing here?"

"I came to see how you were. I-I thought—" Tears again. For heaven's sake, she wished the emotional roller coaster would stop. Taking a seat on the bed, she swiped her face and cleared her throat. Her voice still came out hoarse. "For hours, I thought you were dead."

There'd been so much blood on the grass. His eyes had been open. Unblinking. She shuddered, feeling the grief sweep her again.

"Shit. I didn't realize you saw me." He squeezed her arm briefly, then ran his hand over his short hair in a way that reminded her of Atticus. "I was down; couldn't move. But Slash would have cut my throat if he thought I was alive. It's how he got his handle, right?"

She nodded. The information had been in the inmate's workup. "You faked it."

"Yep. I rolled onto my front to try to hide that I was still gushing blood."

"Well. All my mourning gone to waste." Her smile wavered.

"It's appreciated." His expression said he meant it.

"I hear the governor valued your actions. He's wiping out the rest of your sentence?"

"When this hit the news, the gov got pressure to shortcut the process. And he's coming up for re-election." Sawyer shook his head in wonder. "I'll be a free man. You have no idea how damned fantastic it feels."

"You deserve this," she said softly. "Thank you for my life, Sawyer."

"You know, I can't fix my mistake and bring Ezra back, but maybe I helped balance things a bit."

"Sawyer, you—"

"So." He shifted uncomfortably and—typical man—changed the subject away from anything emotional. "What's been happening at the prison? You keep up with the gossip?"

She let him have his escape. "Some. Jacob Wheeler has a cracked rib and a concussion, but is home. His sister says he's already so grumpy she thinks he should get his butt back to work tomorrow."

Sawyer barked a laugh, groaned, and clutched his side. "Fuck."

"Sorry. By the way, he also has a private practice if you want to remain with him."

Sawyer hesitated. Nodded. "Yes."

"I'll leave his phone number with you." He'd keep up the counseling; progress would continue. Pulling in a relieved breath, Gin continued with the gossip. "Physically, Karen is all right. Mentally—that will take time. Virgil—he's a lieutenant in Bear Flat—says the warden will probably be replaced after an investigation. Apparently, some of the correctional officers were slow to respond, whether from bribes or because a riot earns them extra pay."

"That's ugly. Atticus mentioned a counselor was involved?"

"She's been arrested for aiding and abetting the escape. Her license will be revoked."

"Crazy woman." His keen gaze took her in. "And you? You going to be able to return to the prison after this?"

She shook her head. "If—if I had to, I could tough through it, but I wasn't happy there. I miss working with families and children. Jacob Wheeler offered me a place in his private practice. I can go back to doing what I love." Hearing children laughing. Bringing people closer together.

"Good deal." He eyed her cautiously. "With the kidnapping and those assholes, maybe you should...see someone."

Aww. Her heart warmed. If he could see past his own problems to someone else's, he was really on the road to recovery. "You're right. I'll be on workman's comp for a while, so I'm flying to San Diego where I spent a year after getting my Masters. I can stay with friends and see someone who specializes in after-trauma cases like mine."

"Good enough."

"I..." She chewed her lip for a second and offered, "I'd already sent in a report about Slidell. Now, with an investigation of the mental health department's involvement in a prison break and with my concerns about him on record, I doubt he'll be working there much longer."

Sawyer's smile flickered. "Good."

She patted his hand. "How about you? Have you decided what you're going to do?"

"I'm considering my options as well. Att gave me a few ideas." He gave her a crooked smile. "Ms. Vir—nah, if you're messing with my brother, I get to call you Gin."

She could feel her cheeks heat. *Messing with.* But he was right. "Yes. Call me Gin."

"Good enough." He studied her. "What's going on with you two, anyway?"

"We're"—*messing* wasn't a word she was going to use, thank you very much—"*seeing* each other." She grinned. "I saw him yesterday. He was banged up, bruised, scraped, and all he complained about was the paperwork."

"Bet he's getting grief all right, but nothing a few forms can't overcome."

"He didn't mention having trouble." She scowled. "For what?"

"He took civilians with him after escaped convicts." Sawyer made a disgusted noise. "Because being a superhero, he should've rescued you alone, right? Even worse, he took Fido to a gunfight."

"Fido's name is Trigger, thank you very much. And he's going to be impossible to live with. He was already conceited."

"Must be quite a dog. I hope I'll get to meet him. Damned if that isn't a good thing to be able to say."

"And to hear. Come by anytime." Gin patted his hand. "You'll be welcome."

A *tap, tap, tap* came from the door.

Sawyer tilted his chin toward Summer, who stood in the doorway. "I think Blondie wants to tell you that your time is up."

"I have to catch a plane. Bless you, Sawyer; thank you for my life."

He only managed a nod; she hadn't expected more.

Straightening her shoulders, she headed out. Time to face her fears.

* * * *

Fuck, he hated motel rooms. Stuck in Sacramento for the investigative cleanups, Atticus felt like putting his fist through the hotel room wall. When he wasn't answering inane questions for every bureaucrat in California, he was filling out reports for them.

Next time there was a prison riot, he'd dump the paper-pushers in with the inmates; before nightfall, even hardened convicts would be begging to go into solitary.

Time for a treat. He fast-dialed Gin's number as he had every night since she'd been gone.

"Atticus?" The delight in her voice almost did him in.

"Gin."

"*How are you doing?*" They both spoke the question at the same time.

Her laugh made him smile. "I'm fine. And you? Aren't you supposed to be at the capitol today?"

"I am." He stroked his beard thoughtfully. He'd talked with enough abused women to know she wasn't fine. But he'd give her the play and circle back. Maybe show her how honesty was done. "The trip down almost killed me—felt like I was being stabbed every time we hit a damned bump."

"Oh Lordy, I know. Me too."

Summer and Kallie had taken her to see Sawyer on the way to catch her flight to San Diego. They'd told him about the way she'd winced with every jolt. How stiffly she walked. And yet, his little magnolia had detoured to check on Sawyer in the hospital. How could he not love her?

"Are you all right though?" she asked.

He rested his back against the headboard and ignored the shit-bland artwork on the wall. "Almost back to normal." The docs had said nothing was busted, after all. Inflamed, irritated, a few rips here and there.

"I still can't believe you survived diving off that rock. When I realized... You're lucky I didn't smack you upside the head for doing something so crazy."

Yeah, he'd rather thought she'd been considering it. "Was worth it." When he thought of her in the hands of those bastards, he still felt as if he'd explode with anger. And fear. "When are you coming back from San Diego?"

"After my last session on Friday."

"Seems too fast to be through all the therapy."

"I'll continue with someone in Sonora every week or two for a while, but honestly, I've worked through a lot of the aftereffects already. This type of therapy is like seeing a horror flick over and over until it doesn't have any effect."

Sounded fucking awful. And no therapy would erase his memory of her with a weapon pointed at her back. "Is there anything I can do?"

"Oh, honey, you have. Aside from rescuing me, just knowing there are good men, like you, makes a big difference." She laughed. "And having all the awesome sex before, well…"

Relief eased the constriction around his chest. Damn, she was a strong woman. One who'd hold up against anything life had to offer. "Then I'll see you Friday." He hesitated. "It's probably best if we skip the BDSM camping trip this weekend. You shouldn't—"

"I should," she said firmly. "I've been looking forward to it. I know you agreed to help with the setup in the afternoon, so Summer and I will drive up together, and I'll meet you there."

"Virginia, I'm not sure—"

"Don't you go all Dom on me, Atticus Ware." Her laugh was delightful. "Because it makes me hot, and I'm way too far away."

He could hear the breathiness in her voice. The heat. "In that case, I'll call you tomorrow—and see you at the camp on Friday." Where he'd make his little subbie pay for the erection she'd given him.

Chapter Twenty-One

Gin was late. Very late. Atticus leaned against a tree, arms crossed on his chest, watching the kinksters prepare for the evening. Far down a dirt road behind their lodge, the Hunts had a wide clearing set up for BDSM activities. Split logs formed a St. Andrew's cross. Several actual sawhorses—although modified—created spanking benches. A tipped-over wine barrel with iron bolts welded to the rim was perfect for bending a subbie over the staves and restraining her there.

Chains dangled from tree branches. Ropes wrapped around tree trunks could be used to spread-eagle a submissive.

The night sky was beautifully clear, the waning moon not yet visible.

More people arrived. Still no Gin. With each late-arriving car, he'd expected to see her emerge. How long could it take to dress for the evening? Or had Summer driven them into a ditch or something?

Uneasiness curled in his gut. He might paddle Gin's cute little ass when she got there for making him worry. Making him wait. After all, it'd been six days since he'd had her in his arms. Even longer since they'd made love.

He looked up at the approach of two people. "Hey, deVries. Good to see you and Lindsey here."

"Ware." DeVries was muscular, iron-jawed, and always looked a bit battered. He had both the buzz-cut hair and the arrogance of a Marine drill sergeant.

Made Atticus all nostalgic. As he clasped hands with deVries,

Atticus smiled down at deVries's submissive, Lindsey. Average height and weight. Big brown eyes. Her curly brown hair with colorful red and purple streaks was indicative of her vibrant personality. "How're you doing, pet? Did you get your business settled down south?"

She grinned. "There are a lot of bad guys now stewing in Texas prisons. Life is good."

Excellent. He might not enjoy Gin's girly flicks, but damned if he didn't like a happy ending. The two here had gone through a lot to get theirs.

Speaking of happy endings, once the pleasantries here were done, Atticus was going after his own. If Gin was still trying to figure out what fetwear to put on, he'd haul her ass back up here naked. After he tumbled her in bed first.

They might not make it back here.

Damn, he missed her.

"Always figured the mountains were a quiet place," deVries commented. "Not yours, it seems. You okay?"

"Almost back to normal."

Lindsey smiled at him. "The last time I saw you, you had a goatee. I like the beard better."

"This takes less work." And was softer on his little submissive's inner thighs. Atticus jerked his chin toward a slender young man in a showy black and gold chain harness with matching thong. "I see you brought your whipping boy. You planning to beat on him tonight?"

DeVries glanced over. "We had some fun last night. Stan came late, so I got Dixon all warmed up and ready to welcome him to the mountains."

DeVries and Dixon were into S&M; their partners weren't. So the sadist would give Dixon the pain he needed and return him to Stan. Dixon's partner said he got the best part of the deal with his submissive aroused and ready to fuck. After watching deVries work on Dixon, Lindsey was usually aroused as well…which deVries enjoyed. Apparently, their odd arrangement worked.

"Dixon and Stan are still together?" Which was undoubtedly why the collar around Dixon's neck was a no-nonsense black leather— Stanfeld's style.

"They're so cute." Lindsey gave a reminiscent sigh. "Dixon cried when Stan collared him." Her fingers touched her neck before her hand dropped…and her expression said it all. DeVries's submissive wanted a collar too.

Atticus regarded her. He looked forward to when Gin would show the same longing. She already wanted him. Wanted his command. Eventually, she'd trust him enough to give him...everything.

Before he went to get her, he might as well have some fun with this couple here. DeVries was such a hard-ass, he was a pleasure to torment. So he turned his gaze to Lindsey.

"You look a little naked there, Tex." Chancing his luck—considering his ribs and shoulder were still on the tender side—Atticus stepped between Lindsey and deVries. He took her hands and held them up, looking at her arms. "Naked wrists too."

DeVries growled from behind him.

Ah well, he hadn't done anything foolhardy in a week now. "I could fix that problem for you. Even if it's only for an evening, I like collaring and cuffing a sub. Keeps other Doms from getting too forward." Like he was being right now.

When Lindsey gave him a nervous look, he winked.

She blinked and—smart cookie—dropped her head to hide the laughter in her eyes. "Um..."

"Hands off, asshole." DeVries shoved him away from Lindsey and raised his voice. "Simon, you got a spare set of cuffs in your bag? And a collar?"

"Really?" Lindsey sounded breathless. "A collar too?"

"Babe, you've worn a play collar at Dark Haven." DeVries ran his fingers through her hair.

Lindsey's face fell. "But the staff collar is only to show Xavier is looking out for me, not that I..."

Belong to someone. Atticus could hear what she didn't say. From the dawning comprehension in his face, so could deVries.

Well, my work here is done—although it had become more intense than he'd intended. Silently, Atticus retreated as Simon strolled across the clearing with a set of leather cuffs and collar.

Lindsey went to her knees without being asked.

When deVries buckled on the collar—the tangible signs of his ownership—tears of happiness filled her eyes.

Terse as always, deVries didn't give her any long speeches. "Mine. You're mine." He pulled her to her feet, wrapped her close, and took her mouth. "Fuck, I love you."

Her arms went around his neck. "I love you."

What wouldn't Atticus give to hear the words from Gin? He headed for his pickup.

Halfway across the clearing, a pretty female detached from a group of Doms and submissives. She stopped a few feet from him and politely waited for him to acknowledge her.

"Was there something you wanted?" Atticus strove for politeness, even if his voice came out a growl.

"Yes, Sir." She arched her back, drawing attention to her breasts. "I-I was wondering if you plan to do suspension today, and maybe you need a rope bunny? I'm…I'd love…"

Love. That fucking word.

Well, honestly, leave a Dominant for a few days and look what happened. Gin put her hand over her stomach to silence the butterflies. A minute or so ago, the sight of Atticus taking the hands of a lovely streaky-haired submissive had brought Gin to a complete halt.

But he hadn't done anything other than hold her arms up in the air. When another Dom had given Atticus a territorial scowl and quickly put cuffs and collar on her, Gin knew Atticus had been jerking the Dom's chain.

The man had an evil sense of humor.

Only now, he was being opportuned by a beautiful young woman. And from the way she presented herself, her offer included…everything.

Gin slapped the coil of his heavy hemp rope against her thigh. She was letting last-minute qualms overwhelm her. He'd risked his life for her. He'd even admitted to Wyatt he'd nearly puked on the climb up the boulder. He loved her—she'd heard him.

She was the wimp who hadn't said it to him. She huffed a laugh. Why was opening her heart so much more difficult than facing down death?

With a mental hitching up of her big girl panties—or should she say big girl thong?—she walked across the clearing.

Kallie and Becca noticed and started toward her.

She waved them off, but their concern touched her. Friends. She had friends. Her grip tightened on the rope. Now she had to lasso herself a man. Or, rather, let him do it.

Her steps faltered. The other submissive was truly lovely.

Gin stiffened her spine. *No second thoughts.*

And no fighting. Knocking the young woman on her perky little ass would be ill mannered, so Gin fell back on her mama's lessons. She stopped beside Atticus, facing the young woman, and gave her a smile.

"Oh honey, I'm so sorry. Bless your heart, but this Dom is taken."

A raspy laugh came from beside her.

The woman straightened. "So he told me. Excuse me, please."

Gin managed to close her mouth.

With a slight bow to Atticus, the submissive returned to her friends, leaving Gin to face the Dom she'd claimed.

Atticus turned. Raised an eyebrow.

Uh-oh. Submissives weren't supposed to interrupt conversations. Hopefully that Xavier person wasn't here today. She didn't bother to look. Instead, Gin filled her gaze with all that was her man. A bruise still darkened his left cheekbone; bandages covered the ends of two fingers. He was moving slower and without his usual dangerous smoothness. Because he'd hurt himself saving her life. He wasn't dressed in fancy fetwear like some of the Doms, but wore only a pair of jeans, boots, and a black T-shirt. She'd never wanted anyone so much in her whole life. "Atticus."

Not knowing how to tell him what was in her heart, she handed him the ropes used for suspension. Did the offering tell him enough?

When he studied her without speaking, her hopes sank. "I—"

"Am I?"

"Are you what?"

"Taken?" His thumb and fingers closed on her chin to angle her face toward the moonlight.

This was her chance to tell him how she felt. "You... I—" The words choked in her throat; the planet halted its spinning.

His almost inaudible sigh of disappointment broke her heart. She grabbed his hand and flattened his palm between her breasts. Her heart was pounding madly. "You—you are *taken.*" Sucking in a breath helped. She tried another.

"Gin." When she saw the warmth and pleasure in his gaze, the earth started turning again. "Good. Good girl."

After gathering her senses, she realized his tone held a wealth of satisfaction. Almost too much. *Well.*

She kissed his hand and nipped his finger. "You need to remember, though, Doms who are in exclusive, possessive relationships don't get to play with other submissives."

"Is that right?"

"It's true. Not if they want to keep their essential equipment."

His shout of laughter made people look their way. "Considering I have a fondness for my manly parts, I'll behave myself." He set his hands on her hips. "However, maybe I need something visible to deter all those predatory submissives."

She tipped her head to one side. "Visible?"

"Mmmhmm." He took the rope from her hand, slung it over his shoulder, and stepped close enough that her breasts brushed his chest. An iron-hard arm around her waist pulled her against him until her softness rubbed against a very hard erection. "A nice fat wedding band should do the trick."

Wedding band. Even the stars in the sky seemed to be dancing along the treetops. Her lips curved up and she managed to answer, "I'll find the biggest one available," before he kissed her so thoroughly that wedding vows were superfluous.

* * * *

His little magnolia could steal a man's heart without even trying.

But damn, when she'd handed him the ropes he preferred for suspension, he'd been overwhelmed by her courage. He clearly remembered how she'd reacted the first time she'd imagined being suspended in rope. *"No. No way. Never."*

And then she'd experienced a prison breakout. Kidnapping. Violence.

Now under a massive black oak, she calmly knelt, stripped of all clothing. Patiently accepting of whatever he planned to do.

She humbled him.

Quietly, Atticus walked around her, finishing his preparations. To provide extra light while he worked, he turned up the LED camping lanterns hung around the scene area. The huge branch with a suspended hard point had been tested earlier. Ropes and gear were ready, rescue hook on his belt in case restraints needed to be cut.

He began, enjoying her shiver as the scratchy rope trailed over her smooth skin and the way her face flushed as he wrapped her breasts. Her body turned boneless as he moved her, as he wanted her.

Slowly, he bound her in his ropes. And with every touch, every knot, every kiss, Atticus showed her how much her submission meant to him.

For this first suspension, he'd do nothing fancy, instead he duplicated the pose of a woman leaning back in a swing. Ass lowest, torso angled up, legs temporary stretched outward.

Knot by knot, he took away her freedom, her power, her will...and then he lifted her into the air, putting her completely under his control.

When the ground dropped away, her eyes went as wide as a panicking mare's. Panting, she struggled against the bindings, even though she was only a few inches in the air.

He'd expected this.

"Easy, baby." Taking a knee, he gripped her shoulder and curled his right arm behind her, giving her the illusion of support. "Eyes on me, Virginia. Right here." As he would with a greenie Marine in a first firefight, he sharpened his command enough to slice through her spiraling fear.

Her gaze jerked up to meet his, her breathing still too fast.

"Good. Very good." He lowered his voice to the croon he used with horses—and frightened subbies. "Exactly what are you afraid of, sweetheart? Tell me."

"What am I—" With a click, her mind engaged. She frowned.

"Do you think I'd hurt you?"

"Of course not."

With his hand against her cheek, he nipped at her lips to tease her with what was to come. "Do you think I'd let you fall?"

She swallowed. "Well. No."

But her body's instincts told her she might. He understood that part. What about the other—her deeper fear. "Do you think I'd leave you?"

"No. You wouldn't do that."

She hadn't hesitated, hadn't had to think. His hobbled heart felt as if it had broken free and into a gliding canter. He was in. Finally. "There's my girl."

The way her eyes softened with his approval, his possession, made his arm tighten around her. Fuck, he loved her. And he'd tell her again and again.

But for now...time to fly.

The rope harness he'd created for her torso held some of her weight with the delightful side effect of squeezing her breasts. Her arms were restrained behind her back, forearm to forearm. Webbed rope made a sling for her ass and supported the majority of her weight.

Quietly, he walked around the area and dimmed the lights. The light from the fire pit danced across her skin. The night was cooling. The trilling *who-who-who* of a screech owl joined the sounds of sighing trees and the nearby gurgling creek.

After raising her to groin height, he spread and secured her knees up and apart—opening her for his use. He braided her hair and used a strand of rope to tie it to a vertical line. Her head would be supported—and she'd be unable to see anything except the night sky over the forest canopy.

Suspension was a slow business, sublimely sensuous, and requiring every iota of attention from the Dom. His entire world was tuned to the slow slide of a rope, the feeling of bare skin, of compression and pressure, of the beauty of harsh strands against delicate skin.

"God, you're beautiful." His voice came out hoarse as he finished the last knot.

Her eyes had widened with the first ropes, her body had stilled as he removed her ability to move, and after her initial panic, when he'd lifted her into the air to gently rock above the earth, he'd seen her mind plunge down into the pool called subspace. Even as her body floated, so did her soul.

It was a heady rush to know she trusted him with all of her, body, mind, and soul.

As he circled her to assess her circulation and sensation, he noticed Jake nearby, watching quietly. Even the wilderness had dungeon monitors. Jake gave him a chin lift in acknowledgment before sauntering to the next scene.

Atticus dismissed him from his mind and stepped back to examine his work and his submissive.

Eyes closed, breathing slow and deep, muscles completely relaxed. Someone liked being in ropes.

Smiling, he moved between her raised legs. Yes, the perfect height. He leaned forward. His jeans rubbed against her vulnerable, bare pussy as he ran his palms over her rope-squeezed breasts.

Her eyes popped open, making him grin. "Wh-what are you doing?" Her words came out thick and slow—yep, she'd been pretty deep and wasn't out of la-la-land entirely. Which didn't bother him one bit.

"Playing with the petals on my little magnolia flower." He ran a finger between her drenched folds. Definitely ready for him.

Her whole body quivered.

Her breasts were compressed between the ropes, swollen to a pleasing plumpness. Undoubtedly more sensitive. Testing, he rolled one satiny nipple between his fingers.

She gasped, and her back arched.

Oh yeah.

He'd warned her once what he'd do if he ever had her in suspension. Time to make good his promise.

Unhurriedly, he laved her nipples with his tongue, nibbling and sucking until the peaks were a carnal dark red. When he straightened, the suspension rocked back and forth, but he saw her fear had disappeared.

"Want more?" he asked in a low voice. He moved beside her shoulder so he could taste her mouth. As he traced his tongue over her lips, she sighed.

He nipped lightly, teasing her, before soothing the sting with his tongue.

When he straightened, she tried to lift her head—and couldn't. Her whine was satisfying. She wanted his mouth, but he would give her only what he wanted her to have. What she asked for.

"What, sweetling?"

"More. More, please, Sir."

He pleased them both with long, wet drugging kisses, feeling her submission in the softness of her lips, the willingness to be plundered. Would she surrender everything?

Gin blinked her eyes into focus as Atticus moved away, disappearing from her sight. She tried to watch, but the binding in her hair kept her head from rising.

His palm stroked over her stomach. Down her leg. He always had a hand on her, as if to reassure her that even when she couldn't see him, he was close.

Something moved between her parted legs—a brush of coarse material. His hands closed on her thighs, making her jump with the unexpectedly hard grip.

She stared up into the dark night sky where the waning moon had barely risen over the trees. From the stone pit came the sound of the crackling fire. The flickering yellow light danced over the black tree trunks.

As she rocked in the suspension, the massive branch overhead creaked. The gentle swaying was mesmerizing; the snugness of the ropes over her body comforted and somehow…somehow loosened her grasp on reality. Her mind kept floating away, like a balloon gliding up into the tree canopy.

A zipper rasped, and she felt Atticus's erection slide through her wetness. His fingers made circles around her clit, and as if he were the pied piper of sex, every drop of her blood streamed downward to her pussy.

"Please, Sir." Her plea was mostly a moan. "I want you in me. Please."

The tree branch groaned as he leaned over her, steadying himself with a hand on the ropes.

As his chest rubbed her sensitized nipples, she sucked in a breath. "Please."

His dark eyes were controlled, his jaw determined. "When I'm ready, sweetling."

With his free hand, he traced a finger over her cheek. "You are so beautiful."

The look in his eyes was...was one she'd seen before. One she'd been too scared to recognize.

Today, the knowledge he loved her sent her heart soaring.

Reaching down, Atticus adjusted himself. His cock separated her tissues, entered her, thick and hard and slow, as if he exulted in each micro-inch, each stretch and wakening nerve inside her.

Far more intimate was the way his eyes never left her moonlit face as he pressed deeper.

Exquisite torture. She tried to move...couldn't. He slid in another inch, and her eyes closed. *Ooooh.*

"Eyes on me, baby," he said softly. Firmly.

She forced her heavy lids up, and the keenness of his gaze made her shiver. Made him smile. "Atticus," she whispered, without any reason other than to say his name.

"Shhh."

As he advanced, with excruciating slowness, she panted. Her insides throbbed around his thickness.

And then he was fully in, his coarse pubic hair against her bare pussy, his balls swinging lightly against her buttocks. He gripped her chin—one more restraint, one more symbol of her nakedness before him.

"You're mine, Virginia." His voice was low. Rough. "And you agreed. But I let you evade a step. That time is over." He brushed his lips over hers, never losing her gaze. "I love you, Gin."

He waited a breath, and she swallowed, trying to get the words out.

"Tell me." How could such a quiet voice hold the iron edge of command? "Say it."

His cock slid out, taking her mind away, slid in. Circled and penetrated deeper.

Owned. She was owned. Taken. Held firmly by his ropes and his arms and his will. Another fragment of her defenses slipped away, a wisp of cloud drifting up into the sky.

Mercilessly, his shaft filled her, emptied her, filled her. Her swollen breasts were flattened against his chest, her arms bound and helpless. His gaze never left her face, reading every emotion.

"I—"

"Say the words, Virginia." His kiss was deeper this time, taking her mouth as he had her body.

When he lifted his head, her words poured out, simple and easy. "I love you."

His dimple appeared. Disappeared. His shaft withdrew, drove in harder, wakening need in every nerve. A tremor ran through her.

"Again. Tell me again," he murmured. His hand controlled her face. His ropes, her body. His eyes, her mind. The hot glide of his cock plunging in, pulling out, was the most intimate of caresses.

"I love you, Atticus." The dam was broken; her emotions were unleashed, filling the dry recesses of her soul. "I love you so much."

"Thank fuck," he muttered, surprising a giggle from her.

His grin broke forth. He released her face, straightened, and grasped her hips. "I'm going to take you now, baby." He leaned over her just far enough so she could see his face. The crinkles creased at the corners of his eyes. "I'd say hang on, but—too bad, there's not a thing you can do."

The statement of exactly what her instincts knew—that she was completely immobilized and under his control—sent a quaking through her so hard it shook her body.

He paused, openly enjoying her response. And then he took her, hammering in and out, using the swinging of the suspension to yank her against him.

Her body constricted around him. Each sense wakened to the ropes binding her breasts, the warmth of his hands on her hips, the wet noises, the slap of flesh, and beyond everything, the steely blue of his unyielding gaze.

Like a mountain avalanche, her climax was approaching…and unstoppable. Her muscles tensed, her legs trembled. The rhythm caught her, drove her upward, hung for a beat, another.

He pulled out slower, plunged in, out, keeping her there…there…there.

And then the pulsing started in her recesses as exquisite pleasure burst through, pouring outward along every river of her body. Held helpless in the ropes, her body shook and quivered, unable to halt anything, to do anything except drown in the pleasure.

"That's my Gin," he said softly. And then he pressed deep inside her. His fingers gripped her waist painfully as his eyes went blank, and he took his own release.

His groan of satisfaction had to be the finest sound in the world.

He lowered himself and rested his forehead against hers. "I love you, magnolia. And just so you know, I might remove the ropes, but I'm never going to let you go."

She pressed a kiss to his mouth and whispered, "Good." For she knew to her very core that not even the tightest bondage could prevent her heart from soaring up and into his keeping.

~ The End ~

Sign up for the 1001 Dark Nights Newsletter
and be entered to win a Tiffany Key necklace.

There's a contest every month!

Go to www.1001DarkNights.com to subscribe.

As a bonus, all subscribers will receive a free
1001 Dark Nights story
The First Night
by Lexi Blake & M.J. Rose

Turn the page for a full list of the
1001 Dark Nights fabulous novellas...

1001 Dark Nights

WICKED WOLF by Carrie Ann Ryan
A Redwood Pack Novella

WHEN IRISH EYES ARE HAUNTING by Heather Graham
A Krewe of Hunters Novella

EASY WITH YOU by Kristen Proby
A With Me In Seattle Novella

MASTER OF FREEDOM by Cherise Sinclair
A Mountain Masters Novella

CARESS OF PLEASURE by Julie Kenner
A Dark Pleasures Novella

ADORED by Lexi Blake
A Masters and Mercenaries Novella

HADES by Larissa Ione
A Demonica Novella

RAVAGED by Elisabeth Naughton
An Eternal Guardians Novella

DREAM OF YOU by Jennifer L. Armentrout
A Wait For You Novella

STRIPPED DOWN by Lorelei James
A Blacktop Cowboys ® Novella

RAGE/KILLIAN by Alexandra Ivy/Laura Wright
Bayou Heat Novellas

DRAGON KING by Donna Grant
A Dark Kings Novella

PURE WICKED by Shayla Black
A Wicked Lovers Novella

HARD AS STEEL by Laura Kaye
A Hard Ink/Raven Riders Crossover

STROKE OF MIDNIGHT by Lara Adrian
A Midnight Breed Novella

ALL HALLOWS EVE by Heather Graham
A Krewe of Hunters Novella

KISS THE FLAME by Christopher Rice
A Desire Exchange Novella

DARING HER LOVE by Melissa Foster
A Bradens Novella

TEASED by Rebecca Zanetti
A Dark Protectors Novella

THE PROMISE OF SURRENDER by Liliana Hart
A MacKenzie Family Novella

FOREVER WICKED by Shayla Black
A Wicked Lovers Novella

CRIMSON TWILIGHT by Heather Graham
A Krewe of Hunters Novella

CAPTURED IN SURRENDER by Liliana Hart
A MacKenzie Family Novella

SILENT BITE: A SCANGUARDS WEDDING by Tina Folsom
A Scanguards Vampire Novella

DUNGEON GAMES by Lexi Blake
A Masters and Mercenaries Novella

AZAGOTH by Larissa Ione
A Demonica Novella

NEED YOU NOW by Lisa Renee Jones
A Shattered Promises Series Prelude

SHOW ME, BABY by Cherise Sinclair
A Masters of the Shadowlands Novella

ROPED IN by Lorelei James
A Blacktop Cowboys ® Novella

TEMPTED BY MIDNIGHT by Lara Adrian
A Midnight Breed Novella

THE FLAME by Christopher Rice
A Desire Exchange Novella

CARESS OF DARKNESS by Julie Kenner
A Dark Pleasures Novella

Also from Evil Eye Concepts:

TAME ME by J. Kenner
A Stark International Novella

THE SURRENDER GATE by Christopher Rice
A Desire Exchange Novel

A BOUQUET FROM M. J. ROSE
A bundle including 6 novels and 1 short story collection

Bundles:

BUNDLE ONE
Includes Forever Wicked by Shayla Black
Crimson Twilight by Heather Graham
Captured in Surrender by Liliana Hart
Silent Bite by Tina Folsom

BUNDLE TWO
Includes Dungeon Games by Lexi Blake
Azagoth by Larissa Ione
Need You Now by Lisa Renee Jones
Show Me, Baby by Cherise Sinclair

About Cherise Sinclair

Authors often say their characters argue with them. Unfortunately, since Cherise Sinclair's heroes are Doms, she never, ever wins.

A *USA Today* bestselling author, she's renowned for writing heart-wrenching romances with laugh-out-loud dialogue, devastating Dominants, and absolutely sizzling sex. And did I mention the BDSM? Her awards include a National Leather Award, *Romantic Times* Reviewer's Choice nomination, and Best Author of the Year from the Goodreads BDSM group.

Fledglings having flown the nest, Cherise, her beloved husband, and one fussy feline live in the Pacific Northwest where nothing is cozier than a rainy day spent writing.

Search out Cherise in the following places:

Website: www.CheriseSinclair.com

Facebook: https://www.facebook.com/CheriseSinclairAuthor

Goodreads:
http://www.goodreads.com/author/show/2882485.Cherise_Sinclair
Pinterest: http://www.pinterest.com/cherisesinclair/

Sent only on the day of a new release, Cherise's newsletters contain freebies, excerpts, upcoming events, and articles. Sign up here:
http://eepurl.com/bpKan

Servicing the Target
Masters of the Shadowlands 10
By Cherise Sinclair
Coming July 28, 2015

Raised a tough-as-nails military brat, Anne hates two things—not being accepted as equal to a man, and *change*. So she takes charge of her surroundings, her life, and especially her submissives. As a "bounty hunter," she leads the fugitive recovery team. And if an occasional wife abuser incurs a bruise or two on his return to jail? *Oops.*

A discharged Army Ranger, Ben considers his job as a BDSM club security guard to be an excellent hobby. He has never been tempted to join in...until Anne inadvertently reveals the caring heart concealed beneath her Mistress armor.

Now, he's set his sights on the beautiful Domme. Maybe he'd considered himself vanilla, but she can put her stiletto on his chest any day, any time. He'll trust her delicate hands to hold his heart. And if she wants to whip his ass on the way to an outstanding climax, he's just fine with that too.

Sure, he knows she likes "pretty boy" subs. And he's older. Craggy and rough. And six-five. Minor hindrances. The mission is a go.

* * * *

Ben had been to Anne's house before—chauffeuring her and her friends to a bachelorette party last winter. As he walked around his car, he could see past her cottage-style house to the ocean beyond. How the fuck did she manage a beach house on a bounty hunter's salary?

When he opened the passenger door, the interior light showed she was still asleep in the tipped-back seat. She'd miscalculated the effect of alcohol on pain pills, Z had said.

Her dark brown hair which she'd worn braided back in a severe style had come undone. The loose tendrils softened her aristocratic face. She wasn't a small woman—maybe five-eight—but beautifully formed with small breasts, a tight rounded ass. A darkening bruise marred the sculptured beauty of her right cheekbone.

God fucking dammit, he'd never seen anyone so beautiful.

"Mistress Anne." He unfastened her seatbelt. Hell, she wasn't budging. With a grunt of exasperation, he opened the purse that Z had retrieved from her locker. Her house keys were clipped to the strap. "I hope you don't have a dog, woman, or you'll have a real short ride." He set the purse in her lap and plucked her off the seat.

She was heavier than he expected. Undoubtedly had more muscles than the last lass he'd carried. He kicked the car door shut and carried her up to the cottage.

No dog. He walked through the foyer, took a guess, and headed up the stairs. An opened door showed the master bedroom—or would that be called the mistress bedroom? Using his elbow, he flipped on the overhead chandelier light.

Icy blue walls. A glass-fronted fireplace with an ornate mirror over the mantel. A canopied bed with a ruffled floral bedspread. A white couch with fancy legs in front of a wall of windows. All blue and white, like an airy summer garden, it was the most feminine room he'd ever seen.

She roused when he laid her on the bed, and damned if Ms. Feminine didn't try to punch him.

The candle-shaped lights overhead provided crappy illumination—and hell, she probably only saw a hulking monster over her. He caught her delicate fist in his oversized palm. "Easy, Ma'am."

Her finely arched brows drew together as she tried to sit up. He didn't miss the way her hand grabbed her ribs. Damn foolish woman.

"It's Ben. From the Shadowlands. I brought you home."

"Ah, Ben." She gingerly relaxed back on the mattress. "Thanks for the ride. Please tell Z I said so."

"You're welcome, Mistress Anne." He shifted his weight, uncomfortable as hell. But the garment she wore seemed to be some combination of a corset and a dress. It had obvious ribbing and was way too tight. She couldn't sleep in it. "Uh…you need to get out of that contraption."

He was standing over her—one big ugly guy. She was flat on her back and totally unconcerned. "Do I now?"

The edge of warning in her voice made his cock stir.

"Yes, Ma'am." The honorific came easily to his lips. She reminded him of the elegant captain of Marines in his first deployment. Always in control, and even when covered with blood and filth, still refined.

He smiled at her. "How about you order me to give you some

help?"

Her snort of exasperation sounded like a kitten's sneeze. "Benjamin, if a subbie tells me to order him to do something, then who's in charge?"

"Got me there." And damned if he was going to leave without getting her comfortable. "You going to punch me if I help you strip down?"

She eyed him. Her pupils were still smaller than normal, making her eyes even bluer. "I never realized how stubborn you were."

"Yes, Ma'am."

Her sigh held a note of exasperation. "Help me out of this, then."

He reached for the front and realized her ribbed long dress had no buttons. Stalling, he moved down to unlace her thigh-high boots. When he pulled them off, he heard a sigh of relief.

Damn, her pretty legs had a sexy golden tan. High-arched feet. Her toenails were a pale pink with white stripes. Amazing what women did for fun. Her mutant black dress was next. Thinking to salvage her modesty, he picked up the frilly knitted throw from the foot of the bed and draped it over her lower legs.

Next. He'd have been more comfortable walking into a firefight.

Her fucking dress had toothpick-sized metal studs down the front that poked through metal grommets. Only way to get it off would be to stick his fingers inside and draw the edges together to release each fucking stud. Her breasts were in there. Jesus, he couldn't do this.

Her lips curved up in a wicked smile. "Don't stop now, Benjamin."

"Having fun are we, Mistress?" he muttered and slid his big fingers inside the top.

"Mmmhmm."

She was warm, her skin silky on the backs of his knuckles. And he was harder than a rock. The corset part of the dress came undone, catch by catch. But the tightness increased over her ribs, and when he pulled the edges together, she made a sound of pain.

He stopped. How the fuck could he do this if he hurt her? "Anne?"

"Go on." Her hands were fisted, her fingernails digging into her palms. But her gaze was clear and level. "You're right—I'd have had a hard time getting out of this. I'm not moving as well as I was earlier."

"What kind of damage are we looking at?" His jaw was tight as he continued as ordered. Prong after prong.

Although she controlled her face, she couldn't control the involuntary flinches and tightening of her belly.

"Bruised ribs; nothing broken." Her voice sounded strained, but finally he was past that section.

He undid the looser part over her lower stomach and worked his way...down. As he flipped the dress open, he tried not to look.

Bullshit, he totally looked. His gaze traveled from her thong-covered pussy, up a softly rounded belly, to her sweet, high breasts. Rosy-brown nipples perked up in the cool night air. Her scent was almost edible—like tangerines accompanied by the light musk of a female.

Act like the gentleman you weren't raised as, Haugen. He drew the blanket over her. Turning his gaze away—so he wouldn't see how he hurt her—he slid an arm under her lower back. Shit, her skin there was soft as well. Carefully, he lifted her far enough to slide her dress out.

Now she wore only a thong and a blanket.

The room was far too fucking warm.

"Thank you, Ben. That feels much better."

"I bet." He dared greatly and moved the lower blanket to one side. Her right thigh had a bruise almost the width of his fist. He glanced at her, eyebrows raised. "Boot?"

"The bail fugitive had an overly protective, big brother."

What a fucking job. No wonder she came into the Shadowlands with bruises and gashes. "Wouldn't you rather do something...safer?"

Her blue gaze turned chill as the arctic north. "No."

"Sorry, Ma'am."

"You do say that rather well, you know," she murmured. She had a dimple in her cheek, one he hadn't noticed until he'd seen her at Gabi's bachelorette party.

"I do what?" He needed to leave or he was going to strip that blanket off her again. Find every bruise and kiss them all better.

"*Ma'am.* I thought you were vanilla, Ben."

"I am." And if he'd been daydreaming about her setting a sharp stiletto on his chest, he'd keep those thoughts to himself. "Did a bit of military, is all."

"Ah." She eyed him slowly, still not quite returned to her usual frightening brilliance. "Can I pay you for the time and gas to bring me all the way out here?"

"Yes, Ma'am." He paused a second with a hope that Z never heard. He'd get his ass fired on the spot. "I think I deserve a kiss from the Mistress."

Her eyebrows lifted. "You are just full of surprises tonight."

Her husky voice always sounded like a morning after raw sex, but when it dropped to that throaty tone, he could see why men crawled on their knees in her wake.

He waited while she thought. He'd wait all night—fuck knew, looking at her wasn't a chore.

Rather than answering, she held her arms up.

God loved him. He sat beside her hip, leaned down as she put her hands behind his neck. *More.* He carefully slid a hand behind her shoulders. Her satin skin stretched over her smooth feminine muscles. He opened his other hand behind her head to enjoy the thick mass of silky fine hair. He was used to visual delights—she was a tactile symphony.

He lifted slightly, just enough to draw her against his chest, so he could enjoy the feel of her breasts against him.

Bless Z.

When he gazed down into her face, he could read her surprise at his daring, and then her eyes started to narrow. If he didn't move, he'd lose his treat. So he bent his head and brushed his lips against hers.

Softness. Damned if he'd hurry. He settled his mouth over hers and walked empty-handed into the fire zone.

On behalf of 1001 Dark Nights,

Liz Berry and M.J. Rose would like to thank ~

Steve Berry
Doug Scofield
Kim Guidroz
Jillian Stein
Dan Slater
Asha Hossain
Chris Graham
Pamela Jamison
Jessica Johns
Richard Blake
BookTrib After Dark
InkSlinger PR
and Simon Lipskar